A NEW GRAFT
ON THE FAMILY TREE

THE ALDEN
COLLECTION

Isabella Macdonald Alden

A New Graft
ON THE FAMILY TREE

CREATION
HOUSE
BOOKS ABOUT SPIRIT-LED LIVING
LAKE MARY, FLORIDA

Creation House
Strang Communications Company
600 Rinehart Road
Lake Mary, FL 32746
(407) 862-7565

Originally published in 1880

Unless otherwise noted, all Scripture
quotations are from the
King James Version of the Bible.

First printing, June 1992
Second printing, February 1993

CONTENTS

Introduction 7

   I. Will It Bloom or Wither? 13

  II. The Tree.. 22

 III. Introduced 32

 IV. From Dawn to Daylight 40

  V. Beds and Buttonholes.................................... 51

 VI. A New Service for Sunday 61

VII. A New Sunday Class 71

VIII. New Light... 81

 IX. A New Champion 91

  X. Fishing.. 101

 XI. Grace Sufficient 111

XII. Different Shades 121

XIII. Buds of Promise... 131

XIV. Dust and Doubt 142

XV. Opportunities.. 151

XVI. The Reason of Things 160

XVII. Firstfruits 166

XVIII. Birds of Promise 176

XIX. "Whatsoever" 186

XX. Clouds 196

XXI. "Hedged In" 206

XXII. Cords Unseen.. 216

XXIII. "Forbid Them Not".................................... 226

XXIV. Storm 236

XXV. Unconditional Surrender 246

XXVI. Dorrie's Ambition 256

XXVII. Heartthrobs and Commonplaces 264

XXVIII. "I Don't Know" 274

XXIX. The Old and the New................................ 284

INTRODUCTION

nder the pen name "Pansy," Isabella Macdonald Alden exerted a great influence upon the American people of her day through her writings. She also helped her niece, Grace Livingston Hill, get started in her career as a best-selling inspirational romance novelist.

As Grace tells it in the foreword to *Memories of Yesterdays*, her aunt gave her a thousand sheets of typing paper with a sweet little note wishing her success and asking her to "turn those thousand sheets of paper into as many dollars.

"I can remember how appalling the task seemed and how I laughed aloud at the utter impossibility of its ever coming true with *any* thousand sheets of paper. But it was my first real encouragement, the first hint that anybody thought I ever could write. And I feel that my first inspiration came from reading her books and my mother's stories, in both of which as a child I fairly steeped myself."

On another occasion, a few months before Grace's

twelfth birthday in 1877, Isabella had been listening to her as she told a story about two warmhearted children. As Isabella listened, she typed out the story and later had it printed and bound by her own publisher into a little hardback book with woodcut illustrations. She surprised her niece with the gift on her birthday. That was Grace's first book.

Isabella Macdonald was born November 3, 1841, in Rochester, New York, the youngest of five daughters. Her father, Isaac Macdonald, was educated and deeply interested in everything religious. Her mother, Myra Spafford Macdonald, was the daughter of Horatio Gates Spafford (1778-1832), author and inventor. Isabella's uncle, Horatio Gates Spafford Jr., penned the popular hymn "It Is Well With My Soul" after learning that his wife had survived a tragic shipwreck; his four daughters were lost at sea.

Isabella was home-schooled on a regular daily basis by her father. Her guide and friend, he encouraged her to keep a journal when she was young and to develop a natural affection for writing. Under his direction she acquired the ease and aptness of expression for which her writings became known. When she was only ten, her composition "Our Old Clock," inspired by an accident to the old family clock, was published in the local village weekly.

That first published work was signed "Pansy." Isabella acquired that name partly because pansies were her favorite flower and partly because of a childhood episode. She tried to help her mother get ready for a tea party by picking all the pansies from the garden to decorate the tea table. Not knowing the flowers were to be tied into separate bouquets and placed at each lady's place, Isabella carefully removed all the stems. It resulted in a near-tragedy in her young life.

Years later, while teaching at Oneida Seminary, from which she had earlier graduated, Isabella wrote her first novel, *Helen Lester*, in competition for a prize. She won fifty dollars for submitting the manuscript that best explained the plan of salvation so clearly and pleasantly that very young readers would be drawn into the Christian fold and could easily follow its teachings. She gave the prize money to her parents.

Isabella wrote or edited more than two hundred published works, including short stories, Sunday school lessons and more than a hundred novels. She had only one manuscript rejected, a story sent to a periodical. At one time her books sold a hundred thousand copies annually with translations in Swedish, French, Japanese, Armenian and other languages.

She usually wrote for a young audience, hoping to attract youth to religion and to following the Golden Rule. The themes of her books focused on the value of church attendance; the dangers lurking in popular forms of recreation; the duty of total abstinence from alcohol; the need for self-sacrifice; and, in general, the requirements, tests and rewards of being a Christian.

Reading was more strictly supervised for young people in that day than it was later, and Sunday schools provided many families with most of their reading material. Thus, Isabella's fiction received wide circulation because of its wholesome content.

Readers liked the books. Her gift for telling stories and her cleverness in dreaming up situations, plus just a little romance, held the interest of readers young and old. Isabella was known for developing characters who possessed an unwavering commitment to follow the Master. She portrayed characters and events that anyone might encounter in a small American town during the last quarter of the nineteenth century. One writer was reported to have said in 1932 that "whoever on his ancestral book shelves can discover a stray copy of one of the Pansy books will know more, on reading it, of culture in the American eighties [1880s] than can otherwise be described."

Isabella believed wholeheartedly in the Sunday school movement. She edited a primary quarterly and wrote primary Sunday school lessons for twenty years. From 1874 to 1896 she edited *The Pansy*, a Sunday magazine for children, which included contributions from her family and others. An outgrowth of the magazine was the Pansy societies for self-improvement, made up of young subscribers and aimed at rooting out "besetting sins" and teaching "right conduct."

For many years she taught in the Chautauqua assemblies and, with her husband, was a graduate of what was called the Pansy Class, the 1887 Class of the Chautauqua Literary and Scientific Circle — the first book club in America. The Chautauqua assemblies were an institution that fluorished in the late nineteenth and early twentieth centuries. They combined popular education with entertainment in the form of lectures, concerts and plays and were often presented outside or in a tent.

Throughout her career Isabella took an active interest in all forms of religious endeavors, but her greatest contributions came in her writings. She wanted to teach by precept and parable the lessons her husband taught from the pulpit, in Bible class and in the homes of his parishioners. Her writing was always her means of teaching religious and moral truths as she understood them, and her method was to tell a story.

Her husband, Gustavus Rossenberg Alden, was a lineal descendant of John Alden, one of the first settlers in America. He graduated from Auburn Theological Seminary and was ordained soon after his marriage to Isabella in 1866. He served as a pastor in churches in New York, Indiana, Ohio, Pennsylvania, Florida and Washington, D.C. The Aldens moved from place to place for health reasons and to be near their son, Raymond, during his years of schooling and teaching.

Amidst her many and varied responsibilities as a minister's wife, a mother and a prolific author, Isabella found time to play a significant role in her son's career as a university professor, an author and a scholar in Shakespearean literature.

Her final years were marked by trials and suffering. In 1924, after fifty-seven years of marriage, Isabella's husband died. In that same year her last remaining sister, Marcia Macdonald Livingston, Grace's mother, died. A month later her only son, Raymond, died.

About two years later she fell and broke her hip. Although in much pain and discomfort she continued writing until the end. Her final letters were filled with thoughts of going "Home": "Isn't it blessed to realize that one by one we shall all gather Home at last to go no more out forever! The hours between me and my call to come Home grow daily less...."

Isabella Macdonald Alden died August 5, 1930, at the age of eighty-nine in Palo Alto, California, where she and her husband had moved in 1901.

The following year *Memories of Yesterdays*, her last book, edited by Grace Livingston Hill, was published. In the foreword Grace describes her aunt:

"I thought her the most beautiful, wise and wonderful person in my world, outside of my home. I treasured her smiles, copied her ways and listened breathlessly to all she had to say....

"I measured other people by her principles and opinions and always felt that her word was final. I am afraid I even corrected my beloved parents sometimes when they failed to state some principle or opinion as she had done."

As Grace was growing up and learning to read, she devoured her aunt's stories "chapter by chapter. Even sometimes page by page as they came hot from the typewriter; occasionally stealing in for an instant when she left the study, to snatch the latest page and see what had happened next; or to accost her as her morning's work was done, with 'Oh, have you finished another chapter?'

"And often the whole family would crowd around, leaving their work when the word went around that the last chapter of something was finished and going to be read aloud. And how we listened, breathless, as she read and made her characters live before us."

In *A New Graft on the Family Tree*, you will meet Louise Morgan, a young bride determined to reach her new in-laws with the love of God. It is our hope that, like the thousands of families who read Isabella Macdonald Alden's books in her day, you will be influenced by this release from the Alden Collection to "right feeling, right thinking and right living."

Deborah D. Cole

CHAPTER I

WILL IT BLOOM
OR WITHER?

hat in the world are you going to do with all those doilies?"

The speaker was a girl of sixteen — a fair, bright creature with dancing eyes and that alert expression found on the faces of those to whom the future is an interesting and exciting puzzle.

She was intently watching her sister, who knelt before a half-packed trunk, trying to solve that old problem — how to get twice as much into a trunk as it will reasonably hold. The sister made no answer to the young questioner, for she had just picked up a sheet of paper and was absorbed in its contents. The question was repeated.

"Louise, what do you expect to do with all those doilies?"

"Put them on chairs and sofas," she answered, with a faraway expression in her eyes and a dreamy tone in her voice — studying the paper before her.

The young girl laughed slightly, then her face grew sober. "Louise," she said, hesitating as if she might be on doubtful ground, "has Lewis told you anything about his home and its surroundings?"

"Somewhat, dear." She was still only half-attending to the speaker.

"Well, Addie Dunlap says they live very plainly indeed. She visits the Wheelers, you know, in that vicinity, and she was at their house on two different occasions. She says it is quite isolated from neighbors and is a regular country farmhouse."

This brought a laugh. "What would you have a country farmhouse be but a country farmhouse?"

"Oh, well, Louise, you know what I mean."

If she did she kept the knowledge in silence, and her young sister, after regarding her with a curious look for a moment, drew a heavy sigh.

"It doesn't seem to me that *you* belong to country farmhouses," she said boldly, "with your education and talents. What will you do with them buried among commonplace hills?" She had nearly said *people* but checked herself. "Why should Lewis hide himself in that out-of-the-way place?"

"Well, dear, you know it is a question of health for him. The doctor has told him he must change nearly all his plans in life to protect his health. Besides, farm life agrees with him."

"I don't believe it will with you. I don't like to think of you away off there, miles away from anything to which you are accustomed. Louise, honestly, aren't you afraid you will be homesick?"

Thus solemnly questioned, Louise dropped her engrossing paper and, turning from the trunk, gave the questioner the full benefit of her laughing eyes.

"My dear little grandmother, have you gone and gotten yourself into a fever of anxiety over your young and giddy sister? I'm not a bit afraid of a farmhouse. As for homesickness, of course I shall have that disease. What sort of a heart would it be that could leave such a home as mine without longing for it and the dear faces that belong to it, sometimes many times a day? But, having looked at the matter fairly, it seems to be the right thing to do. And, my troubled little sister, you ought to realize this fully: I am not going 'away off there' alone, but with Lewis Morgan. If I did not love him enough to go to the ends of the earth with him as well as not, I assuredly ought not to marry him."

"And leave Papa and Mama!"

It was impossible not to laugh at the startled, tragic tone in which these words were spoken, as the elder sister repeated them.

"And leave Papa and Mama! And, very important, leave my dear little troubled sister, Estelle. Though it has its sad side, of course, it doesn't seem to be too much of a sacrifice for me to make to be with Lewis. If it did, I should think myself unworthy of him."

How strange! said the younger sister, though she was wise enough this time to say it to herself. I'm sure I don't see how she can do it. Besides Papa and Mama, there is our beautiful home and all the girls and the lectures and the circles and — oh, well, *everything*. According to Addie Dunlap, Louise will just be buried alive, surrounded by snow in winter and haying and harvesting in summer. What is there in Lewis Morgan that should make her want to go? *I* wouldn't like to go anywhere with him. He is nice enough; he is very nice indeed, for that matter. I like him as well, if not better, than any of the young men who call on us. But liking a man and enjoying a half hour's talk with him and going to a lecture or concert with him are one thing. But going away from one's father and mother to spend a lifetime with him is another.

In conclusion to her soliloquy she said aloud, in tones more dismayed than before: "I don't understand it at all! I *never* could go away with Lewis Morgan and leave Papa and Mama and everybody!"

Then the bride-to-be leaned over her open trunk and laughed immoderately. Her young sister's perplexity seemed so funny to her.

"Of course you couldn't, you dear child," she said, when she could speak. "You aren't expected to want to go away from Papa and Mama and live with Lewis Morgan, though I hope you will come and live with us half the time. Farms are very nice places for spending the summer, Estelle. But you mustn't wear a woebegone face over me and think of me as making a sacrifice. If you ever give your heart to a good, true man, you will be entirely willing to go away with him, and, until you are, you must never think of taking marriage vows. Of course you don't understand it, dear; you are much too young. I hope it will be many a year before the thing will seem possible to you."

"It will *never* seem possible," Estelle said stoutly. "I'll never love any man enough to leave Papa and Mama. If that's what I must do to be married, I shall have to be an old maid, for that is all nonsense. I know no man on earth could tempt me to do it."

"Very well," said the bride in much composure, "I'm glad you think so; it is the best way to feel. To be sure, people change their minds sometimes, but at your age it is much the nicest thing to think. Meanwhile, dear, don't you worry about those doilies. I shall find places for them, where they will set the nice old-fashioned rooms aglow with their beauty. I am glad I have so many. Now do you suppose that ebony box would fit in this niche? I would like to take it with me, because we shall keep this trunk with us all the time."

Louise hasn't the least idea how farmhouses look, especially that one, Estelle said again to herself. I wonder if she has the slightest notion how her future brother-in-law looks? Lewis Morgan indeed! I wish he had stayed in Australia! And with another sigh the troubled young sister went in search of the ebony box.

This was not the first time that Louise Barrows had been called upon to vindicate the comforts of her future home. Her father had demurred and hesitated and argued the question with his prospective son-in-law, and the mother had shed some tears in secret over the thought that the daughter of whom she was so proud had chosen so obscure and prosaic a future.

"Think of her getting up at four o'clock in the morning to look after the butter and milk and get breakfast for the workmen!" she had said to her husband in their confidential talks.

"There are worse lots in life than that, I suppose," he had answered.

But he had sighed as heavily as the younger daughter always did when she thought about it, and he had wished from his inmost heart that things had shaped differently. Still he tried to comfort his wife. "He is Louise's own choice, and he is a good Christian man with strong, solid principles. It might have been much worse."

"Oh, yes," the mother assented, "he is a Christian man." The tone in which she said it might almost have justified you in expecting her to add, "but that doesn't amount to much." What she did say was: "But what can Louise do for herself or others, buried alive out there? She is eminently designed for usefulness. You know as well as I that she would grace any circle and that she is a leader among her set; she leads in the right direction, too, which is more than can be said of most girls. But what chance will she have to develop her talents?"

"That's true," the father said, and then he sighed again. Yet these Christian parents had prayed for their daughter every day since she was born, and they professed assured confidence in the belief that God guides His children and answers prayer. Still their faith did not reach high enough to get away from a lurking belief that the Guide of their daughter's life had made a mistake in setting her future among such surroundings. Not that they put the thought into such words; that would have been irreverent. But what did their sighs and regrets mean?

It was rather hard on the prospective bride, even though her parents were wise enough to say almost nothing about their regrets, now that the question was settled. But she felt it in the atmosphere. Besides she had to encounter a like anxiety from another source.

Only the evening before Estelle's cross-examination, Lewis Morgan himself, getting up from one of the luxurious easy chairs that abounded in the Barrows parlors, crossed over to the mantel. Resting his elbow on its edge and his forehead on his hand, he looked down from his fine height on Louise as she nestled in a brown plush chair that harmonized with her soft, rich dress and contrasted with her delicate skin. The gazer beheld a lovely picture, which seemed but to heighten his perplexity.

"After all, Louise," he said, "I don't know but we made a mistake in planning as we did. Somehow, out in Australia where *my* planning was done, the contrast between your present home and our future one was not so sharply defined before me as it is here."

"Shut your eyes, then," said Louise, "and imagine

yourself back in Australia, when you have any planning to do. That is quite as near as I want you to get to that barbarous country again."

Lewis Morgan laughed, and then immediately his brow clouded. "But, Louise, there is a fitness in things, and you fit right in here. Everything matches you." His eyes gave a swift journey up and down the room, taking in its soft and harmonizing furnishings: the richness and glow of the carpet, the delicacy and grace of the lace curtains, the air of ease in the placement of the elegant furniture. Rare paintings looked down on him from the walls, which glowed in the gaslight. His eyes traveled back to the small, graceful figure in the brown chair.

"Louise, you are entirely unfamiliar, you know, with country life, and I don't believe I can give you the least idea of the sharp and trying contrasts."

"Then don't try. Wait, and let me see them for myself."

"Yes, but what if we wait until it is too late to rectify mistakes? Though, for that matter, we can change our plans, of course. But I am really afraid it is a mistake. I seem to feel it more tonight than ever before."

"Lewis," said the little brown-clad figure, "do you really think I am a bird of bright plumage that must have a gilded cage and downy nest and nothing else?"

He looked down on her with unutterable admiration in his eyes.

"Oh, you know very well," he said, half smiling, "that I think you are everything that any mortal woman can be and possibly a little more. But, well, it is not only the house and surroundings, though they are rude and plain enough. I am afraid that you and my mother will not understand each other. She is old-fashioned and peculiar. She is a good mother, and I love and respect her. But, Louise, she is not in the least like your mother, and I am not sure that she will have an idea in common with you."

"Yes, she will. We shall both bestow an undue amount of admiration on, and take an absurd degree of comfort in, your tall self."

He laughed again and shook his head. "I doubt whether even there you will not be disappointed. My mother has a strong, warm love for her family, but she doesn't show it in the way to which you have been accustomed. She is reserved and pent up. She will sit up with my little sister Neelie six nights in succession, but she never caresses and kisses her as your mother does Estelle."

"Never mind," said Louise. "It is not natural for some people to kiss and caress. The sitting up is the most important matter, after all, especially when one is sick — though I will own that I am sorry for poor Neelie without the kisses. Perhaps we can work together. Your mother will do the patient caring for, and I will do the kissing. How will that work?"

"I see you are bent on making everything shine with the brightness of your own spirit. But really and truly I am afraid I have been dreaming a wild dream in supposing that I could transplant you to such a rough atmosphere. It was ridiculous of my father to put in the proviso that we must live at home. I ought to have resisted it. My having to spend my days out of doors working on a farm is no reason why we shouldn't have a home of our own. I think my father is abundantly able to give us a separate start, if he only saw the matter in that light."

"But since he doesn't, we must like dutiful children try to see it in his light, until such time as we can win him over to our notions or become full

converts to his. I know all about it, Lewis. I don't
expect to walk in a garden of roses all the time. I
know, too, that to go into farm life is a trial to you.
All your plans were in another channel. Yet I am
more than glad to give up all those rose-colored
plans for the sake of seeing you look at this moment
as strong and well as your summer on a farm has
made you. I fully intend to be happy on that farm. I
shall have to make a confession to you. Papa talked
seriously to me about trying to rent a farm and stock
it for us, and do you know I opposed it?"

"I should think so," said Lewis Morgan hastily.
"He ought not to spare the money from his business.
And besides, it would be unjust, in his situation."

"Well, I didn't enter into that part of it. I simply
said that I thought your duty to your father obliged
you to yield to his very decided wishes in this matter
and that you and I were both resolved on a thorough
trial of it. And, really, I don't expect any dreadful
consequences. I want to try living with my mother-
in-law and have a thoroughly good time in doing it.
And, Lewis, there is one subject on which we surely
can agree. You forget the most important one of all."

He shook his head, and his voice was low and sad.
"No, I don't, Louise. But you are mistaken on one
count: Not one of the family, except for me, is a
Christian."

The first shadow of the evening flitted across the
face of his bride-to-be. At last he had startled her.

CHAPTER II

THE TREE

ppealing to your Father in heaven to witness your sincerity, do you, Lewis, now take this woman whose hand you hold, choosing her alone from all the world, to be your lawfully wedded wife? Do you trust her as your best earthly friend? Do you promise to love, cherish and protect her; to be considerate of her happiness in your plans of life; to cultivate for her sake all manly virtues, and in all things to seek her welfare as you seek your own? Do you pledge yourself thus honorably to be her husband in good faith, so long as God in His providence shall spare you to each other?

"In like manner, looking to your heavenly Father for His blessing, do you, Louise, now receive this man, whose hand you hold, to be your lawfully wedded husband? Do you choose him from all the world, as he has chosen you? Do you pledge your trust to him as your best earthly friend? Do you promise to love, to comfort and to honor him; to cultivate for his sake all womanly graces; to guard his reputation and assist him in his lifework and in all things to esteem his happiness as your own? Do you give yourself thus trustfully to him to be his wife in good faith so long as the providence of God shall spare you to each other?"

The old story, repeated so many hundreds of times since the world was new — and yet so new a story to each one who becomes an actor in it that it hastens the pulse and pales the cheek.

Estelle Barrows, alert, eager and keen-eared, listened with flushing cheeks and quickened breathing to the interchange of solemn vows. She shivered over the intimacy of the promises and marvelled at the clear steadiness of her sister's voice as she answered, "I do." The same skeptical spirit was in Estelle that had governed her during her talk with her sister. She could not yet see how such things were possible.

It was all very well for Lewis to promise to trust Louise as his "best earthly friend." Of course that's what she was. To promise to love, cherish and protect her — it was the least he could do after she had given up so much for him. "To be considerate for her in his plans for life." Estelle almost thought that he ought to have hesitated over that promise. *Had* he been considerate? Did he think that home in the faraway farmhouse would be conducive to her happiness? He doubtless meant his best, and it was right enough for him to ring out his "I do" in a strong manly voice.

But for Louise, how could she say *he* was her best earthly friend, with Papa looking down on her from his sheltering height and Mama struggling to hold back the tears? How could she promise to assist him in his lifework? Suppose his entire life had to be spent on that hateful farm — must Louise bury herself there and assist him? How would she do it? Would he expect her, sometime, to milk the cows?

Estelle had heard that farmers' wives did these things. Or could Louise be expected to churn the butter or work it or mold it to be ready for market and then to drive into town on a market-wagon and barter her rolls of butter for woolen yarn to knit him some socks? Estelle had stood with a sort of terrified fascination at one of the busy corners of the city, only the day before, and watched a market-woman clamber down from the high seat of her wagon, take a pail of butter on one arm and a basket of eggs on the other and tramp into the store. Afterward she had told it to Louise, who laughed merrily over the discomforted face and asked if the woman did not look rosy-cheeked and happy.

All these and a hundred other commingling and disturbing thoughts floated through Estelle's brain as she watched the quiet face of her sister during the ordeal of marriage. Even after the hopelessly binding words "I pronounce you husband and wife" had been spoken, she still stood, gazing and wondering. She could never, never do it. Marriage was nice enough in the abstract, and she liked to go to weddings — at least she had always liked to before this one. But to single out one man and make him the center of all these solemn and unalterable vows!

Louise seemed entirely unconscious of the necessity for any such mental turmoil on her account. She looked as serenely sweet and satisfied in her white silk robes as she had in the simple gold-brown that had been one of her favorite home dresses. Oh, yes, she was in white silk and bridal veil and orange blossoms. The blinds were closed and the heavy curtains dropped, although it was midday, and the blaze of the gas lighted up the scene; and there was a retinue of bridesmaids in their white robes and their ten-buttoned kid gloves. There were all the *et ceteras* of the modern fashionable wedding!

All these things fitted as naturally into the every-day life of the Barrows family as hard work and scanty fare fit into the lives of so many others. They had not discussed the question at all but had accepted all these minor details as inevitable and made them ready. Mrs. Barrows came from an aristocratic and wealthy family; so also did the father. The family's surroundings and associations had been connected with wealth and worldliness. And, although they were considered among their set to be remarkably plain and economical people, viewed from Lewis Morgan's standpoint, they were so lavish in their expenditures that he knew his father would have denounced their actions as unpardonable.

Isn't it a pity that in this carping world we cannot often put ourselves in other people's places — mentally, at least? Then we might try to discover how we should probably feel and talk and act were we surrounded by their circumstances and influenced by their education. Something of this Lewis Morgan had done. It might almost be said that he occupied halfway ground between the rigid plainness of his country home life and the luxurious ease of his wife's city home life. He had been out into the world and had seen both sides, and his nature was broad enough and deep enough to distinguish between people and their surroundings. Therefore, while he admired and respected Mr. Barrows, he respected and loved his father, who was the very antipodes of his city brother.

Hundreds of miles away from the gaslights and glamour of orange blossoms and bridal veils and wedding favors, on a bleak hillside stood a plain, two-story frame house, surrounded by ample barns.

The barns showed in their architecture and design a more comfortable finish for the purposes for which they were intended than the simple, unpainted house had ever shown. There was even a sense of beauty, or at least of careful neatness, in the choosing of the paints and the general air of the buildings that the house lacked. Whatever Jacob Morgan thought of his family, it was quite apparent that he had a big opinion of his stock.

Within this square, solemn-looking house on a certain dull and solemn fall evening sat the Morgan family, gathered apparently for a special occasion. Although every one of them, down to the old gray cat purring behind the great wood stove, tried to act as usual, a general air of expectancy, indescribable yet distinct, pervaded the room.

The room by the way deserves a passing description. It was at once the sitting room, dining room and kitchen of the Morgans. It was large and square and scrupulously clean. A table with its great leaves turned down was pushed up against the north side of the room and was spread with a dark, flowered, shiny oilcloth over its surface, reaching down nearly to the floor. On the oiled surface a candlestick held a substantial tallow candle.

The flickering light showed Mother Morgan where to put the point of the great darning needle as she solemnly wove it in and out of the gray sock drawn up on her labor-roughened hand. The old-fashioned tray and snuffers stood beside the candlestick. A dreary-faced girl in a dark calico dress, closely buttoned at the throat and collarless, occupied herself in applying the snuffers at regular intervals to the black wick that rapidly formed.

Occasionally the mother hinted that it was a very shiftless way to spend her time and that she would be better off getting out her mending or her knitting. But the girl, with a restless sort of half sigh, replied that she "couldn't mend or knit tonight."

"And why not tonight, as well as any time?" questioned Mrs. Morgan in a half-vexed tone, as one who was fully prepared to combat sentiment or folly of any sort that might have arisen in her daughter's mind.

But the daughter only answered, "Oh, I don't know," and snuffed the candle again.

The darning needle gleamed back and forth in the candle's glow, and no sound broke the stillness for the next ten minutes.

The other furnishings of the room can be described briefly. A square stand in the corner displayed the *Farmer's Companion*, a highly prized weekly paper, and a small copy of Webster's, very much abridged and with one cover gone. A tack in the wall over the stand held the *Farmer's Almanac*, and near it a pasteboard case, gaily decorated with fancy pictures, contained the family hairbrush and comb. The great cookstove, able to hold several chunks of wood at a time, was aglow both with firelight and with polish and was really the only bright and pleasant thing in the room. The floor was painted a good, clear yellow and hadn't even a rug to relieve its bareness.

Behind the stove with his feet on the hearth, his slouched hat pushed back on his head and his pants tucked carefully into his barnyard boots sat the younger son of the family, John Morgan. His hands were shoved into his pockets, and his eyes were fixed somewhat gloomily on the fire.

Just across from him, occupying the other corner of the fireplace, was the father of the family, a bent, prematurely old-looking man. His gray hair stood in disorder on his head — "stood" being the exact word to apply to it, as even vigorous brushing never coaxed it into quietness for any length of time. He was tilted slightly backward in his straight-backed, wooden armchair which boasted of a patchwork cushion and was the only bit of luxury that the room contained.

A few chairs, painted yellow like the floor and with wooden bottoms, kept themselves in orderly condition in the unoccupied corners of the room. They completed its furnishings — unless one included a shelf on the back of the stove where a row of milk pans was stationed waiting for the cream to set; a line on which hung certain towels used in cleaning and drying; the pans; and a hook at a little distance holding the family hand towel.

Sundry other hooks were empty. The sixteen-year-old daughter had taken counsel with herself and then had quietly moved two coats and a pair of overalls to the back kitchen closet.

A door leading into the small, square, bare-floored bedroom of Jacob Morgan and his wife stood open and revealed the six-year-old baby of the family. Fair-haired, soft-faced Neelie Morgan's eyes were wide open and aglow with an excitement which she could not control. Except for the solemn rule that at seven o'clock she must be found in bed, no matter what was happening — even if the town three miles away was on fire — she would have begged to stay out of that trundle bed on this particular evening just one hour more.

John Morgan winked and blinked and nodded assent to his dream thoughts with his mouth wide open. Then he came down on the four legs of his chair with a sudden thud that made him wide awake and rather cross. He looked at the tall, loud-voiced old clock in the corner, which was certainly part of the furniture — and the most important part; it is strange I should have forgotten it. At this moment it was making up its mind to announce the advent of the next hour.

"It seems a pity that Lewis couldn't have come around at a little more seasonable hour," Farmer Morgan said at last, rubbing his eyes and yawning heavily and gazing at the solemn-faced clock. "I can't see why he couldn't just as well have taken an earlier train and gotten here this afternoon. It will be getting-up time before we fairly go to bed."

"I don't see any occasion for being very late to bed," Mrs. Morgan said. She drove the gleaming needle through the sock as though she were vexed at the yawning hole. "We needn't sit up till morning to talk. There will be time enough for that. So long as Lewis went to the expense of getting supper at the village we won't have to be hindered on that account."

"I'm awful glad he did," interposed the candles-nuffer. "I couldn't bear to think of getting supper and washing dishes right before her."

"I wonder why not? She most likely has been used to dishes, and she knows they have to be washed. It isn't worthwhile to go to putting on airs before her, so long as you can't keep them on. The dishes will probably have to be washed three times a day, just as they always have been. Because Lewis has gotten married, the world isn't going to stop turning around."

How fast the darning needle slipped through the hole, shrinking it at every turn and stabbing its sides with great gray threads.

"I 'most wonder why you didn't put a fire in the front room; being it was the first night it would have been less, well — less embarrassing like," the farmer said, hunting in his brain for the right word and apparently not finding it.

"I don't know as there is any call to be embarrassed," Mrs. Morgan said, and the furrows in her face seemed to deepen. "I thought it was best to begin as we would have to hold out, and I didn't s'pose we would be likely to have fires in the front room in the evenings now anymore than we have had. This room has always been large enough and good enough for Lewis, and I suppose we can make a place for one more."

But she looked that moment as though the "one more" were a sore trial to her, which she endured simply because she must, and out of which she saw no hint of comfort.

During this family discussion John Morgan kept his feet in their elevated position on the upper hearth and continued his steady, gloomy gaze into the fire. He was a young man not yet twenty, but already his face looked dismal and spiritless. It was not in every sense a good face. There were lines of sullenness upon it, and there were lines which, even this early, might have been born of dissipation.

Mrs. Morgan had been heard to say many a time that Lewis was a good boy, had always been a good boy, but who John took after was more than she could imagine. He wasn't a mite like the Morgans, and she was sure he didn't favor her side of the house.

But, truth to tell, Lewis Morgan had at last disappointed his mother. Of course, he would get married sometime; it was the way with young men. But he was still quite a young man, and she had hoped that he would wait a few years. And then she had hoped that, when the fatal day did come, he would choose one of the good, sensible, hardworking farmer's girls with which the country abounded, any one of whom would have esteemed it an honor to be connected with the Morgan family.

But to go to New York for a wife and then to plunge right into the midst of aristocracy and actually bring away a daughter of Lyman Barrows, whose brother was a congressman and whose father was once high in power in Washington — ? Mrs. Morgan felt aggrieved. Farmers and farmers' wives and daughters had always been good enough for her. Why weren't they for her son?

This matter of family pride is a very odd thing to encounter. You'll probably not find it so strongly developed anywhere in this country as it is among the thrifty and intelligent classes of farmers. To be sure, there are different manifestations of pride. And Mrs. Morgan knew how to manifest hers.

"There they come!" declared Dorothy. Her face grew red, and she dropped the snuffers into the tray with a bang. It was just as the old clock had finally made up its mind to speak, and it solemnly tolled out eight strokes.

"Dorothy!" said she of the darning needle, severely, "I am ashamed of you. There is no occasion for you to go into hysterics, if they *have* come."

The feet on the upper hearth came down with a louder bang than the snuffers had made. "I'm going to the barn," said their owner promptly. "Lewis will want to have his horse taken care of, and I don't want to see none of 'em tonight. You needn't call me in, for I ain't coming."

He dodged out at the back door, just as the front door opened and a shoving of trunks sounded on the oilcloth floor of the great old-fashioned hall. As Lewis Morgan's voice called out cheerily, "Where are you all?" the mother rolled up the stocking and stabbed it with the darning needle, shook out her checkered apron and stood up to greet them. Louise Morgan had reached her home.

CHAPTER III

INTRODUCED

ow Louise, despite all her previous knowledge of the Morgan family, had done just as people always do: planned their reception at the old homestead after the manner of life to which she had been accustomed, instead of from the Morgan standpoint. She had imagined her husband folded in his mother's arms, his bearded face covered with motherly kisses.

It is not reasonable to suppose that she will care to kiss *me*, she had said to herself. But I will give her one little, quiet kiss to show her how dear Lewis's mother is to me, and then I will keep myself in the background for the first evening. They will be so glad to get Lewis back that they will not have room for much notice of me.

Kisses! Hardly anything could be more foreign to Mother Morgan's life than those. It was actually years since she had kissed her grown-up son. She held out her bared, old hand to him, and her heart beat quickly. She felt a curious tremble all over her that she would have been ashamed to admit, but with a mighty effort she controlled her voice. "Well, so you have got back safe, with all your rampaging around the world; I should think you had had enough of it. And this is your wife."

Then Louise had felt the quick grasp and release of her hand and had not realized the heart beats.

Lewis had shaken hands with his father and his sister Dorothy and had said: "Father, this is my wife."

The old-looking man, with the prematurely gray hairs standing up all over his head, had nodded to her without even a handclasp. "I'm glad you are safe at home. You must be tuckered out; traveling is worse than plowing all day. I never could see why folks who hadn't *got* to do it should take journeys."

This was the homecoming! Two nights before, they had spent in the old home in New York, stopping there overnight, after a two weeks' absence in another direction. How the mother had clasped her to her heart and cried over her. How the father had called her his "precious daughter" and wondered, with a quiver in his lips and a tremble in his voice, how they could let her go again! How Estelle — bright, beautiful, foolish Estelle — had hugged and caressed and rejoiced over her darling sister! What a contrast it was! It all came over her just then, standing alone in the center of that yellow-painted floor — the tremendous, far-reaching, ever-developing contrast between the home that had vanished from her sight and the new home to which she had come. She felt a strange, choking sensation as if a hand were grasping at her throat. The dim light in the tallow candle gleamed and divided itself into many sparks and seemed swinging in space. But for a strong and resolute determination to do no such thing, the bride would have made her advent into the Morgan household a thing of vivid memory by fainting away!

"Lewis!" called a soft, timid voice from somewhere in the darkness. Looking out at them from the bedroom door, poor little Neelie, with her shining eyes and her beating heart, could endure it no longer. She was frightened at her boldness and dipped her yellow head under the sheet the minute the word was out; yet she had spoken that one low, eager word.

"Oh, Neelie!" Lewis had exclaimed. "Are you awake? Louise, come and see Neelie."

Indeed she would. Nothing in life looked as inviting to his young wife at that moment as the darkness and comparative solitude of that inner room. But Lewis had seized the tallow candle as he went. Dorothy, meanwhile, had roused sufficiently to produce another one. As Louise followed him, she caught a glimpse of the shining eyes and the yellow curls. A whole torrent of pent-up longing for home and love and tenderness flowed out in the kisses which were suddenly lavished on astonished little Neelie, as Louise gathered the child in her arms.

"She looks like you, Lewis," was the only comment she made. Lewis laughed and flushed and told his wife she was growing alarmingly complimentary. Neelie looked from one to the other of them with great, earnest, soulful eyes and whispered to Lewis that she loved her *almost* as much as she did him, with a long-drawn breath on the word "almost" that showed the magnitude of the offering in honor of his new wife. On the whole it was Neelie who sweetened the memory of the homecoming and stayed the tears that might have wet Louise Morgan's pillow that night.

As for John, he stayed in the barn as he had planned, until the newcomers were fairly out of sight above the stairs.

"He is a queer fellow," explained Lewis to his wife, as they went about their own room. "I hardly know how to take him. I don't think I have ever understood his character; I doubt if anybody does. He is pent up. There is no getting at his likes or dislikes, and yet he has strong feelings. He has given my father a good many anxious hours already. Sometimes I fear many more are in store for him from the same source."

And Lewis sighed. Already the burden of home life was falling on him.

Louise was by this time so divided between the loneliness that possessed her and the curiosity over every article in and about her room that she could not give to the subject of John the interest it demanded. The room was utterly unlike any she had ever seen before. A brilliant carpet, aglow with alternate stripes of red and green, covered the floor. Louise looked at it with mingled feelings of curiosity and wonder. How had it been made and where? How did it happen she had never seen a pattern like that before? It didn't occur to her that it was homemade; if it had, she would not have understood the term.

The two windows to the room were shaded with blue paper, partly rolled and tied with red cord. A wood fire was burning in a Franklin stove; it snapped and glowed and lighted up the strange colors and fantastic figures of the wallpaper. Two comfortable, old chairs sat in one corner.

A high-post bedstead was curtained at its base by what Louise learned was a valance, though its name or use she could not have told on this evening. The bed itself was a marvel of height; it looked to the bewildered eyes of the bride as though they might need a stepladder to mount it. And it was covered with a tulip quilt! This was also knowledge acquired at a later date. What the strangely shaped masses of color were intended to represent she hadn't the slightest idea.

A very simple dressing table was covered neatly with a towel and had the most common toiletries. A high, wide, deep-drawered bureau and a pine-framed mirror, perhaps a foot wide and less than two feet long, completed the furnishings, except for a couple of patchwork footstools under the windows.

Lewis set down the candlestick on the little dressing table and surveyed his wife with a curious, half-laughing air, behind which was hidden an anxious, questioning gaze. "My mother has an intense horror of the new invention known as kerosene" was his first explanatory sentence, with a comical side glance toward the blinking candle.

"Kerosene," said Louise absently. Her thoughts were so confused that she could not pick them out and answer clearly. "Doesn't she like gas?" And then the very absurdity of her question brought her back to the present. She looked up quickly into her husband's face. Struggling with the pent-up tears, she burst instead into a low, sweet, ringing laugh. He joined in, and their laughter swelled until the low ceilings might almost have shaken over their mirth.

"Upon my word, I don't know what we are laughing at," he said at last. But she's a brave little woman to laugh, he said to himself, and I'm thankful to be able to join her.

He pushed one of the patchwork footstools very close to where she had sunk on the other and sat down beside her. "It is all as different as candlelight from sunlight, isn't it? That blinking little flame over there on the stand furnished me with a simile.

"I haven't done a thing to this room," Lewis continued, "mainly because I didn't know what to do. I realized the absurdity of trying to put New York into

it, and I honestly didn't know how to put anything
into it. I thought you would. Actually, I don't know
but what it fits country life. It has always seemed to
me a nice, pleasant room. But, well — well, the simple truth is, Louise, there is something the matter
with it now that you are in it. It doesn't fit you. But
you will know how to repair it, won't you?" An
anxious look in his eyes, almost a tremble in his voice
and the laughter gone out of them so soon — they
nerved Louise to bravery.

"We will not rearrange anything tonight," she said
brightly. "We are too tired for planning. That great
bed is the most comfortable thing I can think of — if
we can only manage to get into it! What makes it so
high, Lewis?"

Whereupon he laughed again, and she joined in —
laughing in that nervous way which, hilarious as the
laughter appears, for some is but one step from tears.
And thus it was that the first evening under the new
roof was spent.

John, coming from his hiding place and tiptoeing
up the stairs in stocking feet, heard the outburst.

"They feel very fine over it," he muttered sourly,
curling his lip. "I hope it will last."

The poor fellow had not the remotest idea that
it would. Boy that he was, John Morgan was at
war with life. He believed that it had treated him
poorly — that to his fortunate elder brother had
fallen all the joy and to him all the bitterness. He was
jealous because of the joy. He was not sure but he
almost hated his brother's wife. Her low, clear laugh,
as it rang out to him, sounded like mockery; he could
almost make his warped nature believe that she was
laughing at him, though she had never seen him and
perhaps never even heard of him. If she had seen his
face at that moment, doubtless her thoughts would

have been of him; as it was, they revolved around the Morgan family.

"What about your sister Dorothy?" she asked her husband, diving into the bewilderments of the large trunk, in search of her toiletry case.

"Dorothy is a good, warmhearted girl, who has no — well — ," and then he stopped. He did not know how to finish his sentence. It would not do to say she had no education, for she had been the best scholar in their country school and, during her last winter, was reported to have learned all that the master could teach her.

Dorothy had been disappointed, it is true, that the master had not known more, and Lewis had been disappointed because he wanted her to go on, or go elsewhere and get — what? He didn't know. Something his wife had to her very fingertips and Dorothy had not a trace of — what was the name of it? Was it to be learned from books? He had wanted her to try, and she had been willing enough, but Farmer Morgan had not.

"She has book-learning enough for a farmer's daughter," he had said firmly. "She knows more about books now than her mother ever did. If she makes one-half as capable a woman, she will be ahead of all the women nowadays."

So Dorothy had packed away her books and settled down to her churning and baking and dishwashing. She took it quietly and patiently. Lewis did not know whether her disappointment was very great or not; in truth, he knew very little about her. Of late, he had known almost nothing of home.

Lewis seemed unable to add to his unfinished sentence. He bent over the valise and gave himself to unpacking, slightly puzzled though, as if he were trying to solve a problem that eluded him. His wife tried again.

"Lewis, why isn't she a Christian?"

Now, indeed, he dropped the coat he was unrolling and, rising up, gave the questioner the full benefit of his troubled eyes. He was under the impression that he was pretty well acquainted with his wife; yet she certainly asked the most peculiar-sounding questions, perplexing to answer and yet simple and straightforward enough in their tone.

"Why isn't she?" he repeated. "I don't know. My dear Louise, how *could* I know?"

"Well, doesn't it seem strange that a young lady in this day, surrounded by Christian influences, should go on year after year without settling that question?"

Lewis gave his answer very thoughtfully. "It seems exceedingly strange, when I hear you speak of it, but I do not know that I ever thought of it in that sense before."

Then the unpacking went on in silence for a few minutes until Louise interrupted it with another question. "Lewis, what does she say when you talk with her about these matters? What line of reasoning does she use?"

It was so long before she received an answer that she turned from her work in surprise to look at him.

Then he spoke. "Louise, I never said a word to her on this subject in my life. And that seems stranger to you than anything else?" he added at last, his voice low and anxious.

She smiled gently. "It seems a little strange to me, Lewis — I shall have to own. But I suppose it is different with brothers and sisters from what it is when two are thrown together constantly as companions. I have no brother, you know."

Do you know what Lewis thought of then? His brother, John.

CHAPTER IV

FROM DAWN TO DAYLIGHT

ouise had awakened suddenly the next morning, not a little startled at what she supposed were unusual sounds, issuing from all portions of the house in the middle of the night. They dressed by the light of the blinking tallow candle.

"Do you suppose anyone is sick?" she asked her husband. "There has been a banging of doors and a good deal of hurrying around for some minutes."

"Oh, no," he reassured her. "It's time to get up. John is a noisy fellow, and Dorothy can make considerable noise when she wants to. I suspect they are trying to rouse us."

"Time to get up! Why, it must be in the middle of the night!"

"That depends on whether one lives in New York or in the country. I shouldn't be greatly surprised if breakfast were waiting for us."

"Then let's hurry," said Louise, pushing back the bed covers. But Lewis ordered her back to her pillow, while he made vigorous efforts to conquer the Franklin stove and bring some warmth into the room.

"But we ought not to keep them waiting breakfast," Louise said in dismay. "That is very disagreeable, when everything is ready to serve. We have been annoyed in that way ourselves. Lewis, why didn't you waken me before? Haven't you heard the sounds of life for a good while?"

"Yes," said Lewis, "longer than I wanted to hear them. If they don't want breakfast to wait, they shouldn't get it ready at such an unearthly hour. There is no sense in rousing the whole household in the night. During the busy season it is sort of necessary, and I always succumb to it meekly then. But now it is just the result of an idea, and I have waged silent war on it for some time. I suppose I have eaten cold breakfasts about half the time this fall."

"Cold breakfasts! Didn't your mother keep something warm for you?"

"Not at all. My mother would think she was shirking her duty to her son by winking at his indolent habits. She believes it is his sacred duty to eat his breakfast by early candlelight. If he sins in that direction, it is not for her to smooth the punishment of the transgressor."

Louise laughed over the seriocomic tone in which this was said, even though she was a little dismayed. These things sounded so new and odd and unmotherly!

"Louise, dear, I don't want to dictate the least in the world, and I don't want to pretend to know more than I do, but isn't that dress just a trifle too stylish for the country — in the morning, you know?" This question was put hesitantly to young Mrs. Morgan somewhat later.

Her eyes flashed roguishly as she said: "Part of

that sentence is quite correct, Lewis. You are evidently 'pretending to know more' than you do. This dress was prepared especially for a morning in the country and cost just ten cents a yard."

"Is that possible?" he answered, surveying her from head to foot with a bemused look. "Then, Louise, what do you do to your dresses?"

"Wear them," she answered demurely. "And I shall surely wear this, this morning. It fits perfectly."

Did it? Her husband was in great doubt. He would not have liked to admit it, not even to himself, but in fact he lived in fear of his mother's opinions. She was easily shocked and disgusted. The whole subject of dress shocked her perhaps more than any other. She was almost eloquent over the extravagance, lavish display and waste of time as well as money exhibited in these degenerate days in decorating the body. She even sternly hinted that occasionally Dorothy primped altogether too much for a girl with brains. What would she think of Mrs. Lewis Morgan? he wondered.

The dress that troubled him was a soft, neutral-colored cotton, so common and so unfashionable in the fashionable world that Louise had already horrified her own mother and vexed Estelle by her determination to have several of them. Once purchased she had exercised her taste in making the dresses. The patterns and trimming she selected "fit the material perfectly," Estelle had told her, meaning anything but a compliment.

The dress was simplicity itself; yet the pattern was graceful and fit her to perfection. The dress was finished at the throat with a rolling collar, inside of which was basted a very narrow frill of soft, yellowish lace. The close-fitting sleeves were finished in the same way. A very tiny scarlet knot of narrow ribbon at the throat completed the costume, and the whole effect was such that her husband, surveying her, believed he had never seen her better dressed. He was equally certain his mother would be shocked. The bewildered expression on his face struck his wife as ludicrous.

"Why, Lewis," she asked cheerfully, "what would you have me wear?"

"I don't know, I am sure," he answered, joining her laugh. "Only why should ten-cent goods look like a tea-party dress on you?"

Down to breakfast they went. Almost the first thought the young wife had, as she took in the strange scene, was to wonder what Estelle would say if she could look in on them now!

That great, clean kitchen: the kettle was steaming on the stove and the black "spider" was still sizzling with the ham gravy that was left in it. The large-leaved table was spread with a tablecloth, and queer-shaped, blue earthenware dishes were arranged on it without regard to grace certainly, whatever might be said of convenience. In the middle of the table sat the inevitable tallow candle, and another one blinked on the high mantel piece, bringing out the shadows in a strange, weird way.

Seated at the foot of the table was John in his shirtsleeves, the mild winter morning having proved too trying for his coat. His father was engaged in brushing his few spears of gray hair before the little glass in the further end of the room. Dorothy leaned against the window and waited, looking both distressed and cross.

"Come! come! come!" said the mother of this home, as soon as the stair door had closed after the arrival of her new daughter. "Do let us get down to breakfast. It will be noon before we get the dishes out of the way. Now, Father, have we got to wait for *you*? I thought you were ready an hour ago. Come, Lewis, you must be hungry by this time."

The rich blood mounted to Lewis's cheeks. This was a trying greeting for his wife. He felt exactly as though he wanted to say that he thought it was, but she brushed past him at that moment, laying a cool, little hand for an instant on his. Was it a warning touch? Then she went over to the young man in the shirtsleeves.

"Nobody introduced us," she said in a tone of quiet brightness. "I suppose they think that brother and sister do not need an introduction. I'm Louise, and I'm sure you must be John. Let's shake hands on it." And the small, white hand was stretched out and waiting. What was to be done?

John was prepared to hate her, so well prepared that he already half did so. He never shook hands with anybody, least of all a woman, and never came in contact with one if he could help it. He felt the flush in his face deepen, until he knew he was the color of a peony. Nevertheless, he held forth his hard, red hand slowly and touched the small, white one, which instantly seized it in a cordial grasp. Then they sat down to breakfast.

Louise waited with bowed head, startled with how unlike her home it was, as she waited in vain. No voice expressed its thankfulness for many mercies; instead, the clatter of dishes immediately commenced. "Not one in the family except for me is a Christian," she remembered well Lewis's words. But was he of such little consequence in his father's house that the simple word of blessing would not have been received among them from his lips? It had not occurred to her that, because her husband was the only Christian in the household, he sat at a prayerless table.

Other experiences connected with that first meal in her new home were, to say the least, novel. Curiously enough, her thoughts concerning them all connected themselves with Estelle. What would Estelle think of a young lady who came collarless to the breakfast table? Indeed, more than that, who sat down to eat in her father's and mother's presence with uncombed hair, gathered into a frowzy knot at the back of her neck? What would Estelle have thought of Mrs. Morgan's fashion of dipping her own spoon into the bowl of sugar and then back again into her coffee? How would she have liked to help herself with her own knife to butter, having seen the others of the family do the same with theirs? How would she manage in the absence of napkins, and would the steel forks spoil her breakfast? And how would she like fried ham and potatoes boiled in the skin for breakfast anyway?

The newcomer remembered that she had but three weeks ago assured Estelle that farms were delightful places in which to spend summers! Was she so sure of that, even with this little inch of experience? To appreciate the force of the contrasts, one would need only a picture of the two breakfast tables which presented themselves to the mind of this young wife.

Aside from all these minor contrasts, others troubled her more. She had resolved to be very social and informal with each member of the family, but the formidable question arose: What was she to be social about? There was no conversation — unless Farmer Morgan's directions to John about the farm chores and his answers to Lewis's questions as to what had transpired on the farm during his absence could be called conversation. Mrs. Morgan, it is true, contributed by assuring Dorothy that if she did not clean out the back kitchen *this day* she would do it herself and that the shelves in the cellar needed washing off this very morning.

Whatever it was that had put Dorothy in an ill-humor, or whether it was ill-humor or only habitual sullenness, Louise didn't know. Certainly Dorothy's brows were black. Would it be possible to converse with her? She recalled the merry talk with which Estelle enlivened the home breakfast table. The conversation had been so sparkling and flowing that her father had accused her of setting a special snare for him to cause him to miss his train. If Estelle were at this table what would she talk about? It was a new experience to Louise to be at a loss for words. Books? What had Dorothy read? She did not look as though she had read anything or even wanted to. Sewing? Well, the new sister was skilled with her needle. Suppose she said, "I know how to make my own dresses, and I can cut and fit them. Can you?" How abrupt and peculiar it would sound, especially in the midst of the assembled family! She caught herself on the verge of laughing over the absurdity of the thing, but she was as far from a topic for conversation as ever.

Meanwhile, Lewis had finished his question and turned to her. "Louise, did you ever see anyone milk a cow? I suppose not. If it were not so cold you might like to go out and see Dorothy with her pet cow. She is a queer-acting creature — quite a study."

Did he mean Dorothy or the pet cow? It was clear to his wife that he was embarrassed by something in the breakfast scene. But she caught at his suggestion of a subject, even while his mother's metallic voice was saying, "Cold! If you call this a cold morning, Lewis, you must have gotten very tender since living in the city. It is almost as mild as spring."

"Can you milk?" Louise was meanwhile asking Dorothy eagerly. Her eagerness was not assumed; she was jubilant, not so much over the idea of seeing the milking process, as over the fact that she had finally discovered a question she could address to Dorothy, which must be answered in some form.

But, behold! Dorothy, flushing to her temples, looked down at her plate and answered, "Yes, ma'am," and choked herself on a swallow of coffee. The avenue for conversation suddenly closed.

What was she to do? How queer it was to call such distorted attempts at talk by the pleasant word *conversation*! What "familiar interchange of sentiment" could she hope to get up with Dorothy about milking cows? What did people say about cows anyway? She wished she knew something of the domestic habits of these animals. But she was honestly afraid to venture in any direction, lest she should display an ignorance that would either be considered affected or would sink her lower in the family's estimation. Suppose she tried some other subject with Dorothy. Would she be likely to choke again?

Mrs. Morgan tried to help: "Dorothy milked two cows when she was not yet twelve years old!"

Whether it was the words or the tone or the intention, Louise could not tell, but she immediately felt that not to milk two cows before one was twelve years old argued a serious and irreparable blunder in one's upbringing. She was quiet and meek in her reply: "I never had the opportunity of even seeing the country when I was a little girl, only when we went to the seaside in summers, and that is not exactly like the country, you know. All Mama's and Papa's relatives happened to live in town."

"It must be a great trial to a woman to have to bring up her children in a city. Ten chances to one if they don't get spoiled."

Mrs. Morgan did not say it crossly nor with any intention of nettling her. But again Louise felt it to be almost certain that *she* was thought not to belong to that fortunate "one chance" which was not spoiled.

Other trials were connected with this ordeal. She found it almost impossible for her to pretend to eat. She was one of those unfortunate victims to whom pork in any form was utterly repulsive. Therefore she made not the slightest attempt at eating the generous piece on her plate. While potatoes are good, to a delicate appetite in the early morning a large potato, still in its brown coating, is not especially inviting. There were eggs, but they were fried and covered with the offensive ham gravy.

The bread was doughy and reminded Louise of the wicked episodes of her school days at the badly managed boarding school. One of their pastimes was to make little wads of the doughy bread and surreptitiously throw them at each other. What if she should send a tiny ball of dough directly into Dorothy's red and frowning face! Then she would surely choke. Her own mother might laugh at such undignified folly, but would Mother Morgan? She laughed involuntarily over the astonishment into which she might throw this solemn household by such improprieties and then drooped her head over her coffee cup to hide the laugh. The coffee was hot and strong, too strong, but there was no hot-water urn on the table. She might take her cup to that puffing teakettle and weaken the coffee. Perhaps that would be in keeping with the table proprieties of the household, but what would Estelle think of it! What a difference there was in people and in homes!

She glanced at her husband. He was listening respectfully to his father's opinion of the south meadow lot and the "short-horned critter," whatever that was, that inhabited it. He seemed miles away from her. She wondered vaguely if, when they got upstairs to their own room again, she would have any subject for conversation with him.

Mother Morgan startled her out of her wondering. "I hope you will be able to get enough for breakfast. I suppose our living is not what you have been used to."

What could Louise say? It certainly wasn't, and she certainly couldn't affirm that she liked the Morgans' better.

Her husband turned a troubled look on her. "Can't you eat a little?" he asked in undertone.

Did she imagine it, or was he more anxious that his mother should not be annoyed than he was that her appetite should not suffer? Altogether, the young bride was heartily glad when that uncomfortable meal was concluded and she was back in that upper room. She went alone, her husband having excused himself from his father long enough to go with her to the foot of the stairs and explain that Father wanted him a moment.

Do you think Louise fell into a passion of weeping as soon as the door of her own room was shut or that she wished she had never left the elegance of her city home or the sheltering love of her mother? If you do, you have mistaken her character. She walked to the window a moment and looked out on the stubby, partly frozen meadows that stretched away in the distance. She even brushed away a tender tear, born of love for the old home and the dear faces there. But the tear was chased away by a smile as she waved to her husband, who looked back to get a glimpse of her. She knew then, as she had known before, that it was not hard to "forsake all others and cleave to him." Moreover, she remembered that her marriage vows had brought her more than a wife's responsibilities. She was by the vows made a daughter and a sister to those whom she had not known before. They were not idle words to her in terms of these two relationships. She remembered them, each one: Father Morgan, with his old, worn face and his heart among the fields and barns; Mother Morgan, with her cold eyes and cold hand and cold voice; Dorothy and John and the fair, yellow-haired Neelie, whom a special touch of motherliness had left still sleeping that morning. Remembering them, this young wife turned from the window and, kneeling, presented each one by name and desire to her Elder Brother.

CHAPTER V

BEDS AND BUTTONHOLES

ow to fit in with family life at the Morgan farm was a puzzle for Louise. For the first time, she was in doubt as to how to pass her time. Not that she hadn't enough to do. She was a young woman of infinite resources. She could have locked the door on the world downstairs and, during her husband's absence in the field or the barn, have lived happily in her own world of reading, writing, sewing and planning. But the question was, would that be fulfilling the duties which the marriage covenant laid upon her? How in that way could she contribute to the general good of the family into which she had been incorporated and which she had pledged herself before God to help sustain? On the other hand, how should she set about contributing to the general good? Every avenue seemed closed.

After spending one day in comparative solitude, except for her husband's occasional visits to the upstairs front room, she had resolved the problem. The next morning she lingered in the large kitchen. With a pleasant face and kind voice, she said to Dorothy, "Let me help!" and essayed to help clear the family table — with what a dire result!

Dorothy, thus addressed, seemed as frightened as though an angel from heaven had suddenly descended before her and offered to wash the dishes. In her amazement she let slip one end of the large platter which contained the remains of the ham and a plentiful supply of ham gravy, which trickled and dripped in zigzag lines over the clean, coarse linen that covered the table. Dorothy's exclamation of dismay brought the mother quickly from the bedroom. Then and there she gave Dorothy a short, sharp lecture on carelessness.

"Why did you jump like an idiot because you were spoken to?" she said in severe sarcasm to the blazing-cheeked Dorothy. "I saw you. One would think you had never seen anybody before, nor had a remark made to you. I'd try to act a little more as though I had common sense, if I were you. This makes the second clean tablecloth in a week! Now go right away and wash the grease out, and see if you can't keep from scalding yourself with the boiling water."

Then to Louise she said: "She doesn't need your help. A girl who couldn't clear off a breakfast table alone and wash up the dishes would be a very shiftless sort of creature in my opinion. Dorothy has done it alone ever since she was twelve years old. She isn't shiftless, even if she does act like a dunce before strangers. I'm sure I don't know what has happened to her, to jump and blush in that way when she is spoken to. She never used to do it."

It was discouraging, but Louise, bent on belonging to this household, tried again. "Well, Mother, what can I do to help? Since I am one of the family I want to take my share of the duties. What shall be my work after breakfast? Come now — give me a place in the home army and let me look after my corner. If you don't, I shall go out to the barn and help Father and Lewis!"

But Mrs. Morgan's strong, stern face did not relax; no smile softened the wrinkles or brightened the eyes. "We have always gotten along without any help," she said. Her voice reminded Louise of the icicles hanging at that moment from the sloping roof above her window. "Dorothy and I manage to do pretty near all the work, even in summer time, and it would be queer if we couldn't now, when there is next to nothing to do. Your hands don't look as though you were used to work."

"Well, that depends," said Louise, looking down on the hands that were offending at this moment by their shapely whiteness and delicacy. "There are different kinds of work, you know. I have managed to live a pretty busy life. I don't doubt your and Dorothy's ability to do it all, but that isn't the point. I want to help. Then we shall all get through the sooner and have a chance for other kinds of work." She had nearly said "for enjoyment," but a glance at the face looking down on her changed the words.

Then they waited — the younger woman looking up at her mother-in-law with confident, resolute eyes, full of brightness but also full of meaning; and the older face, taking on a shade of perplexity, as if this were a phase of life which she had not expected and was hardly prepared to meet.

"There's nothing in life that I know of that you could do," she said at last in a slow, perplexed tone. "There are always enough things to be done, but Dorothy knows how, and I know how, and — "

"And I don't," interrupted Louise lightly. "Well,

then, isn't it your duty to teach me? You had to teach Dorothy, and I daresay she made many a blunder before she learned. I'll promise to be as apt as I can. Where shall we commence? Can't I dry those dishes for Dorothy?"

Mrs. Morgan shook her head promptly. "She would break every one of 'em before you were through," she said grimly. "Such a notion she has taken of jumping and choking and spilling things! I don't know what she'll do next."

"Well, then, I'll tell you what I can do. Let me take care of John's room. Isn't that it, just back of ours? I saw him coming from that door this morning. While you are at work down here, I can attend to that, as well as not. May I?"

"Why, there's nothing to do to it" was Mrs. Morgan's prompt answer, "except to spread up the bed, and that takes Dorothy about three minutes. Besides, it is cold in there. You folks who are used to coddling over a fire mornings would freeze to death. I never brought up my children to humor themselves in that way."

Louise, not wishing to enter into an argument about the advantages and disadvantages of warm dressing rooms, resolved to cut the interview short and with a quiet nod of her head and a steady tone replied: "Very well, I shall spread up the bed then, if there is nothing else I can do. Dorothy, remember that is my work after this. Don't you dare to take it away from me."

Lightly spoken indeed, and yet with an undertone of decision in it that made Mrs. Morgan senior exclaim wrathfully, as the door closed after her daughter-in-law: "I do wish she would mind her own business! I don't want her poking around the house, peeking into places, under the name of helping — as if we needed her help! We have got along without her for thirty years, and I guess we can do it now."

But Dorothy was still smarting under the sharpness of the rebuke administered to her in the presence of this elegant stranger and did not in any way indicate that she heard her mother's comments, unless an extra bang of the large plate she was drying expressed her disapproval.

As for Louise, who will blame her that she drew a little troubled sigh as she ascended the steep staircase? And who will fail to see the connection between her thoughts and the action that followed. She went directly to an ebony box resting on her bureau and drew from it a small velvet case. When opened, the little case revealed the face of a middle-aged woman with soft, silky hair, combed smooth and wound in a knot underneath the becoming little breakfast cap, with soft lace lying in rich folds about a shapely throat, with soft eyes that looked out lovingly upon Louise and with lips so tender that even from the picture they seemed ready to speak comforting words.

"Dear mother!" said Louise, as she pressed the picture to her cheek. " 'As one whom his mother comforteth....' Oh, I *wonder* if John could understand anything of the tenderness in that verse?" Then she held back the pictured face and gazed at it. Something in the earnest eyes and quiet expression reminded her of words of help and strength and suggestions of opportunity. She closed the case, humming gently the old hymn "A Charge to Keep I Have," and went in search of broom, duster and sweeping cap. Then she penetrated to the depths of John's room. The Christian character in this young wife actually led her to see a connection between that low-roofed back corner known as John's room and the call to duty which she had just sung:

> A charge to keep I have,
> A God to glorify.

What — through the medium of *John's room*? Yes, indeed. That seemed entirely possible to her. More than that, a glad smile and a look of eager desire shone in her face as she added the lines:

> A never-dying soul to save,
> And fit it for the sky.

What if, oh, what if the Lord of the vineyard had sent her to that isolated farmhouse, to be the link in the chain of events which He had designed to end in the saving and fitting for glory of John Morgan's never-dying soul! Possibly you would have thought it was a sudden descent into the prosaic, if you could have stepped with her into the low-roofed room. Can I describe to you its desolation, as it appeared to the eyes of the cultured lady? She stopped on the threshold, stopped her song and looked with dismay!

The floor was bare. The roof on the eastern side sloped down to within three feet of the floor. One western window, small-paned, hung curtainless. One wooden chair held the inevitable candlestick. The way in which the wick of the candle had been permitted to grow long and gutter down into the grease told a tale of dissipation indulged in the night before of which the watchful mother would have sternly disapproved.

There was not the slightest attempt at furnishings, unless one might call the twisted-legged stand that would not stand without being propped, having a ten-inch square glass hung over it, an attempt. The

bundle of very much tumbled and tangled bed-
clothes in the corner, resting on the four-post bedstead, completed every suggestion of furniture in
that long, low, dark room!

"Poor fellow!" said Louise, speaking her thoughts
aloud, as the scene grew upon her. "Why shouldn't
he 'give his father some troubled hours'? What else
could they expect? How absolutely pitiful it is that
this room and that downstairs kitchen are really the
only places where the young man can spend a leisure
hour! How has Lewis submitted to it?"

Yet, even as she spoke that last sentence, she felt
the cold eyes and remembered the stern mouth of his
mother and realized that Lewis was powerless.

At the same moment I shall have to tell you that
the little newcomer into the home set her lips in that
quiet fashion that she had, which communicated this
sentence to those well acquainted with her: "I shall
not be powerless — see if I will." Somehow you
couldn't help believing that she would not. She had
a very curious time restoring order to that confused
bed. It must be noted that she had never before made
up a husk bed. All her experience of bedmaking had
been with the best quality of hair mattress. This being
the case, the initiated will not be surprised to learn
that Louise tugged off the red and brown patchwork
comforter, which did duty as a spread, three times
before she reduced that bed to the state of levelness
which comported with her ideas.

Then the pillows came in for their share of anxiety.
They were so distressingly small! How did John
manage with such inane, characterless affairs? She
puffed them and tossed them and patted them with
all the skilled touches a good bedmaker could bestow, but to little avail. They were shrinking, shame-
faced pillows still. The coarse factory sheet, not yet

bleached, was laid first in a smooth flat and then artistically rolled under the red and brown comforter. While it looked very unlike what Louise would have desired, yet, when she finished, even with those materials, the bed presented a very different appearance from what it had after undergoing Dorothy's "spreading up."

When the sweeping was concluded, Louise stood and thought. What was to be done with that room? How much would she dare to do? She had determined to make no change in her own room at present. She would not even change the position of the great old bedstead. This was a sacrifice on her part only to be appreciated by those who, on first entering a room, can see by intuition the exact spot where every article of furniture should be placed to secure the best effects and to whom the poor arrangement is a positive pain. Louise had seen, even at that first entrance into her room, that the bed was in the most awkward spot possible, but she heroically left it there. She looked, however, with longing eyes on that twisted table in John's room. How she would have enjoyed selecting one of those strong, white, serviceable doilies and spreading it over the marred top. A book or two, a perfume bottle or some delicate knickknack would give the room a habitable air. For fully five minutes she stood shivering in the cold, trying to determine what more she should do. Then she resolutely shook her head and said aloud: "No, it won't do. I must wait," and went downstairs with her dustpan.

During her short absence the dishes had been whisked into their places, the kitchen made clean, and both mother and daughter were seated at their sewing. Mrs. Morgan eyed the trim figure in sweeping cap and gloves, a broom and dustpan in hand, with no approval in her glance.

"I should think you were a little too much dressed up for such work," she said, producing at last the thought which had been rankling for two days. This was Louise's opportunity.

"Oh, no," she said pleasantly. "I am dressed just right for ordinary work. Why, Mother, my dress cost less than Dorothy's. Hers is part woolen, and mine is nothing but cotton."

This remark brought Dorothy's eyes from their work and fixed them in admiration on the well-dressed lady before her. She was utterly unacquainted with materials and grades of quality and judged a dress only by its effects. It was a bewildering revelation that the dress which to her appeared elegant cost less than her own. There flashed just then into her heart the possibility that some day she, too, might have something pretty.

Louise did not wait for her revelation to be commented upon but drew nearer to the workers. Mrs. Morgan was sewing rapidly on a dingy calico for herself.

"Oh, let me make the buttonholes!" exclaimed the new daughter, as though it were to be counted a privilege. "I can make beautiful ones, and I always made Mother's and Estelle's."

Now it so happened that Mrs. Morgan, with all her deftness with the needle, and she had considerable, was not skilled in that difficult branch of needlework, buttonhole making. Moreover, she considered it an element of weakness and would by no means have acknowledged it. But she hated the work with an absolute hatred. It stemmed from an aversion, strong in such natures as hers, toward anything she could not do as well, if not better, than others. The thought of securing well-made buttonholes, over which she did not have to struggle, came with a sense of rest to her soul. She answered more kindly than Louise had heard her speak before: "Oh, I don't want you to bother with my buttonholes."

"I shall not," said Louise brightly. "Buttonholes never bother me. I like to work them as well as some people like to do embroidery."

Then she went to the sink in the kitchen and washed her hands in the bright tin basin and dried them on the coarse, clean family towel.

Presently Louise came, thimble and needlecase in hand, and settled herself on one of the yellow wooden chairs to make buttonholes in the dingy calico. With the delicate stitches in those buttonholes, she worked an entrance-way into her mother-in-law's heart.

CHAPTER VI

A NEW SERVICE FOR SUNDAY

hat time do you start for church?" Louise asked her husband on Saturday evening, as she prepared for the next morning.

"Well," he said, "it's three miles, you know. We make an effort to get started by about half past nine, though sometimes we are late. It makes hurrying work on Sunday morning, Louise. I don't know how you will like that."

"I shouldn't think there would be room in one carriage for all the family. Is there?"

"Room for all who go," Lewis said gravely.

"All who go! Why, they all go to church, don't they?"

"Why, no. In fact, they *never* all go at one time. They cannot leave the house, you know."

Louise's bewildered look proved that she did not know.

"Why not?" she asked, with wonder in her tone and eyes. "What will happen to the house?"

Despite not wanting to do so, her husband was

obliged to laugh. "Well," he hesitated, "you know they never leave a farmhouse alone and go to church."

"I didn't know it, I am sure. Why don't they?"

"I declare I don't know," and Lewis laughed again. "Possibly it is a notion. Ugly-looking fellows prowl around sometimes, and, well, it's the custom anyway."

"Don't they *ever* close the house and all go away?"

Then Lewis Morgan was nonplussed. Before his eyes distinct memories rose of Thanksgiving days, Christmas days, fair days and gala days of several sorts when the house had been closed and darkened and left to itself from early morning until late into the afternoon. How was he to explain why a thing that was feasible for holidays became impractical on Sunday?

"I'm not sure but that is one of the things that no f-f-fellow can f-f-find out," he said, laughing. "Do you know 'Lord Dundreary'? Seriously, Louise, our family has fallen into the custom of not closing a farmhouse except on special occasions. I suspect the custom sometimes grows out of indifference for church. You remember that none of the family has a real love for the service. It is a source of sorrow to me, as you may suppose. I hope for better things."

Then the talk drifted away into other channels. But in Louise's heart there lingered a minor tone of music over the thought that the next day would be Sunday. Shut away for the first time in her life from the prayer meeting, from the hour of family worship, from constant and pleasant interchange of thought on religious themes, she felt a hunger for it all, such as she had never realized before, and closed her eyes that night with this refrain in her heart: "Tomorrow I shall go to church."

The first conscious sound the next morning was the dripping of the raindrops from the eaves.

"Oh, no," Lewis said, with dismay in his voice, "we are going to have a rainy day!"

A careful, critical look from the eastern window confirmed this opinion, and he repeated it with a gloomy face, adding: "I don't know when the weather has succeeded in disappointing me so much before."

"Never mind," Louise said cheerily. "It will not make much difference. I don't mind the rain. I have a rainy-day suit that Mama used to call my coat of mail. It is impervious to all sorts of weather, and with your rubber coat and a good-sized umbrella we shall do almost as well as though the sun shone."

But her husband's face did not brighten. "It is not personal inconvenience that I fear for you," he said gravely, "but disappointment. The truth is, Louise, I am afraid we can't go to church. This looks like a persistent storm. My father has such a love for his horses, and such a dread of their exposure to these winter storms, that he never thinks of getting them out in the rain, unless it is absolutely necessary. And you know he doesn't consider churchgoing an absolutely necessary thing. Could you bear to be disappointed and stay at home with me all day?"

"Why, yes," said Louise slowly, trying to smile over those two words "with me," — "that is, if it is right. But, Lewis, it seems so strange a thing to do, to stay at home from church all day on account of a little rain that would hardly keep us from a shopping excursion."

"I know," Lewis admitted. "Looking at it from your standpoint it must seem very strange. But all the education of my home has been so different that I do not suppose it even seems as strange to me as to you. Still I by no means approve. As soon as I can arrange for a horse of my own, we will not be tried in this way. Indeed, Louise, I can manage it now. Of course, if I insist on it, my father will yield the point, but he will offer very serious objections. What do you think? Would it be right to press the question against his will?"

"Certainly not," his wife said hastily. "At least," she added, with a bright smile, "I don't suppose the command to obey one's parents is exactly annulled by the marriage service. Anyway, the 'honor thy father and thy mother' never is."

And she put aside her church dress and prepared to do what was to her an unprecedented thing — stay at home from church in full health and strength.

When the question was finally settled that, under the circumstances, it was the proper thing to do, it was by no means a disagreeable way of spending Sunday morning. Since their homecoming, Lewis had been so constantly occupied in carrying out his father's plans for improvements on the farm that Louise had seen little of him. After breakfast, when they returned to their own room, he in his robe and slippers replenished the crackling wood fire and opened the entire front of the old-fashioned stove, letting the glow from it brighten the room. Louise admitted then that the prospect was most inviting.

She drew up her own little rocker, which had traveled with her from her room at home, and settled beside him, book in hand. They had a delightful two hours of social communion, such as they had not enjoyed in weeks before.

The reading and talking that went on in that room, on that rainy Sunday morning, were remembered later as pleasant hours. Occasionally the fact that it was Sunday — and she not at church and a picture of the dear church at home and the dear faces in the family pew and the seat left vacant in the Sunday school room — would shadow Louise's face for an instant; but it brightened again. She had chosen her lot, guided, she believed, by the hand of her Lord. And seldom did a shadow linger on her face.

The Sunday dinner had been eaten, and those two were back again, in the brightness of their enjoyed solitude. The grave, preoccupied look on Louise's face told that her thoughts were busy with something outside of their surroundings — something that troubled her.

"Lewis, what shall we do this afternoon?" she asked him, interrupting a sentence in which he was declaring that a rainy Sunday was, after all, a blessing.

"Do?" he repeated. "Why, we will have a delightful Sunday afternoon talk, with a little reading and a good deal of, well, I don't know just what name to give it — heart rest, perhaps, would be a good one. Aren't you enjoying the day, dear?"

She turned a smiling face toward him. "Yes, with a thoroughly selfish enjoyment, I am afraid. I was thinking of the family downstairs. What can we do to help them, Lewis?"

"Oh!" said her husband, and his face clouded. He seemed to have no other suggestion to offer.

"They didn't look as though they were enjoying the day. I think it must be dreary for Dorothy and John. I wish we could contribute something to make the time seem less lonely to them. Suppose we go down, Lewis, and try what we can."

Her husband looked as though that was the thing of all others which he had the least desire to do.

"My dear Louise," he began slowly, then stopped. Finding that she waited, he began again. "The trouble is, wife, I don't know how we can help any of them. They are not good at talking, and the sort of talk in which John and Dorothy indulge wouldn't strike you as being suited to Sunday. In fact, I don't believe you would join in it. They are used to being at home on Sunday. We are always home from church by this time, and the afternoon is the same to them as it always is. I don't believe we can do anything, dear."

The young Mrs. Morgan did not look in the least convinced. "The afternoon ought not to be the same to them as it always has been, should it, Lewis? *We* have come home, a new element in the family. Surely we ought to have some influence. Can't we find something to say that will do for Sunday? What did you talk about with the family before I came? How did you spend Sunday afternoons?"

"Up here in my room when it wasn't too cold — and sometimes when it was, I went to bed and did my reading and thinking there. I rarely went downstairs on Sunday until milking time. You see, Louise, I really don't know my own family very well. The early age at which I left home, coming back only for a few weeks at a time during vacations and then my travels with Uncle John to Australia — all this has contributed to making me sort of a stranger among them. I doubt whether John and Dorothy feel much better acquainted with me than they do with you. They were both little things when I went away. During this last year, I hardly know what is the matter. Perhaps I haven't gone about it in the right way, but I haven't seemed to make any advances in their direction.

"To be very frank with you, Louise, John is always sullen toward me, and Dorothy acts as though she were half afraid of me. Her foolish jumps and blushes seem so out of place, since she is my own sister, that, I confess to you, I sometimes feel utterly out of patience with her. As for my mother and father, while I honor them as truly unselfish, faithful parents, we do not think alike on many subjects. I am often at a loss as to know how to get along without hurting their feelings, so I shirk being social a good deal and devote myself to myself, or did. Now that I can devote myself to you, I am willing to be as social as you please."

The sentence begun in seriousness he had purposely allowed to become lighter. But Louise held with sweet gravity to her former topic.

" 'Even Christ pleased not Himself,' " she quoted gently. Then she added, "You may imagine how pleasant it is to me to sit here with you for a whole quiet day. Nevertheless, Lewis, let's go downstairs and see if we can't as a family honor the day together."

She had risen as she spoke and had drawn her little rocker away from the stove. Very slowly her husband followed her example, reluctance showing in every line of his face.

"I'll go down with you, if you say so. But I never dreaded to do anything more in my life! I can imagine that it seems a very strange thing to you. But I really and truly don't in the least know what to say when we get down there — that will be in keeping with our ideas of Sunday and will help anybody."

"Neither do I," said Louise quietly. "Since we both feel our unfitness, let's kneel down before we go and ask for the Spirit's guidance. Don't you know He promises: 'Thine ears shall hear a word behind thee saying, This is the way, walk ye in it'? I cannot help thinking that He points us down to that family room. Why shouldn't we ask Him to fill our mouths?"

Without another word and with a strange sense of solemnity about him the young husband turned and dropped upon his knees beside his wife.

A few minutes later those in the kitchen were startled by the unexpected entrance of the young couple. Almost any movement would have startled the quiet that reigned therein.

On a dull day with its scarcity of windows, the kitchen was a dark and dingy spot; the clean and shining stove was the only speck of brightness. The family group was complete. Yet Louise, as she glanced around her taking in their occupations, or *want* of occupations, could not keep from feeling the dullness which their positions suggested. Farmer Morgan, with his steel-bowed spectacles mounted on his forehead, winked and blinked over the weekly paper. Mrs. Morgan sat bolt upright in her favorite, straight-backed chair and held in her hands an old family Bible. Neelie had been dutifully spelling out the words in it until her restlessness had gotten the better of her mother's patience. She had been sent to the straight-backed chair in the corner to sit "until she could learn to stand still and not twist around on one foot and hop up and down when she was reading!" How long would poor Neelie have to "sit" before she learns that lesson?

Dorothy was not one whit less restless and lounged from one chair to another in an exasperatingly aimless way. Several times her mother gave a sharp "Dorothy, why can't you sit still when you get a chance? If you worked as hard as I do all week you would be glad enough for a day of rest." But poor Dorothy was not glad. She hated the stillness and inaction of Sunday. She breathed a sigh of relief when the solemn clock clanged out another hour and even looked forward with a sort of satisfaction to the bustle of the coming wash-day morning.

John was there, as silent and immovable as a statue, sitting in his favorite corner behind the stove. He was in his favorite attitude, boots raised high to the stove hearth, slouched hat on and drawn partly over his eyes, hands in his pockets and a deeper shade of sullenness in his face. So it seemed to Louise. Poor fellow! she thought, with compassion. It is a surprise to me that he doesn't do something awfully wicked. He will do it, too. I can see it in his face, unless —

But she didn't finish her thought. These various individuals glanced up in surprise at the entrance of the two and looked their surprise. Then Farmer Morgan, seeing that they meant to take seats, moved his chair a little and motioned Lewis nearer the stove with the words, "A nasty day — fire feels good."

"Yet it hasn't rained much," Lewis said, watching Louise. Finding that she went over to the unoccupied chair nearest Neelie, he took the proffered seat.

"Rained enough to make mean going for tomorrow; and we've got to go to town in the morning, rain or shine. I never did see the beat of this winter for rain and mud. I don't believe it will freeze up before Christmas."

"You can't get started very early for town," remarked Mrs. Morgan. "There was so much to do yesterday that I didn't get around to fixing the butter, and it will take quite a little spell in the morning. Dorothy didn't count over the eggs and pack 'em, either. Dorothy's fingers were all thumbs by the way she worked yesterday. We didn't get near as much done as usual."

"She and John was about a match, I guess," Farmer Morgan said, glancing at the sullen-browed young man behind the stove. "Yesterday was his unlucky day. About everything you touched broke, didn't it, John?"

"That's nothing new." John growled out this contribution to the conversation between lips that seemed firmly closed. Lewis glanced toward his wife. How would she think they were getting on? What would she think of butter and eggs and accidents as topics for Sunday conversation?

But Louise had put an arm around little Neelie and was holding a whispered conversation with her. At this moment she broke into the talk. "Mother, may this little maiden come and sit on my lap, if she will be very good and quiet? My arms ache for the little girl who used to climb into them at about this hour on Sunday."

CHAPTER VII

A New
Sunday Class

eelie is too big to sit on people's laps," her mother said. "But she can get up, if she wants to and can keep from squirming about like a wild animal and act like a well-behaved little girl."

Though she was considered "too big," Neelie, poor baby, gladly availed herself of the permission and curled in a happy little heap in her new sister's arms, whereupon they commenced a low-toned conversation. Lewis watched her and struggled to think of some way of helping Louise in their intended purpose.

"Have you gotten acquainted with Mr. Butler, Father?"

Andrew Butler was the new minister, and Louise, who had heard his name mentioned, was interested in the answer. Farmer Morgan laid down his newspaper, crossed one leg over the other, tilted his chair back a trifle and was ready to talk.

"Acquainted with him? No, I can't say that I am. He knows my name, and I know his. He says, 'How do you do?' to me when he meets me on the street, if he isn't too deep in thought to notice me at all. I reckon that is about as near as I shall get to an acquaintance. I ain't used to any great attention from ministers, you know."

"I thought possibly he had called during my absence."

"No, he hasn't. When it comes to making a friendly call, we live a good ways out, and the road is bad, and the weather is bad, and it is tremendously inconvenient."

"We always live a good ways out of town, except when there is to be a fair or festival, or doings of some kind, when they want cream and butter and eggs and chickens. Then we are as handy to get at as anybody in the congregation." This came from Lewis's mother.

Lewis could not avoid a slight laugh. The degree of social relations the little church in the village had with its country neighbors was so clearly stated by that last sentence.

"Oh, well," he said, "it is a good ways out for those who have no horses to depend on, and many of the church people are in that condition. As for Mr. Butler, he has been here such a short time that he hasn't gotten around the parish yet."

"No," said his father significantly. "It takes a dreadful long time to get around a small field, especially when there's no special motive for going. But, land! We don't care. To hear us talk, a body would think that we were dreadful anxious for a call. I don't know what he would call for — 'pears to me it would be a waste of time."

"You like his preaching, don't you, Father?"

The farmer tore little strips from the edge of his paper and rolled them thoughtfully between his thumb and finger.

"Why, his preaching is all good enough, I suppose. I never heard any *preaching* that wouldn't do pretty well, considering. It's the *practicing* that I find fault with. I can't find anybody that seems to be doing what the preachers advise. What is the use in preaching all the time, if nobody goes and does it?"

This was Farmer Morgan's favorite topic, as indeed it seems to be a favorite with a great many people: the inconsistencies of the Christian world. It is a fruitful topic, certainly, and it is to be regretted bitterly that such unending sarcasm can arise on that subject. Lewis had heard the same sentiment often before and was met — as, unfortunately, so many of us are — by an instant realization of his own inconsistencies; his mouth had been stopped at once. Today he rallied his waning courage and resolved upon a point-blank question.

"Well, Father, why don't you who understand so well how a Christian ought to live set us an example, and perhaps we will succeed better when we try to copy you?"

This question astounded Farmer Morgan. Coming from a minister, he would have considered it pretty sharp; he would have laughed at it good-naturedly and turned it aside. But coming from his own son and spoken in such a tone of gravity and earnestness that there seemed to be no room left for trifling, it startled him. Lewis had never spoken to him in that direct fashion before. In truth, during all his Christian life at home, Lewis had comforted his heart and excused his conscience with the belief that, in order not to prejudice his father against religion, he would do well to make no personal appeals of any sort. Today, in light of the brief conversation which he had held with his wife and, more than that, in light of the brief prayer in which they had asked the guidance of the Holy Spirit, he began to conclude that he had been a coward.

"Well," his father said, after a moment of astonished silence, "that may be a fair question. But then, after all, it is easily answered. There's folks enough trying at it and making failures without me to swell their number. Till I see somebody who is succeeding a little better than anyone I know, I haven't got the courage to begin."

" 'Leaving us an example, that ye should follow *His* steps,' " quoted Lewis Morgan solemnly. "After all, Father, the true pattern is certainly perfect. Why not follow that? Whoever asks the schoolboy to imitate the scrawl of some fellow pupil, so long as the perfect copy is just before his eyes at the top of the page?"

His father regarded him meditatively. Was he touched at last — impressed by the thought of the wonderful life waiting for him to follow? Lewis Morgan's breath came quickly, and he waited in trembling eagerness for the reply. It was the first time that he had attempted anything like a personal conversation on this subject with his father.

Slowly, and with apparently great seriousness, the answer came at last: "It's a pity you had to change your plans. I ain't sure, after all, but you would have made as good a minister as the rest of them. Sometimes I'm a bit afraid that you have got a little too much learning to make a downright good farmer."

The quick bounds of hope that his soul's blood was making receded in dull, heavy throbs, and he counted his first attempt a failure. Lewis looked over to Louise. Wasn't she ready to give up this hopeless attempt at spiritualizing the tone of the conversation

downstairs? He thought he would give almost anything to hide his sore heart just then in the quiet of
their own room with the sympathy of her presence
to soothe him.

But Louise was telling Neelie a story. As he listened and watched her, it became evident to him that
both Dorothy and John were listening. Dorothy had
ceased her restless fidgetings and settled into absolute quiet. Her arm rested on the broad, low window
seat, and her eyes were fixed on Louise. John had
drawn his hat lower so that his eyes were hidden
entirely. But something in the setting of his lips told
Lewis that he heard. Very quietly Louise's voice told
the story; very simply chosen were the words.

"Yes, there He was in the great, gloomy woods for
forty days without anything to eat and nowhere to
rest, and all the time Satan was tempting Him to do
what was wrong. 'Come,' he said to Him. 'If You are
the Son of God, why do You stay here hungry? What
good will that do anybody? Why don't You make
bread out of these stones? You can do it. You could
make a stone into a loaf of bread in an instant. Why
don't You?' "

"And could He?" Neelie asked, her eyes large and
wondering.

"Oh, yes, indeed! Why not? Do you suppose it
would be any harder to turn a stone into bread than
it would be to make a strawberry or a potato or an
apple?"

"Strawberries and apples and potatoes grow,"
said this advanced little skeptic.

"Yes, but what makes them grow? And why does
a strawberry plant *always* give us strawberries and
never plums or grapes? It never makes a mistake.
Somebody very wise is taking care of the little plant.
It is this same person whom Satan was trying to coax

to make bread out of stones."

"Well, why didn't He do it? I don't think it would have been naughty."

"It is very hard to be hungry. It was a great temptation, but perhaps Jesus had promised His Father that He would come here as a man and bear everything that any man could have to. Now a *man* couldn't make bread out of stones. Then, another thing, if He had used His great power and gotten Himself out of this trouble, all the poor hungry boys and girls who are tempted to steal would have said: 'Oh, yes, Jesus doesn't know anything about how it feels to be hungry. He could turn stones into bread. If we could do that, we wouldn't steal, either.' Don't you see?"

"Yes," said Neelie, "I see. Go on, please. He didn't make any bread, did He?"

"Not at that time. He told Satan it was more important that He should show His trust in God than to show His power by making stones into bread. Then Satan coaxed Him to throw Himself down from a great, high steeple so that the people below would see Him and see that He wasn't hurt at all. Satan even reminded Jesus of a promise that God made, about the angels taking care of Him."

"I wish He *had* done that!" Neelie said, with shining eyes. "Then the people would all have believed that He was God."

"No, they wouldn't, for afterward He did just as wonderful things as that. He cured deaf people and blind people and raised dead people to life, and they didn't believe in Him. Instead, some of them were angry with him about these very things. He told Satan that to put Himself in danger, when there was nothing to be gained by it, was just tempting God.

Dear me! How many boys and girls do that! Then Satan told Him that he would give up the whole world to Him if He would just fall down and worship him. I suppose Jesus thought then about the weary way that He would have to travel — all the things He would have to bear."

"Did the world belong to Satan?" Neelie asked. At that question John was betrayed into a laugh.

"Well, yes, in a sense it did. Don't you see how much power Satan has over people in this world? They seem to like to work for him. Some of them are doing all they can to please him, and he is always at work coaxing them to give themselves entirely to him, promising them such great things if they only will. I suppose if he had kept that promise to Jesus and given up leading the world on the wrong road, it would have been much easier for Jesus."

"But Jesus didn't do it."

"No, indeed! Jesus never would do anything *wrong* to save Himself from trouble or sorrow. He said, 'Get thee behind me, Satan.' What a pity that little boys and girls don't refuse in that way to listen to Satan when he coaxes them and offers them rewards! Think of believing *Satan!* Why, the first we ever hear of him he was telling a lie to Eve in that garden, you know, and he has gone on cheating people ever since."

"He never cheated me," said Neelie positively.

"Didn't he? Are you sure? Did he never make you think that it would be so nice to do something that you knew Mother wouldn't like? Hasn't he made you believe that you could have a real happy time if you could only do as you wanted to? Have you never tried it and found out what an untrue thing it was?"

"Yes," said Neelie, drooping her head. "One time I ran away from school and went to the woods. I thought it would be splendid. I got my feet wet and was sick, and it wasn't nice, not a single bit."

"Of course not, and that is just the way Satan keeps treating people. Wouldn't you think that, after he had deceived them a great many times, as they grew older they would decide that he was only trying to ruin them and would have nothing more to do with him?"

"Yes," said Neelie, nodding her wise little head, "I should. But then maybe they can't get away from him."

"Oh, yes, they can. Don't you see how Jesus got away from him? What do you think He suffered those temptations for and then had the story written down for us? Wasn't it just so we could see that He knew all about temptations and about Satan and was stronger than he and was able to help all tempted people? He says He will not let people be tempted more than they can bear but will show them how to escape."

"Then why doesn't He?"

"He does, dear, every single time. He has never failed anybody yet, and it is hundreds and hundreds of years since He made that promise."

"But then I should think that everybody would be good and never do wrong."

"Ah, but you see, little Neelie, the trouble is, people *won't let Him help them*. He takes care of all who trust in Him to do so. But if you think you are strong enough to take care of yourself and won't stay by Him nor obey His directions nor ask His help, how can you expect to be kept out of trouble? When I was a little bit of a girl, I went for a walk with my papa. He said: 'Now, Louise, if you will keep right in this path I will see that nothing hurts you.' We were going through the woods. For a little while I kept beside him, taking hold of his hand. Then I said: 'Oh, Papa, I'm not afraid. Nothing will hurt me.' And away I ran into the thickest trees. I got lost and was in that woods nearly all night! Do you think that was my papa's fault?"

"No," said Neelie gravely. "But — I wish there wasn't any Satan. Does he ever bother you?"

Louise's head dropped lower. The talk was becoming very personal.

"Not often now," she said, speaking low. "He comes to me and whispers thoughts that I don't like, and I say — "

"Oh!" said Neelie, loud-voiced and eager. "I know. You say, 'Get thee behind me, Satan.' "

"No," said Louise firmly, "not that. I heard a lady say once that she was as much afraid of having Satan behind her as she was of having him anywhere else. So am I. Instead I ask Jesus to send him away. I just say, 'Jesus, keep me,' and at the name of Jesus Satan goes away. He *knows* he cannot coax Jesus to do any wrong. But, oh, dear! How hard he fights for those people who will not have Jesus help them. He keeps whispering plans in their ears and coaxing them. They think that the plans are their own, and they follow them, expecting to have good times and never having them. All the while Satan laughs over their folly. Isn't it strange that they will not take the help that Jesus offers?"

"Yes," said Neelie slowly, gravely, with intense earnestness in her voice and manner. "I mean to."

Louise drew her closer, rested her own head against the golden one and began to sing in low, sweet notes:

Take the name of Jesus ever,
As a shield for every snare;
When temptations round you gather,
Breathe that holy name in prayer.

All conversation or attempts at conversation had ceased in the room long before the singing. Some spell about the old, simply told story of temptation and struggle and victory had seemed to hold all the group as listeners. John's face, as much of it as could be seen under his hat and shading hand, worked strangely. Was the blessed Holy Spirit, whose presence and aid had been invoked, using the story told the child to flash before this young man a revelation of the name of the leader he had been so faithfully following, so steadily serving, all the years of his young life? Did he begin to have a dim realization of the fact that his unsatisfying plans, his shattered hopes, were but the mockery of his false-hearted guide? Whatever he thought, he kept it to himself and rose abruptly in the midst of the singing and went out.

"Come," said Farmer Morgan, breaking the hush following the last line. "It is milking time and time for a bit of supper, too, I guess. The afternoon has been uncommon short."

He tried to speak as usual, but his voice was a bit husky. He could argue, but the story told his child had somehow subdued him. Who shall say that the Spirit did not knock loudly that Sunday afternoon at the door of each heart in that room? Who shall say that He did not use Louise Morgan's simple efforts to honor the day by stirring the rust that had gathered about the hinges of those long-bolted doors?

CHAPTER VIII

NEW LIGHT

he little square stand was drawn up in front of the Franklin stove, which was opened to let a glow of brightness reach across the room. Beside it were Lewis and Louise Morgan, seated for an evening of good cheer. She had a bit of needlework in which she was taking careful stitches, and her husband held in his hand, open to a previously set mark, a handsomely bound copy of Shakespeare. He was one of those rare persons who was a good reader of Shakespeare. In the old days at her parents' home Louise had delighted to sit with work in hand and listen to the music of his voice in the rendering.

He had not commenced the regular reading but was dipping into bits here and there, while he waited for her to "settle," as he called the bringing of her small workbasket and the searching out of her work. Now, although she was settled and looking apparently thoughtful enough for the saddest scenes from the great writer, Lewis still continued glancing from page to page, breaking out presently with: "Louise, do you remember this?

> I never did repent for doing good,
> Nor shall not now; for in companions
> That do converse and waste the time to-
>   gether,
> Whose souls do bear an equal yoke of
>   love,
> There must be needs a like proportion
> Of lineaments, of manners, and of spirit.

"Do you remember what a suggestive shrug of her shoulders Estelle gave over the line: 'That do converse and waste the time together'? I suspect she thought it fitted us precisely."

"Yes," Louise said, smiling in a most preoccupied way. That her thoughts were not all on Shakespeare nor even on that fairer object Estelle, she presently evinced by a question: "Lewis, how far did Dorothy get in her studies?"

"Dorothy?" repeated her husband, looking up in surprise and with difficulty coming back from Shakespeare. "I don't know. As far as the teachers in our district school could take them, I remember hearing. That is not saying much, to be sure; though, by the way, I hear they have an exceptionally good teacher this winter. Poor Dorothy didn't have half a chance. I tried to manage it, but I couldn't. Hear this, Louise:

> How he glistens through my rust!
> And how his piety does my deeds make
>   the blacker!

"Isn't that a simile for you?"

"Very," said Louise, and her husband glanced at

her curiously. What was she thinking of, and how did that brief "very" fit in with Leontes' wonderful simile in *The Winter's Tale*?

"Well," he said, "are your thimbles and pins and things all ready, wife? Shall I commence?"

"Not just yet, dear. I want to talk. What do you think about it? Was she disappointed at not having better opportunities?"

"Who? Oh, Dorothy! I thought you were talking about Hermione — she fainted, you know. Yes, Dorothy was disappointed. She wanted to go to the academy in town, and she ought to have had the opportunity; but we couldn't bring it to pass. I was at home only a few weeks, or I might have accomplished more. What is the trouble, Louise, dear? How does it happen that you find poor Dorothy more interesting than Shakespeare tonight?"

"Well," said Louise, laughing, "it is true — I cannot get away from her. Her life seems so forlorn. I can't help being sorry for her. She is losing her girlhood almost before it is time for it to bloom. I have been wondering and wondering all day what we could do for her. I find the real life being worked out before our eyes so engrossing that it is hard to come back to the dead lives of Shakespeare."

Her husband closed the book, putting his finger between the leaves to mark the place.

"I have studied that problem somewhat, Louise," he said earnestly, "in the days gone by. I didn't succeed in making much of it. It is true, as you say, that she is slipping away from girlhood, almost without knowing that she has been a girl. Sometimes I think that she will have only two experiences of life: childhood and old womanhood. Mother cannot realize that she is yet anymore than a child to be governed and to obey. One of these mornings it will be discovered that she is no longer a child but has passed middle life. Her future looks somewhat dreary to me, I confess."

"We mustn't let it grow dreary," Louise said, with a determined tone and a positive setting of her small foot — a curious habit that she had when she was very much in earnest. "What sense is there in it? She's young and in good health and has a sound brain. Why shouldn't she make her life what it ought to be? Why shouldn't we help her in a hundred ways?"

"Yes, but come down to actual, practical truth. What can she do for herself, or what can we do for her? You see, Louise, our family is peculiar. There is no use in shutting one's eyes to that fact.

"It is not because Father is a farmer that we find ourselves situated just as we are. Other farmers have very different experiences. We are surrounded on all sides with men who get their living by cultivating the fields. Their sons and daughters are in college or seminary and in society, and they take as good a position and have as many advantages as town-bred people — at the expense, it is true, of some inconvenience and special labor.

"Of course, it is also true that some of the sons and daughters do not choose to accept all the advantages for cultivation. Equally, of course, some are unable to furnish the means for what they would like their children to enjoy. But no greater proportion of that class is in the country than in town, I think. My father does not belong to any of these classes. He is, as I said, peculiar."

At this point both husband and wife stopped to laugh over the associations connected with that word *peculiar*. It reminded them both of Gough and Dickens, as well as many more common characters which those two geniuses have caricatured.

"It is true, nevertheless," Lewis said, the laugh over. "Let me see if I can explain. In the first place, both Father and Mother had lives of grinding toil and poverty in their youth. Both were shrewd, clear-headed people with much more than the average share of brains. The result is that, despite drawbacks and privations, they made their way, acquiring not thorough educations but a very fair degree of knowledge on all practical subjects. For instance, it would surprise you how much my mother knows concerning subjects she would be expected to know nothing about. Perhaps the result of all this is natural; anyway, it is evident.

"They believe that the rubbing process is decidedly the best way to secure an education or anything else needed in this world. If one makes his way in spite of obstacles, they believe it is because the grit is in him and must find its end. Had Dorothy, for instance, been determined to attend school in town and get a thorough education — had she persisted doggedly against argument and opposition and everything but absolute command — she would have won the prize. Both Father and Mother would have, in a certain sense, respected her more than they do now.

"But Dorothy was not of that mold. She wanted to go on with her studies. If everything had been smooth before her, she would doubtless have gone on and made a fair scholar. But to stem a current with so much against her required more effort of a certain kind than she knew how to make."

"I conclude," said his wife, smiling brightly on him, "that you were one of those who can push persistently."

He answered her smile, partly with a laugh and partly with a shrug of his handsome shoulders: "I did push — most vehemently some of the time! And I worked my way part of the time besides, as you know. But in the end I gained. Father and Mother have a degree of pride in my persistence. It reminds them of their own rugged natures."

"I wonder that Dorothy, thwarted in her desire for education, did not go to the extreme in dressing well and attending social gatherings and wasting valuable time in idle pursuits. That is the rock on which so many girls shipwreck."

"I think she would have done just that thing had she been given an opportunity. I think it is what both my father and mother were afraid of. It has made them draw the reins of family government very tight. They simply commanded that she was to ignore singing schools and country school debating societies and social gatherings in the shape of apple-parings, cornhuskings, quilting bees — any and everything of that nature or those with new names that in more modern days have sprung from their roots. We were all under that command.

"The consequence is, we are almost as isolated from our neighbors as though we had none. My mother did not feel the need of society. She could not understand why anyone should feel that need; consequently, she has no society. Good and pleasant people live around us, people whom you would be pleased to meet. But they never come near us because we have, as a family, led them to believe that we have nothing to do with common humanity."

"What a strange idea! I have wondered why your neighbors didn't call on me. I thought they must have a preconceived dislike for me."

"They have a preconceived belief that you will not care to see them. You would be amused to see how this withdrawal from any friendships has been translated. If Father were a poor man, struggling to get along, it might be set down as queerness or a dislike of mingling with those who were better off in this world's goods than we are. But with his farm stretching before their eyes in so many smiling acres and with his barns, the finest and best stocked in the neighborhood, we are looked upon as a family too aristocratic to mingle with country people. That is so funny, when you consider the fact that we have never been other than country people ourselves and that we live much more plainly than any of our neighbors.

"But you can readily see the effect on Dorothy. She has in a way dropped out of life. Her occasional trips to church on a pleasant Sunday and to market with Mother, when both can on rare occasions be spared from home, are her two excitements. She has hardly a speaking acquaintance with the neighbors about us and no friends whatever."

"Poor girl!" said Louise. There was more than compassion in her voice. There was a curious undertone of determination, which made her husband smile and wonder what this little woman, in whose capabilities he thoroughly believed, would do.

"Haven't I established the validity of our claim to being 'peculiar'?" he asked her.

"I should think you have! What has been the effect of the 'peculiarities' on John?"

Lewis's face sobered instantly, and there was a note of pain in his voice. "John has broken loose from the restraints in a painful way. He has made his own friends, and they are of a kind that he wouldn't care to bring home if he had an opportunity. He is away very frequently in the evenings — it is difficult to tell where. But the daily decrease of anything like manliness attests the unfortunate result.

"I am more than suspicious that he is learning to drink something stronger than cider, and I am sure that he smokes occasionally, at least — two vices that are my father's horror. He looks on with apparently mingled feelings of anger and dismay.

"His pet theories of family government have failed; he honestly desired to shield his children from evil influences. He is comparatively satisfied with the result, both in Dorothy's case and mine. But he doesn't know what to think of John. He has spells of great harshness and severity connected with him, thwarting everything that he undertakes in what must seem to John an utterly unreasonable way. Yet I believe it is done with a sore heart and with an anxious desire for his good.

"And when my mother's face is most immovable," Lewis added, "I have learned to know that she is trying to quiet the frightened beatings of her heart over the wrongdoings of her younger boy."

"Lewis," his wife said, interrupting the next word and with intense earnestness and solemnity in her voice, "we must save John for Christ, and his father and mother."

"Amen. But how, dear — how?"

"Lewis, let's go right downstairs. They are all at home. I noticed it as I came through the room. And they look so gloomy. Why shouldn't we all have a pleasant evening together? Did you ever read anything to them? I thought not. Now don't you know they can't help enjoying your reading? I mean to try it right away."

"Read Shakespeare?" her husband asked dryly, but with dismay in his voice. To talk earnestly over a state of things, to wish that all were different, was one thing. But to plunge right into the midst of existing things and try to change them was quite another. His wife answered his question with a bright little laugh.

"No, I don't believe they would enjoy Shakespeare yet, though I am by no means sure that we can't have some good readings from him sometime. But let me see. I have a book that I am certain they will all like. You never read it, and you ought to. It is worth anyone's while to read it." And she let spool and scissors fall and went in eagerness to the swinging shelves where she had arranged some of her favorite books. She selected from among them *The New Timothy*, by the Rev. William M. Baker.

"Here it is," she said. "Estelle and I enjoyed this book wonderfully. So did Papa. We read it while Mama was away one winter, and we were dreary without her. John will certainly be interested in the bear hunt — being a boy, he can't help it. And I know Mother will like to hear about that poor mother down behind the butterbeans."

"Behind the butterbeans! What an extraordinary place for a mother to be! What was she doing there?"

"Wait until you read it, my dear. You will like the book. People of good sense always do."

"Thank you. But, Louise, dear, do you think it a wise thing to try? Remember what a disastrous failure I made on Sunday. I don't believe I am fitted for aggressive movements."

"I don't believe anybody but Christ knows yet whether your Sunday effort was all a failure, Lewis. And I don't believe that you and I have any right with the results, if we did what we could. Besides, this is different anyway. I *know* you can read. Come."

"I can't see to read from the light of a tallow candle. I always despised them."

"We will take the lamp," she said, with a defiant little nod of her head toward the pretty bronze figure that held a shapely kerosene lamp of newest pattern and improved burner. Lewis had searched the Boston lamp stores for just the right sort of offering for his bride. "We will set it right beside Mother, where it will throw just the right angle of light on her work and yet be shaded from her eyes. And we will not hint by word or glance that she may possibly see better than she does by her candle. Come, Lewis, carry it; it is too heavy for me. I will bring the book and my workbasket."

"Mother despises robes," her husband said, rising slowly. He cast regretful looks at Shakespeare, the open fire and his lounging chair. But it was neither the chair nor yet the book that held him, rather a horrible shrinking from this attempt at innovation and an almost certainty of disastrous failure.

"No, she doesn't. She only thinks so because she isn't used to robes and doesn't realize how much they save wear on other garments. I'm going to make John one for Christmas and a pair of slippers like those Estelle gave you last year, and she will like them very much. You see if she doesn't. Now we're ready."

CHAPTER IX

A NEW CHAMPION

f the Sunday callers to the kitchen had astonished the family group, this descent upon them with workbasket, book and, above all, lamp fairly made them speechless — at least after Dorothy's first startled "Good land!" when she retired into flushed silence.

"Lewis was going to read to me," explained Louise in a tone intended to convey the idea that their proceeding was the most natural and ordinary one imaginable. "I thought it was a pity to waste a new book on one person so we have come down for you all to hear. May I sit by you, Mother?"

Without waiting for an answer, the artful daughter-in-law took her pretty bronze lamp from her husband's hand and set it in "just the right angle." She drew one of the wooden-seated chairs and settled herself near it before the audience had time to recover from its surprise.

"Now, Lewis, we're ready," she added. She had resolved not to venture on the doubtful question as to whether they desired to hear any reading. If their consent was taken for granted, what could they do but listen?

Nevertheless John seemed resolved not to be taken by guile. He drew himself up with a shuffling noise and was evidently making ready for flight. Her husband telegraphed a significant glance to Louise, which said, as plainly as words could, that encouraging sentence: "I told you so; John won't stay." But she saw the whole, and, while her heart beat for the success of her scheme, her voice was prompt and assured: "Oh, John! Do you have to go to the barn so soon? Well, never mind, we'll wait for you. I selected this book on purpose because I was so sure you would like it. It is a special favorite of mine."

Thus addressed, John, who had had no intention of going to the barn but simply of escaping, sat down again simply out of astonishment. Lewis, who was both amazed and amused at his wife's boldness, promptly seized the opportunity to commence his book without further introduction.

All who have had the pleasure of reading that inimitable work of fiction *The New Timothy* know the treat that was in store. It was a book so written that, while the refined and cultured reader thoroughly enjoys it, the untutored and undisciplined mind also grasps enough of the train of thought to be deeply interested, held indeed by the power of description and the vividness of detail. It was nearly eight o'clock when the reading commenced, the usual hour for the family to separate, but for an unbroken hour Lewis Morgan's voice went steadily on. The shade of embarrassment which he felt at first speedily lost itself in his genuine interest in the book, which was new to him; and perhaps he had never shown his reading powers to better advantage.

Louise, to whom the story was an old one, had leisure to watch its effect on the group. She was more than satisfied with the hushed way in which Mother Morgan laid down her great shears on the uncovered stand and finally transferred them to her lap, that their clatter might not make her lose a word; at the knitting which dropped from Dorothy's fingers and lay unheeded while she, unchided by her mother, fixed what were certainly great hungry eyes on the reader and took in every sentence; at the unwinking eyes of Father Morgan, who did not interrupt the hour by a single yawn; but above all at the gleam of intense satisfaction in John's face when the young minister came off victor.

Besides, did she or did she not hear a quick, suddenly suppressed sigh coming from the mother's heart, as she listened to the story of that other mother's wrestlings in prayer in her closet, "down behind the butterbeans"? The loud-spoken clock, as it clanged out the hour of nine, was the first interruption to the reading since it struck eight. Louise, mindful of the lack of wisdom of carrying her experiment too far, hastened to change the program.

"Why, Lewis, it is nine o'clock! It won't do to read anymore."

And Lewis, who had many an evening read until ten and occasionally until eleven to that other family group in the old home, looked up with obtuseness exactly like a man and was about to ask why not. But the warning look in his wife's eyes brought him back to the level of present experiences. Despite Dorothy's hungry eyes and John's utter stillness which indicated he was entirely willing to hear more, the book was promptly closed.

"Well," said Farmer Morgan, drawing a long breath, "that minister in the book was a most likely chap as ever I heard of. If more of 'em acted like that, I should have a higher opinion of them than I do. It's a very well-told story — now that's a fact."

"A pack of lies, the whole of it." This came from Mother Morgan, not severely, but in a deprecatory tone. It was as though she felt herself obliged to say it, as a sort of punishment for having allowed herself to become interested.

"Well, now," said Farmer Morgan, dropping his head to one side, with a thoughtful air, "I don't know about that. There is nothing so dreadfully unlikely about it. And that smart chap had a streak of good luck and a streak of common sense. I've known myself exactly such a family as that set of boys, father and all, hard as they were. Whether it is lies or not, it is told exactly as though it all might have happened. I don't object to hearing it anyhow. It takes up the time, though. I had no idea it was nine o'clock."

"Nine o'clock isn't late," ventured Dorothy. "Jamie Stuart's folks sit up till ten almost every evening. I always see a light in their front room when I go to bed."

"Yes, and they don't get up till long after daylight and don't have breakfast until it's 'most time for dinner. I never brought up my children to habits of that kind, thank fortune." There was a good deal of sharpness in the mother's tone by this time. She was growing vexed to think she had allowed her heart to throb in sympathy with the trials of a mother whose experience was only a "pack of lies." She forgot for the moment that touches of the bitterness of that mother's experience over her youngest born had already come to her. If only she would make the experience of prayer her own — !

Louise arose promptly. She was satisfied with her experiment and judged it wise to beat an immediate retreat.

"Come, Lewis," she said, her hand on the pretty lamp. "If I am late to breakfast tomorrow morning, Father will think it is a bad book. Isn't that a dainty design for a lamp handle, Mother?"

"It's a dangerous thing to carry around," the mother said grimly, meaning the lamp and not the handle. "I never take up the paper that I don't read about an accident of some sort with kerosene lamps. If I could have had my way, there should never one of them have come into this house."

"Oh, but this is a new patent. If Lewis should stumble and drop it, the light would go instantly out. Look! Just a little motion, such as the lamp would get if it fell, and the light is gone." Suiting the action to the word, the flame was instantly extinguished.

"There!" Lewis said. "Now we are in darkness."

"I didn't mean to have it go quite out," Louise laughed. "I was only going to move it a little to show Mother. Never mind. John will get us a candle — won't you, John?"

Thus appealed to, John arose slowly from his corner. He went slowly to the high mantel, where shone several beautifully polished candlesticks, and took from the paper holder a paper match. Applying it to his mother's candle, he solemnly lighted the other candle and as solemnly handed it to Louise. This was the first act of simple courtesy for a lady that he had ever done in his life.

"Thank you," she said, quite as a matter of course. Yet it was actually the first "thank you" of his grown-up life!

There were certainly two sides to John's gruffness. Louise would have been amazed to know how that simple "thank you" thrilled him!

"If I had dared," began Louise, as soon as they

were in the privacy of their own room, "I would have substituted that big, old Bible for this book during the last ten minutes and asked you to read a chapter and pray with us all. I believe your father would have liked it. I don't believe he is as indifferent to these things as he seems."

"It is well you don't dare," her husband said gravely. "I'm afraid I should have disappointed you, Louise. I don't believe I could have done that. It looks to me like an almost impossible thing."

"Why, Lewis, you led at family worship at home right before Papa and Mama and Estelle — and sometimes when the house was full of company!"

"That was a very different thing," he answered earnestly. "I felt then that the head of the house was in sympathy with me and joined in the reading and the praying. It was like a company of brothers and sisters talking together with their father. Here it is different. My father's tendency would be to make light of the whole thing."

"I don't believe it," she said positively. "I can't believe that he would make light of an earnest, simple prayer such as you would offer. It is the profession of godliness and an absence of the fruit that he naturally expects to see in lives which inclines him to ridicule. That sounds harsh, Lewis, but I don't mean harshness. He evidently expects great things of Christians, and their lives naturally enough disappoint him. How do you know, dear, but that your very silence, or reserve, toward him on these subjects leads him to question the degree of anxiety you have for his conversion?"

Whatever Lewis Morgan thought of this direct question he made no definite answer, and the subject was dropped.

All things considered, Louise was well pleased with the result of one evening's sacrifice. To give up the delightful privacy of their own room and their own plans and listen to a book that she had heard before was somewhat of a sacrifice. Its result elated her. She felt that her position in the family was on a more assured footing, and she looked forward to the accomplishment of other little plans with a greater degree of certainty of success than she had felt heretofore. What a pity that her feelings should have been put to rout through the intervention of a boiled dinner!

A victim to old-fashioned boiled dinners once explained to a novice how to make them: "Take a few of everything that grows in the garden and dump them all together with some slab-sided beef and a little pork and let them boil for hours and hours. That will send a remarkable odor through the house, which penetrates every tightly closed door and window. Then serve with quarts of slush!" Whether this recipe would be acknowledged by the lovers of such dinners or not, it exactly describes the state of nerves in which a few people sit down to partake of them. Now I beg you not to fall into the mistake of supposing our friend Louise to be an epicure or unreasonably dainty as to the food she ate. On the contrary, if her friends had but known it, she had the comfortable, natural appetite which a healthy condition of stomach and brain are likely to produce.

She was not one of those unhappy beings to whom the sight and smell of food which they do not happen to like is positive torture. On the contrary, Mother Morgan might have had a boiled dinner three days out of every week had she chosen. So long as the bread tray was piled high with generous slices of good, sweet, homemade bread and the butter dish held its roll of hard, yellow, glistening butter and the generous-sized pitcher brimmed with creamy milk,

Louise in her own estimation would have made a dinner fit for a queen. For when did a healthy city maiden other than rejoice over real country butter and cream?

The trouble lay in the fact that poor Mother Morgan herself had nerves. She despised the name and considered all such matters as modern inventions of fashionable society. But it was just as surely an overwrought and undisciplined state of nerves which caused her to express harsh displeasure on certain innocent tastes which differed from her own, as though she had expressed it with a burst of tears. Did you ever have a hostess who accepted it as a personal insult if you declined any dish of her preparing? If not, you are fortunate. But just such a one was Mother Morgan. Her family had for years and years with some enthusiasm partaken of cabbage, turnips, potatoes, beets, beef, parsnips and pork, all dwelling in friendly nearness in the same large pot. They had even appreciated sometimes the little round, yellow balls, known to the initiated to be cornmeal balls, but tasting to the ignorant like nothing so much as sawdust wetted up with a little pork gravy.

With some dismay Louise watched the lading of the plate which she knew was intended for her! How was she ever to dispose of that mass, which from the unmashed turnip down to the yellow cannon balls she disliked? If she might only say, "No, thank you," and take the inviting looking bread and butter and milk! Why must people have nerves which lead straight to their palates and in this world of infinite variety take the trouble to be aggrieved because tastes differed? Meekly she received the well-laden plate; meekly she sliced bits of potato and minced at the turnip, even taking delicate nibbles of the stump of cabbage which she detested. All to no purpose. Mrs. Morgan was watching her with sharp eyes. What right had this newcomer to dislike so savory a dinner? Presently her indignation found vent in words.

"I don't see but we shall have to set a separate table for you. It seems you can't stand the dishes we are used to. I don't want you to starve on our hands, I'm sure."

Despite the fact that Louise had just received a letter full of tenderness from the dear mother at home — a tenderness which made this mother a distinct contrast — she was enabled to laugh as she answered pleasantly: "Oh, Mother, I'm in no danger of starving. It seems to me that I like your bread and butter better than any I ever tasted. I suppose I am somewhat peculiar in my tastes, but I always find plenty to eat."

If people could see into each other's hearts or if they could keep still when they ought, it might have gone well. But life had gone awry with the young husband that morning. He had had a discussion with his father concerning certain farming plans, and a decided difference of opinion had developed, during which the son expressed himself warmly and positively. The father, waxing indignant, had informed him sharply that going to college and to Australia and marrying a fine lady for a wife didn't make a farmer. Had Lewis found a moment's leisure and privacy with his wife, and he had spoken his thoughts, they would have been somewhat like this: "I am discouraged with the whole thing. We never can belong here. If it were not for you, I should be miserable. You are the joy of my heart, and my rest." Then Louise would have comforted and encouraged him.

As it was, believing in her wholly and being just then desirous that she should appear perfect in the eyes of his father, he addressed her in a disturbed, not to say almost vexed tone, albeit a low one: "Do,

Louise, pretend to eat something, whether you accomplish it or not."

Louise could never understand how it was; she had not supposed herself one of the nervous sort. But just then and there arose such a lump in her throat that to have taken another mouthful would have been impossible. To her dismay and chagrin, actual tears rushed into her eyes!

Then up rose John to the emergency of the situation. "Why in the name of common sense can't you all let folks eat what they like without nagging at them all the time? I never touch cabbage and won't no more than I will touch a frog, and you let me alone. Why can't you her?"

Whereupon Dorothy was so amazed that she continued pouring milk into the bowl long after it had brimmed, her eyes fixed on her brother John's face. As for Lewis, he seemed stricken with remorse for his words, apparently realizing at this moment how they sounded. But Louise was so pleased with John's evident desire to champion her and so amused that it should seem to be necessary to shield her on a question of cabbage or not cabbage that the ludicrous side of the matter came uppermost. As she laughed, the lump in her throat vanished.

"Thank you," she said cheerfully to John. "Don't you like cabbage, either? I'm glad of it. We'll form a compact to stand by each other for freedom without cabbage."

Something approaching a smile hovered over John's face, and Dorothy giggled outright.

CHAPTER X

FISHING

unday morning dawned at last, with as bright a sunshine as ever a summer day may have produced. The air was crisp and clear, and the level road was frozen hard. Try as he might, Farmer Morgan would have found it hard to produce an excuse for why the family should not appear in church. To be sure, he often said that he didn't "feel like going." As John wouldn't go, that had heretofore settled the matter for the mother and Dorothy, whether they would or not.

But on this morning Louise and Lewis came from their room evidently dressed for the day, and Louise remarked with confidence: "What a nice morning for a ride! If one didn't care for churchgoing, it would be pleasant to get out today."

In Lewis's mind were some doubts as to who of the family could go, as the small spring wagon would not accommodate more than four. But Farmer Morgan settled it by saying in a positive voice: "You'll have to go today, John, and drive. I've got a stiff neck, and I don't feel like going out."

"I guess Lewis hasn't forgotten how to drive," John began sullenly. "I ain't going to church."

"You can go to church or not, just as you like, when you get down there, I s'pose. But you will have to drive the horses, for the filly has got to go. She isn't used to Lewis, and I won't have him drive her. It would look more decent to go to church, I think, but you've got so you don't care much about decency. I s'pose you'll do as you please. You going, Mother?"

"No!" said Mrs. Morgan promptly. "I'll get the dinner. Dorothy can go if she likes."

And the instant glow on Dorothy's cheek told that she "liked." Only John was sullen. He did not recover during the entire ride. He spoke only to the horses, except when Dorothy gave little frightened jumps when the filly seemed to her not to be moving with propriety. Then the driver snapped at her to "sit still and not act like a simpleton."

Arriving at the church door, he sat still, allowing Lewis to alight and wait on the ladies.

"Let's wait for John," Louise said, as her husband turned from the wagon. "It's nicer for us all to go in together."

John opened his lips. If ever lips were going to say, John isn't coming, his were, but he hesitated. He looked down at the young, earnest face turned with a confident air toward him, then turned away, snapped his whip and said nothing.

"You'll be here in a minute, won't you, John?"

"Yes," he said, or rather snapped, as though he was disgusted with himself for the answer. Then he gave the filly a smart touch with the whip. She curveted around the corner in a style which would surely have made Dorothy scream, had she been behind her.

"That is only a little short of a miracle," Lewis said, in surprise. "I never knew John to compromise his

dignity by going to church, after he had announced
that he wasn't going. That announcement is the rule
rather than the exception."

"I felt as though he must come to church this
morning," Louise answered in a low tone. "I couldn't
give it up. It has been the burden of my prayer all the
morning."

To which remark Lewis Morgan had no reply. He
remembered, with a sudden sting of conscience, that
he had not so much as thought of his brother's name
in prayer that morning. Based upon common-sense
principles, how much could he have desired his
presence in the church?

It was a quiet, little village church, looking natural
enough to the eyes of the usual worshippers. But
what a strange feeling it gave Louise! She was accustomed to broad, soft-carpeted aisles; richly carved
and upholstered seats; costly pulpit furnishings; a
massive organ, with solemn tones filling the church.
Here her feet trod on bare floors, and the pew to
which she was ushered had neither footstool nor
cushion, though it was high enough to demand the
one and hard enough to suggest the other. The odd
red and yellow tassels which hung from the pulpit
cushion were frayed and faded; the sun streamed in
unpleasantly from windows that boasted of neither
shades nor blinds; and there was a general air of
dilapidation about everything.

Louise looked around with curious eyes on the
congregation. Their appearance was not in keeping
with the surroundings. They looked well dressed
and well bred, as if most of them might have come
out from comfortable homes to spend this hour together. To all such, what a painful contrast between
the comforts and luxuries of their own homes must
the house of God have presented. While to those who

came from desolate homes, if there were any such, what attractions did the place offer?

It isn't even clean, the newcomer said to herself, her lip almost turning up as she saw the stray bits of paper and card scattered over the floor and the dust lying loosely everywhere. If they care for the church at all, why don't they keep it in order? she wondered.

When the service commenced, the feeling of discomfort was not removed. The little choir, perched high in the air at the back of the church, would not at that distance and height have been able to "lead the congregation" had they been so disposed. Their voices were clear and in harmony, and the little parlor organ was originally sweet-voiced. But the whole was so marred by a high-keyed, distressing squeak that Louise found it difficult to keep from frowning. She bowed her head during the prayer and succeeded in getting into the spirit of communion, then waited eagerly for the sermon.

The words of the text rang with a suggestive thought: "The life is more than meat, and the body more than raiment." But, alas, for the sermon! What was the matter with it? It was true. It was well written and well read. It was carefully logical. It sought to impress upon the minds of the hearers what a wonderful and glorious and endless thing was life! And John and Dorothy, those two for whom Louise had a most anxious desire, listened — or appeared to listen — to the wonderful possibilities of this life and the wonderful certainties of the future. And they were as indifferent to the one as the other, neither serving to lift the bored look from their faces.

As Louise watched and saw how little they were getting, Satan appeared to her, suggesting to her heart that perplexing and harassing question with which he delights to weary those who try: "What

good," said he, "will it do to have those two young
people come to this church and listen to this sermon?
Do you believe they have gotten a single new idea or
aspiration? Don't you feel nearly certain that they
will go home less impressible than they came? You
must remember that every presentation of the truth
either helps or hardens. Of what use were all your
plans and prayers? What availed your little thrill of
thanksgiving over the success of your scheme? Don't
you see it will amount to less than nothing?"

Isn't it strange that the followers of Christ will go
on year after year bending a listening ear to Satan
while he rings the charges of that old, long-ago vanquished falsehood: "If thou be the Son of God — "?

"If the Lord had cared anything about your efforts
to serve Him," said the tempter on this Sunday morning, "wouldn't He have planned this whole service
differently? You believe that He could have done it.
Why didn't He? You know very well that nothing has
been said that would help these two persons."

What should Louise do? Here she was in the house
of God, and here was this tempting demon at her
elbow! Who was it that said, "Whoever else stays
away from church, Satan never does"? Whoever said
it, the thought flashed over this tried soul suddenly,
and she bowed her head to speak a word to that
triumphant conqueror, who passed through the conflict centuries ago, and is "able to succor them that
are tempted." Did He speak again the word of command: "Get thee hence, Satan"? Assuredly He came
Himself and stood beside her. She was enabled to
remember that her part was to plant and water as she
could, the fruit of her work being God's part, and His
unchangeable "doubtless" was added to the promise
of success. In the hymn and prayer that followed the
sermon, heart and spirit joined. As Louise Morgan

raised her head after the benediction, she felt that this was indeed the house of God and the gate of heaven. He had verified His promise yet again and met her in His temple.

Nevertheless, her first spoken words after the service would not have seemed to many to be in keeping with the hour: "John, what on earth is the matter with that organ?"

Despite the habitual frown on John's face, he was betrayed into a laugh; there was so much intensity in the questioner's voice.

"Why, it needs a drop or two of oil," he said promptly, "and has needed it ever since I can remember. Anybody would think they considered the squeak an addition to the music by the way they hang on to it."

"Is it possible that a little oil is all that is needed to stop that horrible sound? Why don't you fix it?"

"I?" said John, turning full, astonished eyes on her, surprised out of his reserve and his frowns.

"Why, certainly. How can you endure it for so long? Do, John, fix it before next Sunday. It spoils the music. I could hardly enjoy even the words because of that dreadful sound. How many things there are that ought to be done here! Why do they leave the church in this shape? Isn't there a sexton?"

"Why, yes," said John, "I suppose so. Of course, there must be. He rings the bell and makes the fires."

"But never sweeps," added Louise, smiling, "nor dusts. John, if you can prevail on him to do some sweeping this week, I'll come down with you, when you come to oil that organ, and do the dusting. Wouldn't that be an improvement?"

When you come to oil that organ! The sentence had so strange a sound that John repeated it to himself. Was it possible that he was coming to oil the church organ? She spoke very confidently, quite as though it were a settled matter. And yet he would almost as soon have expected to see himself coming to preach the sermon! What would the people think of his going into the church on a weekday? No one remembered better than he that of late his presence on Sunday had been a rarity. He had been on the verge of telling her that he hadn't been hired to keep the church in order, but neither had she been hired to dust it. He was quick-witted enough to see that, after the dusting scheme was proposed, his subterfuge wouldn't do.

Oh, well, he said to himself, she'll forget it. Catch me oiling the church organ! If it groaned loud enough to be heard ten miles off I wouldn't touch it! And he honestly thought he wouldn't. He had a vindictive feeling for that old organ.

This conversation had consumed much less time than it has taken me to give it. They were only just passing down the aisle. John had been withheld from his usual habit of rushing out the instant the amen was spoken by the sudden question that had been put to him. Now Louise turned his thoughts into another channel. Her husband had been waylaid by a gentleman who seemed anxious to have his opinion on some church matter; therefore she was at leisure to fish for John.

"I don't want to go home without being introduced to the minister," she said. "There he comes now. Will you introduce me, John?"

"I don't know him," answered John shortly. His tone added, And I don't want to.

"Don't you? Oh, he's a newcomer. Well, then, let's introduce ourselves."

He was just beside them now and aided her plans, holding out his hand with a genial "Mrs. Morgan, I believe." He was a young, bright-faced man, cheery of voice and manner and more winning, apparently, anywhere else than he was in the pulpit.

Louise returned his handclasp cordially and hastened to say: "My brother, Mr. Morgan; my sister, Miss Morgan. We are all strangers together, I believe. You have been here but a short time, I understand?

"Why, yes," the minister said, flushing slightly. He was comparatively a "newcomer." He was remembering the embarrassing fact that he had been there quite long enough to get acquainted with that portion of his flock which seemed to him worth cultivating. "I have not gotten out to Mr. Morgan's yet, but I hope to do so this week. What day will you be most at leisure, Mrs. Morgan?"

"Oh," said Louise brightly, "we shall be glad to see you at anytime. Suppose you come on Tuesday." She was thinking of one or two little pet schemes of her own. "Shall we expect you to tea? John, we would like to have him take tea with us, wouldn't we? You haven't an engagement for Tuesday, have you?"

Thus appealed to, what was there for John but to stammer out an answer, over which he ruminated half the way home. Was it possible that he had engaged to be at home on Tuesday to meet the minister and had actually seconded the invitation to tea? How did he come to do it? What were the words he said? How did he happen to say them? He felt very much bewildered, somewhat vexed and just a very trifle interested. There was certainly nothing in the minister to like, and he didn't like him. Moreover, he didn't mean to like him. What was it then that interested him? He didn't quite know. He wondered what loophole of escape he could find for Tuesday. Also, he wondered whether he really and truly was determined to escape. Altogether, John didn't understand his own state of mind.

"Oh, Lewis," said Louise, just as they were nearing home, "do you suppose anybody would object if you were to cut those dreadful looking yellow tassels from the pulpit and tack a neat little braid, such as upholsterers use, around it? John and I are going down there some day this week to fix up things, and you may go along and upholster the pulpit if you want to."

"John and you!"

The astonishment in her husband's voice made Louise's eyes laugh, but her tones were steady. "Yes; he is going to stop that dreadful squeak in the organ. Isn't that terrible? It just spoiled the music, and it would have been good but for that. I've promised to dust, if there can be some sweeping done. Oh, John, did you speak to the sexton? No? Well, I'm not sure that it's really Sunday work. But when can you see him?"

Then Dorothy roused to the occasion. "The sexton comes every morning to get a can of milk for some of his customers at the village."

"Oh, does he? Then you can see him. John, you will attend to it tomorrow morning, won't you? And have it done before Wednesday, because then the church will be warmed for prayer meeting, and we can get it ready more comfortably. I wonder if those lamps don't smoke? They look as if they might."

"They used to smoke fiercely enough when I knew them last," her husband said. "I haven't been down in the evening since I came home from Australia."

Here was certainly a revelation to Louise. Her husband had not been to the church prayer meeting since he came from Australia eight months before! But she made no comment.

Dorothy having once determined to speak had more to say: "They look as though they hadn't been washed in forty years! I never saw such black things in my life!"

"Suppose you enlist with us, Dorothy? Go down on Wednesday, and let's put the lamps in order. We'll let Lewis buy some wicks and chimneys for his share. I saw that two of the chimneys were broken; those two lamps will smoke, of course."

John laughed outright. "I believe you saw every crack and corner of the church," he said, speaking almost good-naturedly.

And Dorothy spoke her troubled thought. "I don't know anything about kerosene lamps. I don't suppose I could fix one to save my life."

"I know all about them. Papa used to have one in his office that I took care of, and Mama used one for sewing. I can show you all about them in five minutes. Will you go?"

"Well," said Dorothy, veiling her eagerness as well as she could, "I'd be willing, but I don't believe Mother will."

"Yes, she will. I'll look out for that."

It was neither Lewis nor Louise that made this startling promise, but John himself!

"Was it quite according to Sunday observance to make all those plans?" Louise asked her husband, smiling, but with a shade of anxiety in her voice, when they were upstairs in their room. "Sometimes those things trouble me. I had Sunday plans at heart, but I'm afraid they didn't show very plainly."

"Well, I don't know. To brighten the church so that it shall be a more tolerable spot is important, certainly. It is a very desirable thing to accomplish, Louise. But I don't see how you coaxed John into it."

"I want the church to look better — it is true," Louise said thoughtfully. "But, after all, that is secondary. Lewis, I want John and Dorothy."

CHAPTER XI

GRACE SUFFICIENT

rs. Morgan senior, with her long, checkered apron reaching to within an inch of the hem of her dress, her sleeves rolled to her elbow and her arms akimbo, stood in the kitchen door. She regarded Dorothy with an air of mute astonishment for about two minutes, then her thoughts found vent in words: "And did she invite him to tea her own self?"

"Yes," said Dorothy, a curious mixture of satisfaction and glumness in her tones, "she did, with her own lips. I didn't say a word, and Lewis wasn't there. He was talking with Deacon Spaulding just behind us, and John didn't speak, of course, till he spoke to him."

"Well, I never!" said Mrs. Morgan. Then, after a somewhat lengthy pause, she added, "Seems to me she is taking things into her own hands most amazing fast. Nothing but a stranger herself and gone to inviting company! Without even waiting to see if it would be convenient, either. There's extra work, too.

I suppose, though, she thinks she can sit in the front room and entertain him, and we can do the work."

"I s'pose she is so used to company that she doesn't think anything about it and doesn't know that other folks do. It isn't a dreadful thing to have the minister come to tea. For my part I'm glad he is coming." This came as a sudden outburst from Dorothy.

Her mother turned and surveyed her again in bewildered fashion. Who had ever before heard Dorothy express an outright opinion contrary to her mother's? While she was meditating on how to treat this stranger development, the hall door opened, and Louise, broom and dustpan in hand and a quaint little sweeping cap set on her head, appeared on the scene.

She dashed into the subject in mind at once: "Mother, has Dorothy mentioned that Mr. Butler is coming to tea? We didn't think about the extra ironing or we might have chosen some other night. Why didn't you remind me, Dorrie? You must let me do all the extra work to pay for my carelessness. I have come down now to put the front room in order, or shall I help in the kitchen first?"

What was a woman to do who had managed her own household with a high hand for more than thirty years and was thus unceremoniously taken by storm? She turned her gaze from Dorothy to Louise and stood regarding her for a second, as if in no doubt what to say. Then, with a bitterness of tone that Louise did not in the least understand, she said: "Do just exactly what you please — which I guess is what you are in the habit of doing without asking permission."

Then she dashed into the outer kitchen and set up such a clatter with the pots and kettles there that she surely could not have overheard a word had any been said.

Louise, with honest heart and desiring to do what was right, was by no means infallible, but she was quick-witted. She discovered at once that she had blundered. It flashed before her that Mother Morgan thought she was trying to rule the household — trying indeed to put her, the mother, aside. Nothing had been further from her thoughts. She stood transfixed for a moment, the rich blood rolling in waves over her fair face at the thought of this rude repulse of her cheery effort to play that she was at home and act accordingly.

It was as Dorothy had said: She was so accustomed to the familiar sentence, "Come in and take tea," that it fell from her lips as a matter of course, regarding one's pastor. Her invitation to Mr. Butler had been unpremeditated and, she now believed, unwise. Yet how strange a sense of loneliness and actual homesickness swept over her, as she realized this. How difficult it was to step at all. How she must guard her words and her ways. How sure she might be of giving offense, when nothing in her past experience could foreshadow such an idea to her! Was it possible that in her husband's home she was not to feel free to extend hospitalities when and where she chose? Could she ever hope to grow accustomed to such a trammeled life?

She stood still in the spot where her mother-in-law had transfixed her, the dustpan balanced nicely so that none of its contents could escape. The broom swayed back and forth slowly by a hand that trembled a little. The fair pink-trimmed, cambric sweeping cap that was so becoming to her and so useful in shielding her hair from dust heightened the flush on her face. If she had but known it, that sweeping cap was one of her many sins in the new mother's eyes.

"The idea of prinking up in a frilled cap to sweep!" that lady had exclaimed the first time she saw it. She drove the coarse comb through her thin gray hair as she spoke, regardless of the fact that much dust had settled in it from that very morning's sweeping.

"It keeps her hair clean, I'm sure," Dorothy had interposed. "You are always for keeping things most dreadfully clean."

"Clean!" the mother had exclaimed, vexed again at she hardly knew what. "So will a good washing in soap and water and look less ridiculous besides. Why do you catch me up in that way whenever I say anything? Attend to the dishes, and don't waste your time talking about hair. If you ever stick such a prinked-up thing on your head as that, I'll box your ears."

What could there be in the little pink cap to drive the mother into such a state? She rarely indulged in loud sentences. It was unfortunate for Louise that this episode had occurred but a short time earlier. And it was fortunate for her that she did not, and could not, guess what the innocent cap made by Estelle's deft fingers had to do with Mrs. Morgan's state of mind. Had she known that such a trifle had power over the mother's nerves, it might have appalled her.

We grieve sometimes because we cannot know other people's hearts and foresee what would please and what would irritate. Sometimes in our blindness we feel as if some other way certainly would have been wiser. Yet I doubt if Louise's courage would not have utterly forsaken her could she have seen the heart of her husband's mother as she rattled the pots and kettles in the outer kitchen. Hearts calm down wonderfully sometimes. What need is there then to know of their depths while at the boiling point? But what sights

must the all-seeing God look down upon, sights in
tenderness shut away from the gaze of His weak
children?

Poor Louise! It was such a little thing, and she felt
so ashamed for allowing herself to be ruffled. Several
states of feeling seemed knocking for admittance.
She almost wished that she could go to that outer
kitchen, slam the door after her, set the dustpan
down hard before the cross lady and say to her:
"There! Take your broom and your dustpan and do
your own sweeping up in John's room after this, and
let Lewis and me go home to Mother. *You* are not a
mother at all. The name does not fit you. I know what
the word means. I have had a mother all my life, and
I begin to think Lewis has never had one."

What if she should say something like that! What
a commotion she could make! It was not that she had
the least idea of saying it. It was simply that she felt,
What if I should? — Satan's earliest and most spe-
cious form, often times, of presenting a temptation.
Also, there was that unaccountable tendency to burst
into tears. She felt as though she could hardly keep
them back, even with Dorothy's gray eyes looking
keenly at her. Just a little minute allowed all these
states of feeling to surge by.

Then Dorothy broke the stillness, roused out of her
timidity by a struggling sense of injustice: "You
mustn't mind what Mother says. She speaks out
sometimes sharp. Anybody who didn't know her
would think she was angry, but she isn't. It is just her
way. She isn't used to company either, and it kind of
flurries her. But she will be real glad to have had Mr.
Butler here after it is all over."

Such a sudden rush of feeling came to Louise,
borne on the current of these words. She knew the
words cost Dorothy an effort for she had been with

her long enough and watched her closely enough to
realize what a painful hold timidity had on her. But
these eager, swiftly spoken words, so unlike
Dorothy's usual hesitation, evinced a tenderness of
feeling for Louise herself that the lonely young wife
reached after the words and treasured them gratefully. The tears rolled down her cheeks; they had
gotten too near the surface to control and were determined for once to have their way. But she looked
through them with a smile at Dorothy. In fact, she set
down her dustpan suddenly, dropped her broom
and went over to the astonished girl and kissed her
heartily.

"Thank you," she said brightly, "you good sister
Dorrie. You have helped me ever so much. Of course
Mother doesn't mean to scold me. If she did, mothers
are privileged and should be loved so much that little
scoldings can be taken gratefully — especially when
they are deserved, as mine is. I ought to have asked
her whether it would be convenient to have company. But never mind — we'll make the best of it and
have a good time all around. Dorothy, let's be real,
true sisters and help each other and love each other.
I miss my sister, Estelle."

It was the last word she dared trust herself to
speak. Those treacherous tears desired again to
choke her. She turned abruptly from Dorothy and
ran upstairs, leaving the dustpan a central ornament
of the kitchen floor. Hidden in the privacy of her own
room with the door locked on the world below,
Louise sat down in the little rocker and did what
would have thoroughly alarmed her own mother
because of its unusualness. She buried her head in
her hands and let the tears have their way.

She had managed to control herself before
Dorothy, to smile brightly on her, and to feel a thrill

of joy over the thought that she had touched that
young person's heart. But all this did not keep her
from being thoroughly roused and indignant toward
her mother-in-law. What right had she to treat her as
though she were an interloper? Was she not the wife
of the eldest son, who toiled early and late, bearing
burdens at least equal to, if not greater than, his
father?

"What that woman needs," said a strong, decided
voice in her ear, "is to realize that there are other
people in this world besides herself. She has been a
tyrant all her life. She manages everybody; she thinks
she can manage you. It is for her good, as well as your
own, that you straighten her out. You owe it to your
self-respect to go directly down to that outer kitchen
where she is banging the kettles around and say to
her that you must have an understanding. Are you
one of the family, with rights as a married daughter,
to invite and receive guests as it suits your pleasure,
or are you simply a boarder? In which case you are
entirely willing to pay for the trouble which your
guests may make."

Every nerve in Louise's body seemed to be throbbing with the desire to help her carry out this advice.
It was not merely the sting of the morning, but an
accumulation of stings which she felt had been gathering ever since she came into the house. But who
was the bold adviser? It startled this young woman
not a little to realize that her heart was wonderfully
in accord with his suggestions. As usual there was
war between him and another unseen force.

That other one said: "It is a trying position, to be
sure. You have many little things to bear, and it is
quite probable that, since your life has been so
shielded before now, they seem to you great trials.
But, you will remember, I never promised that you

should not be tried. I only pledged myself that your strength should be equal to your day. And really no temptation has taken you but such as is common to men, and I am faithful that I will not allow you to be tempted above that which you are able to bear."

Surely she knew *this* voice and recognized this message sent to her so long ago, which had proved true to her experience so many times.

"But," said that other one, "you really are not called upon to endure insults. It is a perfectly absurd position. If you had gone out West as a home missionary or were among uncouth people who had had no advantages and to whom you were not in any sense related, it would do to talk of bearing trials. But in this case what right has your husband's family to put trials of this sort upon you? You have a perfect right to please yourself, and they ought to know it."

"Yes," said that other voice, "there are undoubtedly some things they ought to know. But then 'even Christ pleased not himself.' "

"But it is so absurd! She is evidently vexed because you have invited her own pastor to take tea with her! The most natural and reasonable thing in the world. She ought to want him to come. The idea of having trouble over such a trifle as that!"

"Yes, but, after all, are there not two sides to even that? How did you know that it would be extremely inconvenient for your new mother to see her pastor just at the time you set?"

"I never thought of such a thing. In our house it was always convenient to see people."

"Why not tell her that you didn't think of it, omitting the reference to the different conditions of your own home? You know you never like to have people suggest uncomplimentary comparisons to you. By the rule which you profess to have accepted, you must not hint them to others."

"But," said that other one, "it is an unnecessary humiliation for you to go to her and apologize, as though you had done something wrong! The idea! You should certainly have some regard for your position. Because you came here full of schemes for usefulness, eager to do her good, is no reason why you should tamely submit to such treatment as this — least of all, offer an apology for what you had no idea would be disagreeable. Besides you almost apologized, and how did she receive it?"

Then that other voice: "Remember the word that I said unto you. The servant is not greater than his lord."

Straightway there surged over Louise Morgan's soul such a sense of "remembrance" of that other's patience and meekness and forgiveness and humiliation, such a remembrance of His thirty years of sorrowful cross-bearing for *her*, that there surely was verified to her another of the promises: "He shall bring all things to your remembrance." Moreover when her eyes were opened by the searching Spirit, she saw who that counselor was, with his suggestions of self-respect and wounded dignity and position. Always at variance with that other one, always directly contradicting, always eagerly putting "self" between Christ and His work. The tears came down in showers, but they were shed in a lowly attitude, for this troubled young soul sank on her knees.

"Oh, Lord Jesus," she said, "You conquered him years ago. He desires to have me. Mighty One, bid him leave me, for You are pledged that You will with the temptation provide a way of escape. And now, dear Christ, help me to show such a spirit of meekness and unfaltering cheerfulness of spirit before Lewis's mother that she shall be led, not to me, but to You."

It was a very peaceful face which presented itself in the kitchen not many moments thereafter, and the voice that spoke seemed to Dorothy, who looked on and listened, the very essence of the morning sunshine.

"Mother, it was certainly very careless of me to invite anybody to tea without first learning whether it would be convenient for you. If you will forgive me this time, I won't do it a 'bit more.' That is what my little sister says when she gets into trouble. Now I want to know if you will let me hang some of my pictures in the parlor. I've been unpacking them, and I don't know what to do with half of them."

"Of course," said Mother Morgan. "Fix the parlor as you want it. It never was called a parlor before in its life, but I daresay that is as good a name as any. The extra ironing is no consequence, anyhow. We always have enough to eat. He might as well come today as any time, for all I know." Then she dashed out at that end door again and set the outer kitchen door open and stood in it, looking off toward the snowy hills. Nobody ever apologized to her before; it gave her a queer feeling.

"Well!" said Dorothy, addressing the dustpan after Louise had vanished again. "I never could have said that in the world! After what Mother said to her, too. I don't care — I like her first rate. There now!"

CHAPTER XII

Different Shades

ouise surveyed the front room; it was square and bare. At least that last word expresses the impression it made upon her. She felt sure she could do several things to brighten it, but the question turned on expediency. How much would it be wise to undertake?

It is a curious fact that the people who, from choice or necessity, have contented themselves with paper window shades have also been the people fated to choose for these ungainly creations colors that would fight with the shades of carpet and wallpaper. Those shades in the Morgan household were the ugliest of their kind. The background was blue. Whoever saw a tint of blue that would harmonize with a cheap ingrain-carpet? They were embellished by corner pieces done in dingy brown with streaks of red here and there. The design looked like something without enough distinction to have a name; the whole of it was grotesque. In the center was a bouquet of flowers so ugly that it was a positive relief to

121

remember that nature never produced anything in the least like them.

A piece of furniture known as a settee suggested possibilities of comfort, if it had not been pushed into the coldest corner of the room and been disfigured by a frayed binding and a broken spring. The chairs, of course, were straight-backed and stiff and set in solemn rows. But the table with its curious, clawed legs and antique shape filled Louise's heart with delight.

"What a pity," she said aloud, "that they couldn't have put some of the grace into the old-fashioned chairs which they lavished on those delightful old tables. How that bit of artistic twisting would delight Estelle's heart!"

She was surveying her present field of operations after the sweeping and dusting were over, and she was trying to settle the momentous question of what to do next.

The door leading into the kitchen was swung open, and Mother Morgan presented herself in the doorway, her arms still in their favorite, reflective attitude, holding to her sides.

"The curtains do look scandalous," she said, her eyes lighting on them at once. "I've been going to get new ones for I don't know how long, but I never seem to get at such things. I declare I didn't know they were so cracked."

Instantly Louise's wits sprang to grasp this opportunity. Who could have expected such an opening, in accord with her present thoughts: "Oh, I hope you won't get new ones! I have a set of curtains that my mother gave me for my room, so I might have a reminder of home, and they are altogether too long for my windows. But I think they will just fit here. I should so like to see them in use. May I put them up?"

What was the mother to say? She possessed that unfortunate sort of pride which is always hurt with the suggestion of using other people's things. Yet she had herself opened the door to this very suggestion. How was she to close it?

"Oh, it isn't necessary to bring your curtains down here. I mean to get new ones, of course. I've just neglected it, that's all. There's been no need for it."

"I'm so glad then that you have neglected it," Louise said quickly. "It has made me feel sort of lonely to see those curtains lying idle in my trunk. I wanted to put them somewhere. How fortunate it is that they are just the right color to match nicely with the carpet. You are real good to let me have them up here."

Whereupon Mrs. Morgan, with a vague feeling that she had been "good" without in the least intending it, kept silent.

Louise gave her little chance for reflection. "You can't think how much I like that sofa. Wouldn't it be nice if they made such shaped ones so long and wide nowadays? It suggests rest to me. I can't think of anything more comfortable than this corner, when the fire is made, with that nice, hospitable sofa wheeled into it."

This sentence brought Dorothy from the kitchen to gaze with wide-eyed wonder first at the sofa and then at the speaker. The object of her intensified hatred for many a day had been that old, queer-looking, widespread, claw-footed settee. She was not accustomed to seeing such an article of furniture anywhere else and was keenly alive to the difference between her home and that of the few other homes into which she had occasionally penetrated. She had unconsciously to herself singled out the old settee

and the old table and concentrated upon them her
aversion to the whole.

There was something about Louise that gave a
stamp of sincerity to everything she said. Dorothy
found herself believing implicitly just what had been
said. Therefore this surprising eulogy of the old settee was the more bewildering. Louise's next sentence
completed the mystification.

"But the prettiest thing in this room is that table. I
never saw anything like that before. It must be very
old, isn't it? And it looks like solid mahogany."

There was no resisting the impulse. Mother Morgan's heart swelled with a sense of gratified pride (if
it were not a nobler feeling than pride). "It is solid,"
she said quickly, "every inch of it. It belonged to my
mother. It was one of her wedding presents from my
grandfather. There isn't another table in the country
as old as this."

"Isn't that delightful!" said Louise, genuine eagerness in tone and manner. "To think of your having
one of your own mother's wedding presents! My
sister, Estelle, would like to see that. She has such a
wonderful feeling of reverence for old things — especially when she can hear about the hands that
touched them long ago. Did your mother die a good
many years ago?"

"She died when I was a girl like Dorothy there,"
said Mrs. Morgan, her voice subdued. She gathered
a corner of her large apron and carried it to her eyes.
"I always set great store by that table. I've seen my
mother rub it with an old silk handkerchief by the
half hour to make it shine. She thought a great deal
of it on Grandfather's account, let alone its value,
and it was thought to be a very valuable table in those
days. I have always thought I would keep it for
Dorothy. But, land! She don't care for it. She thinks it

is a horrid, old-fashioned thing. She would have it put into the barn loft along with the spinning wheel, if she could. Your sister must be different from other girls, if she can stand anything old."

Poor Dorothy, her cheeks aflame, stood with downcast eyes. She was too honest to deny that she had hated the claw-footed table, as one of the evidences of the life to which she was shut up, different from others. Louise turned toward her with a kindly smile.

"I think Estelle is different from most girls," she said gently. "Our grandmother lived until a short time ago, and we loved her very dearly. That made Estelle like every old-fashioned thing more than she would. Mother says that most girls have to get old and gray-haired before they prize their girlhood or know what is valuable."

"That is true enough," said Mother Morgan emphatically.

Then Louise turned the conversation in a different direction. "I wonder if I can find John anywhere? I want him to help me hang pictures and curtains. Do you suppose Father can spare him a little while?"

"John!" said the wondering mother. "Do you want *his* help? Why, yes, Father will spare him, I daresay, if John will do anything. But I don't suppose he will."

"Oh, yes," said Louise, "he promised to help me. Besides he invited the minister here himself or at least seconded the invitation heartily, so of course he will have to help get ready for him."

"Well, there he is now in the shed. You get him to help if you can; I'll risk his father. And move things about where you would like to have them. I give this room into your hands. If you can make it look as pleasant as the kitchen, I'll wonder at it. It was always a dreadful, dull-looking room somehow."

And the mollified mother went her way. An apology was a soothing sort of thing. It was very nice to have the long-despised old settee and table (dear to her by a hundred associations — so dear that she would have felt it a weakness to admit it) not only tolerated but actually admired with bright eyes and eager voice. But to engage her younger son in any enterprise whatever, so that there might be hope of his staying at home with the family the whole of Tuesday was a thought to take deep root in this mother-heart. (On Tuesday evening a certain club in the village met; he was then more than at any other time exposed to temptation and danger.) She didn't choose to let anybody know of her anxiety concerning this boy. But it was the sore ache in her heart. The miseries of the morning had developed when she thought of the brightness of Louise's carefree face in contrast with her own heavyheartedness. After all, to our limited sight it would seem well once in a while to peep into each other's hearts.

Greatly to his mother's surprise and somewhat to his own, John strode at first call into the front room, albeit he muttered as he went: "I don't know anything about her gimcracks. Why don't she call Lewis?"

"Are you good at driving nails?" Louise greeted him. "Lewis isn't. He nearly always drives one crooked."

"Humph!" said John disdainfully. "Yes, I can drive a nail as straight as any of 'em, and I haven't been to college, either."

"Neither have I," said Louise, accepting his sentence in the spirit of banter, "and I can drive nails, too. If I were only a little taller I'd show you. But how are we going to reach up to the ceiling? Is there a stepladder anywhere?"

"Yes, make one out of the kitchen table and the wood box."

And he went for them. Then the work went on steadily. John could not only drive nails but could measure distances with his eye almost as accurately as with a rule and could tell to the fraction of an inch whether the picture hung "plumb" or not. Louise, watching, noted these things and freely commented upon them until despite himself John's habitual gruffness toned down.

"Who is this?" he asked. Perched on the table and wood box, he stopped to look at the life-size photograph of a beautiful girl.

"That," said Louise, pride and pleasure in her voice, "is my sister, Estelle. Isn't she pretty? With the first breath of spring I want her to come out here, and I want you to get ready to be real good to her and show her all the interesting things in field and wood."

"I?"

"Yes, you. I look forward to your being excellent friends. There are a hundred delightful things about nature and animal life of which she knows nothing, and she is eager to see and hear and learn. I look to you for help."

At this astounding appeal for "help" John turned and hung the picture without a word. What was there to say to one who actually expected help from him for that radiant creature!

Louise, apparently busy in untangling cord and arranging tassels, watched him furtively. He studied the picture after it was in place. He had difficulty in getting it to just the right height and tied and untied the crimson cord more than once in his precision. The bright, beautiful, girlish figure was full of a nameless fascination and grace that shone out at you from every curve! Louise hardly knew how much she wished for the influence of the one over the other. If Estelle could help, would help, him in a hundred ways, as she could, and if he would help her — ! Yes, Louise was honest. She saw ways in which this solemn-faced boy could help her pleasant young sister, if only he would.

Oh! she said to herself with great intensity of feeling, if only people would influence each other just as much as they could, and just as high as they could, what a wonderful thing this living would be!

It was for this reason among others that she had selected from her family group, hanging in her room, the picture of this beautiful young sister and sacrificed her to hang between the windows in the front room. There were other pictures, many of them selected carefully, with an eye to their influence. Among others was a brilliant illuminated text worked in blues and browns, and the words woven into it were such as are rarely found in mottoes. In the center was a great, gilt-edged Bible and circling over it were these words: "These are written that ye might believe on the Son of God," then underneath in smaller letters, "and that believing, ye might have life through his name."

"That is Estelle's work," Louise said. "Isn't it pretty?"

"I suppose so. I don't know anything about pretty things," John replied.

"Of course you do. You know perfectly well what you think is pretty. I venture to say that you know what you like and what you dislike, as well as any person in this world."

He laughed, not ill-pleased at this. Louise, with no apparent connection, branched into another subject.

"By the way, where is that church social that was

announced for Friday night? Far away?"

"No, just on the other hill from us, about a mile or a bit more."

"Then we can walk, can't we? I'm a good walker, and if the evening is moonlit, I should think it would be the most pleasant way of going."

And now John nearly lost his balance on the wood box, because of the suddenness with which he turned to bestow his astonished gaze on her.

"We never go," he said at last.

"Why not?"

"Well," he said, with a short laugh, "that question might be hard to answer. I suppose I don't because I don't want to."

"Why don't you want to? Aren't they pleasant gatherings?"

"Never went to see. I grew away from them before I was old enough to go. Mother and Father don't believe in them, among other things." There was a suspicion of a sneer in his voice now.

Louise was a persistent questioner. "Why don't they believe in them?"

"Various reasons. They dress up, and Mother doesn't believe in dressing up. She believes women ought to wear linsey-woolsey uniforms the year round. And they dance, and neither Mother nor Father believes in that. They think it is the unpardonable sin mentioned in the Bible."

"Do they dance at the church socials?"

"Yes," he said, an unmistakable sneer in his tones now, "I believe they do. We hear so anyway. You will look upon the institution with holy horror after this, I suppose?"

"Does Mr. Butler dance?"

"Well, reports are contradictory. Some say he hops around with the little girls before the older ones get there, and some have it that he only looks on and admires. I don't know which list of sinners he is in, I'm sure. Do you think dancing is wicked?"

"I think that picture is crooked," said Louise promptly. "Isn't it? Doesn't it want to be moved a trifle to the right? That is a special favorite of mine. Don't you know the face? Longfellow's 'Evangeline.' Lewis doesn't like the picture nor the poem, but I can't get away from my girlhood liking for both. Don't you know the poem? I'll read it to you some time and see if you don't agree with me. Now about that social — let's go next Friday and see if we can't have a good time. You and Lewis and Dorothy and I. It is quite time you introduced me to some of your people, I think."

"You didn't answer my question."

"What about? Oh, the dancing? Well, the truth is, though a short question, it takes a very long answer, and it is so involved with other questions and answers that I'm afraid if we should dip into it, we shouldn't get the curtains hung by teatime. Let me just take a Yankee's privilege and ask you a question. Do you expect me to believe in it?"

"No."

"Why not?"

"Because — well — because you religionists are not apt to."

"Don't you know any religionists who seem to?"

"Yes, but they are the counterfeit sort."

"Then you think real, honest Christians ought not to believe in dancing?"

"I didn't say any such thing," returned John hotly. He quickly realized his position and, despite his attempt not to, laughed.

"I think we'd better go after those curtains now," he said significantly. And they went.

CHAPTER XIII

BUDS OF
PROMISE

ell," said Dorothy, and she folded her arms and looked up and down the large room, a sense of great astonishment struggling with one of keen satisfaction on her face. "Who ever thought that she could make this look like this!"

This mixed and doubtful sentence indicates the bewilderment in Dorothy's mind. No wonderful thing had been done, but Dorothy belonged to that class of people who do not understand what effects little changes might produce. Still she belonged, let us be thankful, to that class of people who can *see* effects when the changes have been produced. Not a few in this world are as blind as bats about this latter matter.

The place in question was the large, square front room of the Morgan family. The heavy crimson curtains of rare pattern and graceful finish hung in rich waves about the windows, falling to the very floor and hiding many a defect in their ample folds. The walls were hung with pictures and brackets and text cards. The brackets were filled, one with a pretty antique vase, hiding within itself a small bottle of prepared earth which nourished a thrifty ivy. One held a quaint old picture of Dorothy's mother's mother, for which Louise's deft fingers had that morning fashioned a frame of pressed leaves and ferns.

The settee was drawn into exactly the right angle between the fireplace and the windows. The torn braid had been mended, and John of his own will had repaired the broken spring. The heavy mahogany table rejoiced in a wealth of beautifully bound and most attractive-looking books. A little stand brought from Louise's own room held a pot of budding and blossoming pinks, whose spicy breath pervaded the room.

Perhaps no one little thing contributed more to the holiday air which the room had taken on than did the doilies of bright wools and clear white, over which Estelle had wondered when they were being packed. Louise thought of her and smiled and wished she could have had a glimpse of them. They adorned the two rounding pillow-like ends of the sofa, hung in graceful folds from the small table that held the blossoming pinks, adorned the back and cushioned seat and arms of the wooden rocking chair in the fireplace corner, and even lay smooth and white over the back of Father Morgan's old chair. Louise had begged the chair for the other chimney corner, and Mrs. Morgan, with a mixture of indifference and dimly veiled pride, had allowed it to be taken thither.

These were all little things, yet what a transformation they made to Dorothy's eyes!

For Louise the crowning beauty to the scene was the great artistic-looking pile of hickory logs which

John had built up scientifically in the chimney corner. The blaze of those logs, when set on fire, glowed and sparkled and danced and burnished with a weird flame every picture and book. It played at light and shade in the heavy window drapery in a way that was absolutely dazzling to the eyes of the newcomer.

"What a delightful room this is!" she said, standing with clasped hands and radiant face, gazing with genuine satisfaction upon it when the fire was lighted. "How I wish my mother could see that fire! She likes wood fires so much, and she has had to depend on black holes in the floor for so long a time! I do think I never was in a more homelike spot."

It was fortunate for Louise that her education had been of that genuine kind which discovers beauty in the rare blending of lights and shades and the tasteful assimilation of furnishings, rather than in the richness of the carpet or the cost in dollars and cents of the furniture. It was genuine admiration which lighted her face. The room had taken on a touch of home and home cheer.

Mrs. Morgan senior, eyeing her closely for shams, felt instinctively that none was veiled behind those satisfied eyes and thought more highly of her daughter-in-law than she had before.

As for Dorothy, she was so sure that the fairies had been there and enchanted the great, dreary room that she yielded to the spell, nothing doubting.

It seemed almost strange to Louise herself that she was so deeply interested in this prospective visit from the minister. She found herself planning eagerly for the evening, wondering whether she could draw John into the conversation; whether Dorothy would rally from her shyness sufficiently to make a remark; and whether the bright-eyed young minister would second her efforts for these two.

During a bit of a confidential chat which Louise had with her husband at noon, she said, "I can't help feeling that there are serious interests at stake. Mr. Butler *must* get hold of the hearts of these young people. There must be outside influences to help us, or we cannot accomplish much. I wonder if he has his young people very much at heart?"

"I may misjudge the man," Lewis said, leisurely buttoning his collar and speaking in an indifferent tone, "but I fancy he hasn't a very deep interest in anything, outside of having a real good, comfortable time."

"Oh, Lewis!" His wife's note of dismay caused Lewis to turn from the mirror and look at her inquiringly. "How can you think that of your pastor? How can you pray for him when you say such things?"

"Why," Lewis said, smiling a little, "I didn't say anything very dreadful, did I, dear? He really doesn't impress me as being thoroughly in earnest. I didn't mean, of course, that he is a hypocrite. I think him to be a good, honest-hearted young man, but he hasn't that degree of earnestness that one expects in a minister."

"What degree of earnestness should a minister have, Lewis?"

"More than he has," said her husband positively. "My dear wife, really you have a mistaken sort of idea that because a man is a minister, he is perfect. Don't you think they are men of like passions with us?"

"Yes, I do. But from your remark I thought you were not of that opinion. No, really, I think I am on the other side of the argument. I am trying to discover how much more earnest a minister should be than you and I are, for instance."

"Rather more is expected of him by the church," her husband answered, moving cautiously and becoming suddenly aware that he was on slippery ground.

"By the church, possibly — but is more really expected of him by the Lord? Sometimes I have heard persons talk as though they really thought there was a different code of rules for a minister's life than for the ordinary Christian's. But after all he has to be guided by the same Bible, led by the same Spirit."

"There's a bit of sophistry in that remark," her husband said, laughing, "but I shall not stay to hunt it up just now. I suspect Father is waiting for me to help with matters that he considers more important."

"But, Lewis, wait a moment. I don't want to argue. I just want this: Will you this afternoon pray a good deal about this visit? I do feel that it ought to be a means of grace to our home and to the pastor. There should certainly be a reflex influence in visits between pastor and people. I have been for the last two hours impressed to almost constant prayer for this, and I feel as though I wanted to have a union of prayer."

Her husband lingered, regarding her with a half-troubled, half-curious expression. "Sometimes," Lewis said slowly, "I am posed to think that you have gone way beyond me in these matters, so that I cannot understand you. Now about this visit. I can see nothing but an ordinary, social cup of tea with the minister. He will eat bread and butter and the regulation number of sauces and cakes and pickles, and we will keep up a flow of talk about something. It will not matter much what to any of us, just so we succeed in appearing social. Then he will go away, the evening will be gone, and, so far as I can see, everything will be precisely as it was before."

"No," she said, with a positive setting of her head. "You are ignoring entirely the influence which one soul must have over another. Don't you believe that all of our family, by this visit, will have been drawn either to respect religion more, to feel its power more plainly, or else will have been repelled from the subject? They may none of them be aware that such is the case. Yet when they come in contact with one so closely allied to the church and the prayer meeting, I think that either one influence or the other must have its way."

"That's a new thought to me, put on that broad ground. If it is true, it proves, I think, that the minister has more influence over the community than private Christians have. Certainly it is possible for you and me to go out to tea and have a pleasant, social time and not change any person's opinion of religion one-half inch."

Louise shook her head. "It proves to me that the outward position helps the minister by the law of association to make a more distinctly realized impression. But, dear Lewis, the question is, is it right for any servant of the King to mingle familiarly for an afternoon with others who either are, or should be, loyal subjects and not make a definite impression for the King?"

"I don't know," he said slowly, gravely. "I don't believe I have thought of social gatherings in that light."

Louise realized with a throb of pain, as he went away, that she wanted the minister to make a definite impression for good, not only on Dorothy and John, but on her husband. Perhaps she never prayed more constantly for the success of any apparently small matter than she did for this tea drinking.

Her interest extended even to the dress that Dorothy wore. She knew well it would be a somewhat rusty black one. The door of that young lady's room was ajar. She was visible, adding to her dress an ugly red scarf that set her face aflame. Louise ventured a suggestion.

"Oh, Dorrie, if you would wear some soft laces with that dress, how pretty it would be!"

"I know it," said Dorothy, snatching off the red scarf as she spoke. "But I haven't any. I hate this scarf. I don't know why, but I just hate it. Mother bought it because it was cheap!" Immense disgust registered in her tone and manner. "That is surely its only recommendation."

"I have some soft laces that will be just the thing for you," Louise said in eagerness, and she ran back to her room for them.

"These are cheap," she said, returning with a box of fluffy ruchings. "They cost less than ribbon in the first place and will do up as well as linen collars."

These were new items to Dorothy. The idea that anything so white and soft and beautiful could also be cheap! This young woman had the mistaken notion that everything beautiful was costly.

"Let me arrange them," Louise said, in a flutter of satisfaction, lifting her heart in prayer as she worked.

Praying about a lace ruffle! Oh, yes, indeed — why not? If they are proper to wear, why not proper to speak of to the Father who clothes the lilies and numbers the very hairs of our head? Actually *praying* that the delicate laces might aid in lifting Dorothy into a reasonable degree of self-appreciation and so relieve somewhat the excessive timidity which Satan was using successfully against her. I wonder, has it ever occurred to young people that Satan can make use of timidity as well as boldness?

"There," said Louise, as she arranged the puffy knots, giving those curious little touches which the tasteful woman understands so well and finds so impossible to teach. "Aren't they pretty?" And she stood back to view the effect.

The happy glow on Dorothy's face showed that she thought they were.

With the details of the supper Louise did not in the least concern herself. She knew that food would be abundant and well prepared, and the linen would be snowy and the dishes shining. What more need mortal want?

As for the minister, truth to tell, he spent his leisure moments during the day dreading his visit. He had heard so much of the Morgans — of their coldness and indifference, of their holding themselves aloof from every influence, either social or spiritual. The few sentences that had ever passed between him and Farmer Morgan had been so tinged with sarcasm on the latter's part and had served to make him feel so thoroughly uncomfortable that he shrank from all contact with the entire family. This was with the exception of the fair-faced, sweet-voiced stranger, but not her husband. Something about the grave, rather cold face of Lewis Morgan made his young pastor pick him out as a merciless, intellectual critic. However, it transpired that most of his forebodings were unrealized.

Mrs. Morgan senior arrayed herself in a fresh calico, made neatly and relieved from severe plainness by a very shining linen collar. Though her manner was nearly as cold as the collar, yet there was a certain air of New England hospitality about it that made the minister feel not unwelcome. Dorothy, under the influence of her becoming laces, or some other influence, was certainly less awkward than usual. And fair, curly-haired, sweet-faced Neelie caught the young man's heart at once and was enthroned upon his knee when Farmer Morgan came to shake hands before proceeding to supper. If there was one thing on earth more than another that Farmer Morgan did admire, it was his own, beautiful, little Neelie. If the minister saw that she was an uncommon child, why then, in his heart he believed it to be a proof positive that the minister was an uncommon man.

Altogether, Andrew Butler's opinion of the Morgan family was very different by six o'clock from what it had been at four. Louise had just a word alone with him, when Farmer Morgan suddenly remembered an unforgotten duty and went away, and while Mrs. Morgan and Dorothy were putting the finishing touches to the supper table. Lewis was detained with a business caller at one of the large barns, and John had not presented himself at all. This was one of her present sources of anxiety. She turned to the minister the moment they were alone.

"We need your help so much," she began eagerly. "My husband and I are the only Christians in this family. I am specially and almost painfully interested in both John and Dorothy. They need Christ so much and apparently are so far from Him. Is the Christian influence of the young people decided in this society?"

"I hardly know how to answer you," he said, hesitating. "If I were to tell you the simple truth, I seem better able to influence the young in almost any other direction than I do in anything that pertains to religion." And if the poor young man had but known it, he was more natural and winning in regard to any other topic than he was with that one. "I have hardly a young man in my congregation on whom I can depend in the least," he continued sadly, "and I do not see any improvement in this respect."

He is in earnest, thought Louise in answer to this. He wants to help them but doesn't quite see how. If he is willing to be enough in earnest, his Master can teach him. Then, before there was opportunity for the half dozen other things that she wanted to say, they were summoned to the tea table.

John was there in his Sunday coat and his hair brushed carefully. It was more than could have been expected. Moreover, almost immediately by one of those chance remarks that seem of no importance, an item of political news was started for discussion.

Behold the father and Lewis were staunchly on one side, and the minister and John on the other. John, roused by a nettlesome speech of his brother, boldly uttered his opposing views and was strongly approved and supported by Mr. Butler. The interest deepened, and the arguers waxed earnest.

But all the while in Farmer Morgan's face, veiled to any but a close observer such as Louise was that day, there was a sense of surprised satisfaction over the fact that his boy John had such clear views of things and could talk as well as the minister. And the minister, whether he was to win souls or not, surely knew one step of the way — he was winning hearts. They went, all of them together, to the bright parlor again.

Presently, when the discussion calmed, and the subject changed to the delights of corn-popping and apples roasted in the ashes, Mr. Butler said with zest: "John, let's try some. Suppose you get the apples and superintend the roasting. Miss Dorothy, can't you and I pop some corn?"

Dorothy's cheeks were aflame. But the corn was brought, and the evening waned before even Neelie knew it was late.

"He's a good deal likelier chap than I thought from his sermons," Farmer Morgan was heard to remark to his wife when the minister had finally bade them good evening and departed.

"Oh, Lewis," said Louise, when they were alone again, "if he had only asked to read a few verses in the Bible and offered prayer before he went. I surely thought he would do it. Isn't it strange that he did not?"

"Why, yes," said Lewis, "as a minister, it would have been entirely in keeping. I wonder that he did not suggest it."

"Why didn't you suggest it, Lewis? I was hoping you would. That was what I meant by all those telegraphic communications I was trying to make."

"My dear Louise," said her husband, "that was my father's place, not mine."

CHAPTER XIV

DUST AND DOUBT

ouise's scheme to visit the dingy church on Wednesday afternoon and contribute to its cheer was carried out to the very letter. Mrs. Morgan senior made sundry dry remarks about not being aware that any of her family had been hired to put the church in order. But Farmer Morgan declared that it certainly needed it as much as any place he ever saw and that he would be ashamed to have a barn look as that did. John declared that he had promised to stop the squeak in that old organ, and he meant to do it, hired or not hired.

Louise, who had not heard him promise and who had felt much anxiety lest he would refuse to perform, was so elated over this declaration that, with her husband's help, she parried her mother-in-law's thrusts with the utmost good humor. She was also helped by the fact that whatever she might say, that strange woman actually felt glad over the thought of her young people going off together like other folks.

Mrs. Morgan had spent her life in keeping her

children from being "like other folks." Yet with
strange inconsistency she liked to see these ap-
proaches to other people's ways of doing things. If
she could have explained what her sore and disappointed heart had meant, it would have revealed the
fact that she intended her children to be superior to,
not isolated from, the society around them.

Wednesday afternoon proved a real gala time to
Dorothy. She entered with zest into the lamp cleaning and, after a few lessons from Louise, developed
a remarkable talent for making the chimneys glitter
in the sunlight. The surprised and smiling sexton
had done his share, and the dust from the long
unswept room lay thick on pulpit and seat-rail. The
room was comparatively warm, too, which, if Louise
had but known it, was a rare thing on Wednesday
evening. John swung the old organ around in a busi-
ness-like manner and applied a drop of oil here and
another there. Then he gave himself to mending one
of the organ stops, while Lewis tacked away on the
new binding for the desk and whistled softly an old
tune. Altogether, Louise's plans were working roy-
ally. She had managed a difficult bit of business in
the shape of a basket of food, which had been smug-
gled into the buggy with them.

"What on earth do you want of that!" Mrs. Morgan
had exclaimed when she had been appealed to. "You
don't expect to work so hard that you will get hungry
before supper, do you?"

"Why, we want it for our supper," explained
Louise. "You know we shall not have time to come
back before prayer meeting, and that will make us
late for supper."

"Prayer meeting?" No words on paper can express
to you the surprise in the questioner's voice. "Are
you going to stay to prayer meeting?"

"Why, certainly. We want to see whether the lamps are improved. If Dorrie leaves lint on the glass it will show splendidly when they are lighted. Besides, I want to hear how that organ will sound when it doesn't squeak."

"And what is going to become of John while you are staying to meeting?" Mrs. Morgan's face had taken on a deeper cloud of disapprobation, and her voice was glumness intensified.

"Why, John will stay to meeting with us, of course." This came from Louise in a positive tone, even though she was painfully uncertain about that very thing. She was certain only of this, that if John wouldn't stay, the rest of them wouldn't. It was no part of her plan to carry him down to the village simply to be tempted of Satan as he always was at the street corners.

"Humph!" said Mrs. Morgan senior, and she went her way. She gave no sign of relief or approval, except that the food she prepared and packed for their united suppers was bountiful and inviting.

So Louise dusted and advised as to lamps and pulpit and prayed heartily meanwhile. How was she to prevail on John to stay for the prayer meeting? Was it a foolish scheme? Would it be better to abandon it and go home? What if, at the last moment, he should rebel and go away and spend the evening in that horrid corner grocery! Recent though her introduction into the family was, she had already learned how they dreaded the influence of that corner grocery. She lingered near her husband and consulted. "Lewis, how can we prevail on John to be willing to stay tonight until after the meeting?"

"Oh, he'll be willing enough — no danger of him. He hasn't had an opportunity to visit his friends at the corner for some time. He will jump at the chance."

"Oh, but we mustn't have that kind of staying. I mean, how can we coax him to stay here at the prayer meeting?"

Her husband regarded her curiously. "I don't believe even *you* can accomplish such a result as that," he said at last, "and I am willing to admit that you do accomplish some very extraordinary things."

"Lewis, why do you speak in that way, as though I were trying to do anything wonderful? Can any work be simpler than to seek to get one interested in prayer meeting, who has no natural interest in such things? I want you to ask him to stay. You said yesterday that you had never invited him to attend. Tell him we have a nice supper and want him to stay with us and enjoy the meeting. Perhaps all he is waiting for is an invitation."

"Louise, dear, you don't know John. He would have no enjoyment from this meeting even if he stayed, which he will not do. In all sincerity I believe he would be much less likely to stay if I were to ask him than he would under almost any other circumstances. It is a humiliating fact that he doesn't care to do anything that I want him to do."

Louise turned away with a sigh. Her work was growing complicated. The dusting and cleaning went steadily on. When all was accomplished, the church was certainly improved.

A somewhat weary but cheerful little company gathered under one of the renovated lamps just at nightfall. Louise and Dorothy folded away their large aprons and sweeping caps and donned hats and shawls again, and they all sat down to eat the generous supper.

"Queer way of having a picnic," said John. "I've always supposed the woods was the place for such gatherings. We might as well go home, for all I can see. Our work is about done."

Lewis glanced at his wife; her face expressed doubt and anxiety. Certainly it would be better for them all to go home at once rather than for John to spend his evening at the corners. Just what should she say at this juncture? She hesitated but a moment, then said quickly: "Why, we are going to stay to prayer meeting. Don't you suppose we want to see the effect of these improvements on the people?"

"To prayer meeting!" echoed John. Then, beyond a low, suddenly suppressed whistle, he said no more.

Their departure for the church had been delayed, and the work there had taken more time than was planned. As the short winter day drew rapidly to its close, the meal had finally to be disposed of in haste so that two or three unfinished matters might be accomplished before the hour for prayer meeting. With very little idea as to what she should say or whether it would be wise to say anything, Louise followed John to the organ corner, while he struggled to make the organist's broken seat less objectionable.

"The idea of allowing a church to run into shabbiness in this fashion!" he said with energy, a sneer in his voice. "Shows how interested the people are in it."

"Why doesn't the sexton light the lamps on the other side?" questioned Louise. She was unwilling to enter into a discussion concerning the inconsistencies of the church and was really curious to understand the movements of that worthy person, the sexton.

"I don't know. They are all filled and trimmed, I am sure; perhaps he doesn't know that. He probably economizes by using the lamps on one side until they are empty and then taking the other row."

"No," said Louise, "I see what it is done for — so people will sit close together and not have to speak over the entire church. It is a good idea, too."

"Yes," said John. "Shows how many they expect!"

What strange power John had to throw meaning into a few words. This simple sentence startled Louise. She glanced over the large church. What a very small corner of it was lighted and made habitable. Yet she felt her own faith was equal to even less than that amount of room. She struggled for some satisfying explanation. "But, John, you know this room has to be large enough for the entire congregation. A great many of them are in the country and could hardly be expected, I suppose, to attend prayer meeting."

"I know it," said John. "Twice as far down to the village on Wednesday evening as it is Saturday. On Saturday evenings the stores have to be kept open until eleven o'clock, so many country people are in town. But none of them is affected in that way on Wednesday."

"Well," said Louise, trying to speak lightly, "our party will count four more than are usually here. That is one comfort."

John regarded her furtively from under lowering eyebrows.

"Have you any kind of a notion that I intend to stay to this meeting?" he asked at last, a curious mixture of sarcasm and sneer in his tones. Something in John's voice was constantly reminding one of sneers.

A sudden reaction swept over Louise, or rather the feeling that she had held in check rose to the surface. A vision appeared before her of John at the corner playing cards, smoking, drinking beer; of the mother at home, sick at heart when she saw him and smelled his breath; and of the father's anger and Lewis's gravity. Her voice faltered, and her eyes were full of tears as she answered from a full heart: "No; I am afraid you are *not* going to, and I am so disappointed about it that I feel as though I could hardly — "

Here the words stopped, and the tears actually dropped — one of them on John's hand that was outstretched just at that moment to grasp the hammer lying beside her. He withdrew it suddenly, a strange expression crossing his face. He looked at his hand doubtfully, gravely, then looked back at Louise. "Why in the name of common sense do you care whether I stay for prayer meeting, or where I go?"

"I care," said Louise, brushing away the treacherous tears and raising earnest eyes to his face, "a great deal more than I can explain to you. I never had a brother. I have always wanted one, and I looked forward to having pleasant times together with my brother, John. But you are unwilling to do something that means so much to me."

"How do you know I won't?" His voice was gruff now, gruffer than it had been during the day, and he seized the hammer and pounded so vigorously that she could neither speak nor hear. She turned from him in doubt and anxiety still and immediately joined her husband who had come to say that the pounding must cease. The people were beginning to come to prayer meeting. Nevertheless, the pounding did not cease until two more nails were in place. Then did John without any effort to be quiet stalk down the uncarpeted aisle and seat himself in the Morgan pew. Dorothy followed, showing her astonishment.

Louise tried to feel triumphant. But as the hour dragged its slow length along, her heart was very heavy. What a strange meeting it was — strange, at least, to her who had been used to better things. In the first place the number, counting the four who filled the Morgan pew, amounted to twenty-three. Now when twenty-three people are placed in a room designed for three hundred, the effect, to say the least, is not social. These twenty-three seemed to have made a study of seating themselves in as widespread a manner as the conditions of light and darkness would admit. Dorothy saw this and lost herself in trying to plan where the congregation would have been likely to sit had the other lamps been lighted.

The condition of inability to sing, which seems to be the chronic state of many prayer meetings, was in full force here. Mr. Butler announced a hymn, read it and earnestly invited a leader. None responded. Louise felt her cheeks flushing in sympathy with the minister's embarrassment. Never more earnestly had she wished that she could sing. Even Dorothy, conscious that *she* could sing, was so far roused by sympathy that she felt the bumpings of her frightened heart caused by the courageous question, What if I should? Not that she had the least idea of doing so, but the mere thought made her blood race through her veins at lightning speed. At last a quavering voice took up the cross and made a cross for everyone who tried to join in the unknown and uninviting melody.

This prayer meeting does not need a lengthy description. There are, alas, too many like it. Two long prayers were called for by the pastor between two silences which waited for someone to "occupy the time." A few dreary sentences came from "Deacon Jones," who is always in every meeting detailing his weary story of how things used to be when Mr. Somebody Else was our pastor. Another attempt was made at a song of praise, which made John's lip curl more emphatically than the first one had. Then the pastor arose to make some remarks.

How interesting he could be at the supper table! How bright and pleasant he could be when roasting apples and popping corn! These things the Morgans knew; so did nearly every one of the other nineteen. Why was he so uninteresting in the prayer meeting?

Louise tried to analyze it. What he said was true and good. Why did it fall like empty bubbles on her heart or vanish away? His theme was prayer. Did he mean the words he was repeating, "If ye ask anything in my name, ye shall have it"? Did he understand what those words meant? If so, why didn't he explain them to others?

Dorothy wondered at this, too. She had not gotten so far as to doubt them — that is, she knew they were Bible words. She saw Mr. Butler open his Bible and read them from it. Of course it didn't mean what it said. If it *did*, said poor Dorothy to herself, I would ask — oh, I would ask for ever so many things. And then her mind went off in a dream of what it would ask for, if only those words meant what they said!

And Mr. Butler talked, generalized, told wonderful and blessed and *solemn* truths, much as a boy might tell about the words of his spelling lesson. Did the pastor feel those words? Did he realize their meaning? Had he been asking? If so, for what? Had he received it? If he had not received and still believed the words he read, why didn't he set himself to find the reason for the delay? Poor Louise! Her mind roved almost as badly as Dorothy's, only over more solemn ground.

As for John, his face told to a close observer just what he thought. He didn't believe a word, not a word of what had been read nor of what was being said. More than that, he did not believe that the minister believed it. Was there any good in getting John to stay to prayer meeting?

CHAPTER XV

OPPORTUNITIES

church social had been one of the places against which the senior Morgans had set their faces like flints. Not that there had been much occasion for peremptory decisions. When John arrived at the proper age for attending, he had grown away from the church into a lower circle. Dorothy was frightened at the mere thought of going anywhere alone. So occasional sharp criticisms as to the proceedings — reports of which floated to them from time to time — were the extent of their interference. But Louise had weighed the matter carefully and was determined upon an attendance at the church social. Had she taken time to notice it, she might have been amused over the various forms of objection that met her plans.

"I'm afraid they will think the Morgan family has turned out *en masse*," her husband had said when he listened to the scheme. "I'm in favor of *our* going, because I think the people will like to meet you, and you will like some of them very well. But wouldn't it be better to get acquainted with them ourselves before bringing Dorothy into society? She will be frightened and awkward and will be very far from enjoying it. John won't go, of course."

"Lewis," his wife said impressively, "I believe John *will* go. I am very anxious to have him, and I feel impressed with the belief that God will put it into his heart."

The curious look on her husband's face emboldened her to ask a question which had been troubling her. "Lewis, you sometimes act almost as though you didn't believe such matters were subjects of prayer at all. Are these things too small for His notice when He Himself refers us to the fading wildflowers for lessons?"

Lewis studied his answer carefully. He admitted that of course we had a right to pray about everything. But then, well, the truth was, she certainly had a way of attaching importance to matters which seemed to him trivial — for instance, that tea. He had not understood then — did not now — why she should have been so anxious about it. As for this matter, what particular good was it going to do to take John to the church social?

"Don't you see," his wife asked earnestly, "that we must get John into a different circle, if we would draw him away from the one that he has fallen into?"

Yes, he admitted that. In fact, he admitted everything that she could possibly desire. Yet she knew he went away feeling that it was, after all, of exceeding little consequence whether John went or stayed.

Nevertheless her desire to accomplish this matter remained firm. She studied many ways for winning John's consent to the plan, seeking counsel on her knees, and wondering much that no way opened to her. But on the day in question she discovered that there was no need for an opening. John had settled the matter, for reasons best known to him, and broached the subject by inquiring whether she still believed that the pleasantest thing she could do was to walk.

"Walk where?" questioned the mother, and the subject was before them.

"Why, to the social this evening," explained Louise quickly. "I propose a walk. The evenings are perfect now, and I'm a first-class walker. I feel anxious to show my skill in that line."

"To the social — fiddlestick!" said Father Morgan, with more asperity than he generally spoke.

And Mother Morgan added: "I wonder if you and Lewis are going to sanction those gatherings."

"Why," said innocent Louise, "of course we must sustain the social gatherings of our church. I think them very important aids."

"Aids to what, I'd like to know? They are just dancing parties, and nothing else. I'm not a church member, to be sure, but I know what church members ought to be. To see them standing up for the world in that way and helping it along is sickening, to say the least." This came from Farmer Morgan.

Then Mrs. Morgan senior said: "They stay until 'most morning and dress up and gossip and giggle and dance. If that is sustaining the church, the less it is sustained the better, according to my notion."

Then Louise said: "May not part of the trouble be that those who do not approve of such management stand aloof and let Satan manage it his own way and lead the young people whither he will?"

"Humph!" said Farmer Morgan (and there is hardly in our language one syllable more expressive than that in the mouths of some people). "The minister goes."

"I know, but he cannot do much alone."

"In my opinion," said Mrs. Morgan firmly, "he enjoys it all too well to want to do anything." Her lips and eyes said as plainly as words could have done: You will do as you like, no doubt — but you won't get my Dorothy to help sustain any such thing.

"Well, Mother, we are going tonight, to see what we can do toward sustaining or something else — I hardly know what we *are* going for, I'm sure. But I know this much: we are going." Perhaps of all the group, none was more surprised than Louise at this statement from John's lips.

She hesitated, and her heart beat high with anxiety and doubt. John meant to go then, but ought he to speak so to his mother? And ought she to seem to approve of such speaking? After only a second of thought she said: "Oh, John, we wouldn't go if Mother disapproved, would we? Lewis says he always minds his mother, and I'm sure I always minded mine." This sentence, half-laughing, yet inwardly wholly earnest, was sent forth in much anxiety. The speaker remembered the fifth commandment, even though she wished most earnestly just then that it were not made so difficult a duty by the mother in question.

But a change had suddenly come over that mother. To have the boy John even at a church social, disreputable as she believed those places to be, was much better than to have him at the corner grocery or in any of his favorite haunts. The moment the idea dawned upon her that *he* really meant to go, her objections softened.

"Oh, I don't want to keep any of you from going, I'm sure. Go if you want to, of course. A church gathering ought to be a nice place; and if it isn't what it ought to be, it isn't your fault, I suppose. I shan't

make any objections." This was a remarkable conces-
sion when one considered the woman who made it.

So they went to the social, and they walked. Lewis
and Louise stepped briskly along together over the
moonlit earth. They enjoyed every step of the way —
as only those can who have little opportunity for
long, quiet walks together, even though they are
bound by the closest ties.

The large, modern farmhouse where the gathering
was held was a surprise to Louise. Unconsciously
she had gauged all farmhouses by her father-in-
law's. But here she was introduced to one of those
fair country homes with which New England
abounds — bright and tasteful and in its free and
easy, home-like way beautiful. The large rooms were
carefully arranged, and little works of art and souve-
nirs of celebrated spots and scenes were freely scattered. The books, displayed lavishly, spoke of
cultured tastes and leisure for their indulgence.

A large company was gathered, and the scene was
social in the extreme. The newcomers were greeted
very heartily. It was evident to all but her that Mrs.
Lewis Morgan was considered an acquisition to the
society, much to be desired. As for that lady, she was
engrossed in making Dorothy feel at home and have
a good time and anxious that John should not slip
away in disgust before the evening was over. She
forgot her position as a stranger and, with a purpose
in mind, made acquaintances eagerly and search-
ingly, looking everywhere for the helpers that she
hoped to find in these young people.

Meanwhile, she studied the actual scene, trying to
fit it to the reports which had come to her. The
company was very merry. They talked a good deal
of nonsense, no doubt, and it was possible that a sort
of giggly, good-natured gossip came in for its share.

They were, at least the younger portion, too much dressed up for a church social. Though the evening was advancing, she had as yet seen no indications of the amusement which Father and Mother Morgan found so objectionable.

During a moment's leisure Andrew Butler came over to her. He had been among the young people all the evening, the favorite center of the merriest circles. It was evident that these young people enjoyed their pastor at a church social, whatever opinion they might have of him elsewhere.

"I am so glad you came out to our gathering," he said to her cordially. "It was very kind of you to overlook our lack of courtesy in the matter of calls. Our ladies will call on you promptly enough now. Some of them had the impression that you might not care to make new acquaintances."

"I wonder why?" said Louise in surprise. "My old friends are too far away to be made available. Mr. Butler, what a great company of young people! Do these all belong to your congregation? Where were they on Wednesday night?"

"Well," said Mr. Butler, "the plain and painful truth is that wherever they are on Wednesday evenings, at one place they are not, and that is the prayer meeting. Some of them are church members, but it never seems to be convenient for country people to come to town on Wednesdays nor to be out so late as it is necessary in order to attend prayer meeting."

"Yet they come to the church socials?"

"Oh, yes, indeed. That is another matter. They have no objection to being social."

"Then what a pity it is that we couldn't have our prayer meeting social, isn't it?"

Mr. Butler laughed, then grew grave. "But, Mrs. Morgan, you do not suppose it is possible to make prayer meetings into places where those who have no love for Christ will like to come?"

"Perhaps not; though more might be done even for them, I suspect, than is. But some of these young people belong to Christ, don't they?"

He shook his head. "Very few. I never knew a church with such a large class of indifferent young people in it. Oh, some of them are members, to be sure. But the large majority of those here tonight, the young ones, have no sympathy with the church except in its socials."

"What a doubly important opportunity this church social is," Louise said with glowing eyes. "This is really almost your only chance with the young people, then, beside calls. How do you manage the work, or is that too close a question to answer?"

The bright eyes of the young minister dropped before her. He felt indeed that the question was too close though not in the sense that she meant it. He wished that he could just let her think that his ways of working were too intermingled to be explained. But whatever faults he may have had, deception was not one of them. He hesitated and flushed, then met her gaze squarely: "The simple truth is, Mrs. Morgan, I am doing just nothing with these young people, and I don't know what to do."

"I know," she said quickly. "The work is immense, and little, patient efforts sometimes seem like 'just nothing.' But, after all, how can you tell? The earnest words dropped here and there, even in such soil as this, may spring up and bear fruit. So long as you meet your people in this way once a week and can gather them about you as you do, I wouldn't get discouraged."

Evidently she did not understand him. He was

leaving her to suppose that he was moving quietly around among them dropping seeds. In reality he had been chatting with them about the skating and the sleighing and the coming festival and the recent party. He had dropped no earnest, honest seeds of any sort. His honest heart shrank from bearing unmerited approval.

"I am being literal," he said earnestly, "though you are kind enough to translate it figuratively. I don't feel that I am saying anything to help these young people, except to have a pleasant evening. I don't know how that is going to be a help for the future, and I don't know what I can do to aid toward *that*. I cannot get someone into a corner and preach a sermon to him at such a time as this, now can I?"

"I shouldn't think it would be a good place in which to read sermons," said Louise with smiling eyes and grave mouth. "But then we who never preach at all won't allow you to profess that the sermon is the only way of seed sowing."

"I didn't mean literal preaching, of course," he said, a trifle annoyed. "What I mean is, there is no opportunity here for personal effort of any sort. I am always afraid to attempt anything of the kind, lest I may prejudice people against the whole subject. Don't you think there is danger of that?"

"Well, I don't know," Louise said thoughtfully. "If I were to talk with one of my friends who isn't acquainted with you and tell her how kind you were, how interested in all young people and how pleasant and helpful you were, it doesn't seem to me that I should prejudice that friend against you. Why should I feel afraid of prejudicing them against my Savior?"

He looked at her doubtfully. "Don't you think young people look upon this question differently from any other? Aren't they more afraid of hearing it talked about?"

"Aren't they more unaccustomed to hearing it talked about?" was Louise's earnest answer. "Have we as Christians tried the experiment fully of talking freely, brightly, socially about this matter, about our joys and hopes and prospects? What do you suppose the effect would be? Suppose, for instance, Mr. Butler, you and I were in the midst of that circle across from us where there is just now a lull in the conversation, and you should say to me: 'Mrs. Morgan, what have you found today that affects our plans for day-to-day living?' and I should answer: 'Why, I found that our Father loves us even better than I had supposed. I found today that He says He blots out our transgressions for His own sake!' I did find that today, Mr. Butler, and it is as news to me. He really loves us so much that, for His own sake, He forgives us. What if I should say that to you in the presence of these others?"

"They would consider us a couple of fanatics," said Mr. Butler quickly.

"Well," said Louise with bright eyes and smiling mouth, "that certainly wouldn't hurt us. But why should we be called fanatics? I heard you telling what Professor Proctor says he has recently decided in regard to a scientific matter, and the young men about you listened and questioned and didn't act as though you were a fanatic at all."

CHAPTER XVI

THE REASON
OF THINGS

ohn came over to her, speaking abruptly to her and ignoring the presence of the pastor other than by a nod: "They want to know whether you dance."

The minister flushed over the question, as though it had been personal.

Louise laughed. "Can't you tell them, John?"

"How should I know?" he replied in his gruffest tones.

"Now, John! Didn't you tell me only a few days ago what you expected of me in that regard? Do you think I want to disappoint your expectations?"

"Well, then, what is the reason that you don't?"

"Mr. Butler, think of my being called upon to answer such an immense question as that at a church social! John, you will have to be my champion and explain, if you are hard-pressed, that the reasons are too numerous to be given now and here. Meanwhile, you may vouch for me that I have excellent ones."

John turned away, a grim smile on his face. Louise

looked after him, feeling much less bright and undisturbed than she appeared. She saw that he was not displeased with her answers, but she wondered uneasily what he might be enduring in the way of banter for her sake. She had grown to have that degree of confidence in him. She believed that he would endure something for her sake. She need not have been disturbed; there had been no bantering. Mrs. Lewis Morgan was at present held in too great respect for that.

Still, John had been surprised into some abrupt admissions, which he had felt obliged to have corroborated by her. "Does your sister dance?" had been asked of him abruptly by one of the pretty visions in curls, whom his eyes had been following half the evening. He had given a confused little start and glanced instinctively at the corner where Dorothy sat, while a nice old lady was talking kindly to her.

"Dorothy?" he exclaimed, with surprise. How absurd it seemed to suppose such a thing! "No, she never dances."

"Oh, I don't mean Dorothy," and the pretty vision echoed his surprise in her voice. "I mean your brother's wife."

Then John turned and looked at Louise, as she stood a little to one side conversing animatedly with the minister. How pleasant she was; how unlike anyone that he knew. What a strange sound that phrase, "your sister," had to him when he applied it to this fair young woman! She was his acknowledged sister, then, in the eyes of all these people. He had not realized it before. To be sure she had called him her brother, and it had pleased him. At the same time, the idea that other people might so speak had never occurred to him. It certainly was by no means an unpleasant idea. He was in danger of letting his mind wander off over the strangeness of this relationship and its possible pleasantnesses, unmindful of the small questioner who waited.

"Well," she said inquiringly, with a little laugh closing the word, "are you trying to decide the momentous question?"

"No," he said with emphasis, "she doesn't dance."

"Never?"

"Of course not."

"Dear me! Why 'of course'? You speak as if it were the unpardonable sin!"

They were the very words John had used in speaking of this very subject; yet he disliked this speaker for these words which slipped so smoothly from her pretty lips.

All unconscious of this, she continued: "I shall be greatly surprised if you are not mistaken. She is from the city, and in cities all the young people dance. The old fogy, country ideas on that subject are thought to be absurd. I believe she would like a little refreshment from this dullness. And really I think she looks too sensible to have any such silly notions as some of our deacons indulge. I don't suppose you ever asked her point blank, did you?"

John did not choose to tell how nearly he had done just this nor did he choose to be catechized any longer. He turned from her with this parting sentence: "If you are anxious about the matter, it is easy enough to ask her. She can speak for herself."

No sooner was he left to himself than it occurred to him that he had been very emphatic. After all, what ground had he for his positive statements? He recalled the brief conversation which he had held with Louise on the subject. What had she said? Not much besides asking him a question or two. He did not believe that she ever joined in that amusement; he felt positive about it. At the same time he could not have told why he felt so. Suppose he should be mistaken? Suppose they should get up a dance here and now and she should join them? He grew hot over the thought. She needn't try to cajole me into her prayer meetings or organ mendings after that, he told himself in indignation. But then, John Morgan, why not? You believe in dancing. You know you have sneered at your mother for her views on this subject.

Never mind what he believed — he assuredly did not believe in having this new sister of his take such a position before this public. A desire to have the proof of her own words added to his feelings sent him across the room to interrupt the conversation between her and the minister. And though she certainly did not say much, he had turned from her satisfied that, "city lady" though his new sister was, that pert little yellow-curled girl would find herself mistaken.

Meanwhile, Mr. Butler regarded the lady with a curious blending of amusement and anxiety on his face.

"Your brother has evidently assumed your defense," he said lightly.

"Yes," Louise said hesitantly. Then, with a smile, she turned her full attention upon the minister. "Now tell me, please, who is that young man who seems to stand aloof? I have noticed him several times this evening. He appears to be a stranger. He is standing quite alone near the sitting room door."

"I don't know who he is," said Mr. Butler. "I have noticed him at the socials once or twice before, but I don't know his name and can't imagine where he comes from."

"Won't you please find out for me, if you can, and introduce us?"

Thus commissioned, the minister turned away with heightened color. Not a word had Mrs. Morgan said about the strangeness of a young man's appearing in his church socials two or three times without his discovering who he was. Nevertheless, an uncomfortable sense of having seemed indifferent to his flock haunted the minister, as he looked about for ways of meeting the stranger.

"That?" said Deacon Shirley's son, Ben, to whom he appealed. "Oh, that is Carey Martyn. He is a farm hand in summer and a — well, anything he can find to be in winter. He is doing odd jobs for Mr. Capron now on the farm. He is working for his board, I believe, and attending the school in the village. I don't know him. Queer chap, I guess — keeps to himself."

"Hasn't he been to our socials before?"

"Oh, yes — twice, I think. Jennie Capron has to depend on him for an escort. He comes in the line of his work, just as he does everything else. He doesn't seem to enjoy them much."

"Suppose you introduce me?" said the minister. Ben, much amazed, complied.

While they were making their way to his side, little Jennie Capron, who had been standing near them, sped away to the young man, who was a friend of hers, and whispered: "Carey! Oh, Carey! Mr. Butler has been asking Ben Shirley all about you, and he wants to be introduced to you, and they are coming now."

"All right, little one," said the young man cheerily. "Only don't tell them we know it." And he received the promised introduction with a broad smile on his face.

Nobody knew better than Mr. Butler how to be genial when he chose, or actually when he thought of it. Carey, who had felt somewhat sore that even the minister had overlooked him, thawed under the bright and cordial greeting and was presently willing to cross the room to Louise and receive another introduction.

"Mrs. Morgan wants to meet you," said the minister as they went toward her. "She especially desired an introduction."

The young fellow's heart warmed at the idea. He was not to be left out in the cold then, after all, even if he did drive Mr. Capron's horses and work for his board. That is how he had interpreted the thoughtlessness of the young people. He was proud, this young man. A good many young men are, intensely and sensitively proud, about a hundred little things of which no one else is thinking. Thus they make hard places in their lives which might just as well be smooth.

Mr. Butler, having performed his duty, immediately left the two to make each other's acquaintance. He went himself to hunt out a new face that he had seen in the crowd. He was beginning to feel that there were ways of making church socials helpful.

A little touch of pride, mingled with a frank desire not to sail into society under false colors, made Carey say in answer to Louise's kind questioning: "Oh, no, I don't live here. My home is a hundred miles away. I am really only a servant."

"To be a servant under some masters is a very high position," Louise answered quickly. "May I hope that you are a servant of the great King?"

Then you should have seen Carey Martyn's gray eyes flash. "I believe I am," he said proudly. "I wear His uniform, and I try to serve Him."

"Then we are brother and sister," said Louise. "Let us shake hands in honor of the relationship."

She held out her fair hand and grasped the roughened one. The young man's heart warmed, and his face brightened as it hardly had since he left his mother.

CHAPTER XVII

FIRSTFRUITS

ewis," said his wife as she came to him in the hall with her coat on. "I have a little plan. I want you to walk home with Dorothy tonight and let me go with John. I would like to have a talk with him. More than that, I want you to have a talk with Dorothy. You never get an opportunity to see her alone."

"Oh, Louise!" said her husband, with clear dismay. He tried to disguise it — he did not want her to know how entirely he shrank from such a plan. "I don't think, dear, that it will be wise. Dorothy is at all times afraid of me, and a long walk alone with me would be a terrible undertaking in her eyes. Besides, Louise dear, I am not like you. I cannot talk familiarly with people on these topics as you can."

"Don't talk anymore than you think wise. Get acquainted with Dorrie, and drop one little seed that may spring up and bear fruit. I want you to try it, Lewis."

Something in her face and voice when she said

such things had often moved Lewis to go contrary to
his own wishes. It worked the same effect in him
now. Without another word of objection he turned
away — though the walk home in the starlight had
been a delightful prospect — and went to do what
was a real cross to him. What had he and Dorothy in
common? What could they say to each other?

"What is all this?" John questioned sharply, as
Lewis strode out of the gate with the frightened
Dorothy tucked under his arm. He suspected a trap,
and he had all of a young man's horror of being
caught with cunningly devised plans. If this were
one of Louise's schemes to lecture him under the
pretense of enjoying a walk, she would find him very
hard to reach.

Louise knew he was not one to be caught with
guile — at least, not guile of this sort. She answered
his question promptly and frankly. "It is a plan of
mine, John. I wanted to talk with you, and it seemed
to me this would be a good opportunity. You don't
mind walking with me, do you?"

Thus squarely met, what was John to say? He said
nothing, but he reasoned in his heart that this was a
straightforward way of doing things, anyhow — no
"sneaking" about it.

After offering his arm they walked over the frozen
earth for a little while in silence. "Well," he said,
"what have you got to say to me? Why don't you
begin your lecture?"

"Oh, John! It isn't in the least like a lecture. It is a
simple thing very easily said. I wish you were a
Christian man. That comprises the whole story."

What a simple story it was! What was there in it
that made John's heart beat quicker?

"What do *you* care?" he asked her.

"Why, isn't that a singular question? If I love my

King, don't I want all the world to be loyal to Him? Besides, if I love my friends, don't I want for them what will alone give them happiness?"

"What do you mean by being a 'Christian'?"

"I mean following Christ."

"What does that mean? I don't understand those odd phrases, and I don't believe anybody else does."

"Never mind 'anybody else.' What is there in the phrase that you don't understand?"

"I don't understand anything about it and never saw anything in anyone's religion to make me want to. I believe less in religion than I do in anything else in life. It is a great humbug. Half your Christians are making believe to their neighbors, and the other half are making believe, not only to their neighbors, but to themselves. Now you have my opinion in plain English." John drew himself up proudly, after the manner of a young man who thinks he has advanced some unanswerable arguments.

"Never mind 'other people's religion' just now, John. I don't want you to be like anyone you ever saw. I am not anxious just now to know whether you believe in religion or not. Do you believe there is such a person as Jesus Christ?"

Then there was utter silence. John had a hundred ways of twisting this subject and was ready with his lancet to probe the outer covering of all professions. He who believed that he could meet all arguments with sneers was silenced by a name. He did not believe in religion or churches or ministers or the Bible; at least he had sharply told himself that he didn't. But was he prepared to say plainly, here in the stillness of the winter night under the gaze of the solemn stars, that he did not believe there was such a person as Jesus Christ?

Foolish disciple of that orator Robert Green Ingersoll though he thought he was, something, he did not know what, some unseen, unrealized power, kept him from speaking those blasphemous and false words. Yes, he knew in his heart that to deny his belief in the existence of such a person would be as false as it was foolish. He would have been glad for Louise to advance her arguments, press the subject or be as personal as she pleased — *anything* other than this solemn silence. It made him strangely uneasy.

But Louise only waited, then repeated her question.

"Why, of course, I suppose so" was at last John's unwilling admission.

"Are you very familiar with His character?"

Another trying question. Why couldn't she *argue* if she wanted to like a sensible person? He was willing to meet her halfway. But these short, simple, straightforward questions were very trying.

"Not remarkably, I guess," he answered at last, with a half laugh. What an admission for a man to have to make who was expected to prove why he didn't believe in *anything!*

But apparently Louise had no intention of making him prove anything. "Well," she said simply, "then we have reached our starting point. I wished that you were a follower of Christ. To follow Him, of course you will have to know Him intimately."

"Who follows him?"

The question was asked almost fiercely. Oh, if Louise could only have reminded him of his mother — could have brought her forth as an unanswerable argument against this foolish attempt at skepticism! She knew mothers who could have been brought forward, but, alas for him, John Morgan's mother was not one of them. The minister? She thought of him quickly and as quickly laid his name aside. He was a "good fellow," a genial man. John already half fancied him. But it would not do to bring him forward as a model of one who was following Christ. Alas, again, for John that his pastor could not have been a satisfactory pattern! She thought of her husband and with a throb of wifely pain realized that she must not produce *his* name. Not indeed because he was not a follower, but because this unreasonable boy could so readily detect flaws and was fiercely claiming a perfect pattern. She must answer something.

"Oh, John!" she said, and her voice was full of feeling. "Very many do follow Him in weakness and with stumblings, but what has that to do with the subject? Suppose there is not a single honest follower on earth. Does that destroy you and Christ? To point out *my* follies to Jesus Christ will not excuse *you*, for He does not ask you to follow me. John, let's not argue these questions that are as plain as sunlight. You believe in Jesus Christ. Will you study Him and take Him for your model?"

"Not until I see somebody really accomplish something." He said it with his accustomed sneer. He knew it was weak and foolish and was in a sense unanswerable because of its utter puerility. All the same, he repeated it in varied forms during that walk, harping continually on the old key: the inconsistencies of others. In part he believed his own statements. In fact, he was at work at what he had accused Christians of doing: "making believe" to himself that the fault lay all outside himself.

Louise said very little more; she had not the least desire to argue. She believed that John, like many other young men in his position, knew altogether too little about the matter to be capable of honest argument. She believed he was, like many another, very far from being sincerely anxious to reach the truth. Otherwise he would not have had to make that humiliating admission that he was unacquainted with the character of Jesus Christ.

He talked a good deal during the rest of the way, waxing fierce over the real, or fancied, sins of his neighbors. He presented numerous examples and seemed surprised and provoked that she made not the slightest attempt to counter his statements.

"Upon my word!" he said at last. "You are easily vanquished. You have never lived in such an interesting community of Christians as this, I fancy. So you haven't a word to say for them?"

"I didn't know we were talking about them," she answered quietly. "I thought we were talking about Jesus Christ. I am not acquainted with them, and in one sense they are really of no consequence. But I do know Jesus and can say a word for Him, if you will present anything against Him. Still, as you seem very anxious to talk of these others, I want to ask one question: Do you believe these traits of character which you have mentioned were developed by religion?"

"Of course not — at least I should hope not. It is the absurdity of their professions in view of such lives that I was trying to point out."

"Well, suppose we grant that their professions are absurd. What have you and I gained? What has that to do with the personal question that rests between us and Christ?"

"Oh, well," he said sneering, "that is begging the question. Of course, if the life is such an important one, the fruit ought to be worth noticing. Anyhow, I don't intend to swell the army of pretenders until they can make a better showing than they do now."

It was precisely in this way that he avoided the subject, always moving away from a personal issue. You have doubtless heard them, these arguers, going over the same ground again and again exactly as though it had never been touched before. Louise was sore-hearted; she began to wonder miserably if she had made a mistake. Wasn't this talk worse than profitless? Wasn't he even being strengthened in his own follies? She had so wanted to help him, and he really seemed farther away from her reach than when they had started on this walk. She was glad when they neared their own gate. John had lapsed into silence, whether sullen or otherwise she did not know. They had walked rapidly at last and gained upon Dorothy and Lewis, who were coming up the walk.

"Good night," said Louise gently.

"Good night," he answered, then added with some hesitation: "I'm rather sorry on your account that I am such a good-for-nothing. Perhaps if I had had a specimen of your sort about me earlier, it might have made a difference. But I'm soured now beyond even your reach. I'd advise you to let me go to decay as fast as possible." And he pushed past her into the hall and up the stairs, leaving her standing in the doorway waiting for her husband.

Meanwhile, in silence and embarrassment Lewis and Dorothy had trudged along. At least he was embarrassed. He didn't know what she was feeling, except that the hand which rested on his arm trembled. This very fact disturbed him. Why did she need to be afraid of him? Was he a monster that she should shrink and tremble whenever he spoke to her? Still, conscience told him plainly that he had never exerted himself to make her feel at ease with him. Then he fell to thinking over her dull weariness of a life.

What was there for her anywhere in the future more than in the present? She would probably stagnate early, if the process were not already completed, and settle down into hopeless listlessness.

Still his view of it gave him a feeling of unutterable pity for his sister. Until now he had thought little of significance about her, except to admit a general disappointment in her. Now he began to wonder: What if she should awaken to a new life in Christ? What a restful, hopeful life it might give her! She will never be able to do much for Him, but what wonderful things He could do for her!

This was a new angle from which to look at it. Before now he had thought of her as one who would be nothing but a passive traveler to heaven, even if she were converted, and therefore not of much consequence! Was that it? Oh, no! He shrank from putting it that way. He had really not been so indifferent as he had been hopeless. If he had put the thought into words, he would have had to admit that there hadn't seemed to him enough of Dorothy for Christ to save! Something very like that, at least.

Still he had honestly meant to try to say a word to her — not so much for her sake, nor even for the Master's sake, but because of his wife's eager face and earnest voice. He had determined to talk pleasantly to her, to tell her some bright and interesting thing connected with his long absences from home. Then, when he got her interested and no longer self-conscious, he would drop just a word for Christ with a very faint and faithless sort of hope that it might possibly some time bear fruit.

He did nothing of the sort. Some new feeling took possession of him. It gave him a desire for fruit and made him eager to brighten Dorothy's desolate outlook on life with Christ. The first words he spoke very soon after the walk commenced were: "Do you know, Dorothy, I can't help wishing with all my heart that you belonged to Christ?"

Then the hand on his arm trembled violently. While he was thinking how he should quiet her tremor and chiding himself for having been so abrupt, Dorothy answered with a burst of tears: "Oh, Lewis, I never wished anything so much in my life! Will you show me how?"

"Did you know how Dorothy felt?" Lewis said, beginning the moment the door of their room closed behind him and his wife.

There was a new look on his face — an eager, almost exalted look — and a ring to his voice that made Louise turn and regard him half curiously as she said: "Nothing beyond the fact that she has seemed to me very impressible for a day or two and that I have had strong faith in praying for her. Why?"

"Why, Louise, she melted right down at the first word. She is very deeply impressed and wonderfully in earnest, and I half believe she is a Christian at this moment. I found her bewildered as to just what conversion meant, but she grasped at my explanation like one who saw with the eyes of her soul. I was so surprised and humiliated and grateful!"

All these emotions showed in his prayer. Louise, who had believed him much in earnest for years, had never heard him pray as he did that evening for his sister Dorothy. As she listened and joined in the petitions, her faith grew strong as she realized a new name was written in heaven that night and rejoiced over among the angels. And yet her heart was sad. In vain she chided it for ungratefulness and dimly suspected selfish motives at the bottom. But it did seem so strange to her that John, for whom she had felt such an increasing anxiety and for whom she had prayed as she could not pray even for Dorothy, remained aloof. He was even farther away tonight than she had felt him to be before, and Dorothy, at a word from the brother who had hardly given her two connected thoughts in years, had come joyfully into the kingdom!

Was Louise jealous? She would have been shocked at the thought. Yet in what strange and subtle ways the tempter can lead us unaware, even when we believe ourselves to be almost in line with Christ.

CHAPTER XVIII

BIRDS OF PROMISE

ne moment, Mr. Butler," said Louise, detaining the minister. He had greeted her cordially in the church aisle, bowed to Dorothy and shaken hands with Father Morgan, and was turning away. "We have something to tell you — something that will make you glad. Our sister Dorrie has decided for Christ."

Simple words enough. I suppose even Dorothy, though her cheeks glowed and her eyes were bright with joy, did not recognize the tremendous import of their meaning. Louise was surprised at their effect on Mr. Butler. He was a young minister, you will remember. While he had not been doing all that he could, he had scarcely realized that he could do more — at least, not until very recently. This was really his first experience in greeting a newborn soul among his flock. It came to him with a joyous, almost overwhelming, surprise. True, he had prayed that he might have "souls for his hire." Yet he had prayed as many another does, without realizing that possibly his prayer would be answered. Souls would actually come into the kingdom, whom he could welcome to his Father's table!

There was an instant flush over his handsome face, an eager flash in his eyes. He turned to Dorothy again and held out his hand. "Welcome," he said.

Not a word more, but the quiver in his voice said that words were beyond him just then. Dorothy turned from him with the belief that it certainly meant a great deal to the minister to have a person "decide for Christ." She was very much surprised, and not a little confused. It had not occurred to her that others, outside of Lewis and Louise, would ever know about her new hopes and intentions. I am not sure that it had occurred to her that anyone would care! She had seen very little of this before.

So it was another surprise to her when Deacon Belknap shook her hand heartily, as he said: "So you have experienced religion, have you? Well, now, that's good! That's good!" And his face shone, and he shook the smaller hand until it ached.

Poor Dorothy did not really know whether to laugh or cry. She had always been a good deal afraid of Deacon Belknap. He was a solemn-faced, slow-speaking man. She had not known that his face could shine or that he believed anything anywhere was good. Moreover, she was not sure that she had "experienced religion." Indeed, she was by no means sure what those words meant. It was true that she had decided for Christ, or — no, was that it? It almost seemed to Dorothy that instead it should be said that Christ had decided for her! How wonderfully He had called her! How almost she had heard His voice! How tenderly He had waited! How He loved her! And how sure was she that she loved Him! But to

experience religion was some wise and solemn thing
that it did not seem to her she understood.

But Deacon Belknap had something further to say:
"You're very happy now, I suppose? Yes. Well, young
converts always are. But I want to warn you: you
mustn't expect to have that feeling last. It is like 'the
morning cloud and the early dew.' You must expect
trials and crosses and disappointments and unhap-
piness. It is a hard world. Some people expect to be
'carried to the skies on flowery beds of ease.' But I
tell you it is a 'straight and thorny road and mortal
spirits tire and faint.' "

And Deacon Belknap either forgot or had never
learned the very next line in that grand old hymn.
He assured her that the sooner she realized this
world was full of troubles and conflicts, the easier
it would be for her, and went away to his waiting
class.

Dorothy's brow clouded; she was troubled. She
felt so innocently glad and happy, so sure of a
Friend, so certain that He loved her and that she
loved Him. Was it possible that she must lose this
feeling and be lonely and dreary and unsatisfied,
as she had been ever since she could remember?
Was that what was the trouble with Christians that
the feeling didn't last? Dorothy almost felt as if she
had been deceived! Her face was not nearly so
bright as before, when Carey Martyn came toward
her. He had been introduced at the church social
and had not seen her since, but he grasped her
hand — as eagerly as Deacon Belknap had.

"I hear good news of you," he said simply, with a
glad look on his face. Something in his tones made
Dorothy understand what he meant.

"Is it good news?" she asked him doubtfully.

"Is it? The very best in the world. You don't doubt

it, I hope. Are you going to stay to Sunday school? Come over and join our class. We are getting up a new class, and we are going to ask Mr. Butler to take it. I never thought I should care to have him, but it seems to me now that he would be a good teacher. Do you believe he will take a class?"

Then Dorothy, remembering his handclasp and the light in his eyes, said: "Yes, I should think he would. But I can't stay, I suppose. Oh, how I should like to!"

"Like to what?" Louise questioned, just at her side. "Oh, you are talking about Sunday school. I think we can manage it. Lewis has been asked to take a class, and I am wanted to supply a vacancy. Father said to stay if we wanted to — he was in no hurry."

Then Dorothy went over to the new class that was forming. The minister came presently and shook hands with them all and said he felt honored to be chosen as their teacher. He wondered that none of them had thought of it before. To Dorothy it seemed as though the millennium were coming, or so it would have seemed had she known anything about that word or its meaning. Many were surprised as to where that new class suddenly came from or who started it. The simple truth was, what had been lingering in Carey Martyn's heart for weeks took shape and form along with the handclasp of his pastor at that church social. He was used to Sunday school, and his old class had been taught by his old pastor.

All in all, it was a good day for Dorothy Morgan. It was her first Sunday in a new world — a Sunday in which she had received greetings from the brothers and sisters of the kingdom and been counted in; a Sunday in which she had actually joined in the hymns and the prayers and the readings, and attempted to follow the sermon. Truth to tell, Dorothy had gotten very little from the sermon. Try as she would to become interested, her thoughts would wander. But they wandered constantly to the hymn that had just been sung, the words of which she felt, and to the prayer of the pastor, the spirit of which she understood.

Why can't ministers preach just as they pray? wondered Dorothy.

The ride home in the brightness of the winter day was not unpleasant. Father Morgan, whether subdued by his long wait or by the white world glistening in the sunlight, certainly had nothing to say that was jarring and seemed not dissatisfied with the condition of things.

Dorothy stole little glances at him from under her wrappings and wondered whether he would ever know that everything was different to her from what it had been last Sunday. What would he say if he ever did know? Suddenly, like the leap of a new emotion into her heart, she wondered if he knew for himself what it all meant. Oh, how she wished that Father were a Christian! Where did the sudden intense desire come from? She had never felt anything like it before.

Sometimes indeed she had drearily wished that they were more like other people who went to church regularly or even went occasionally as did the Stuarts, who lived no farther away and had the social assigned to be at their house. But it had been a dreamy, faraway sort of wish, with little desire in it, and nothing at all like this sudden longing.

Then there came to Dorothy the sweet thought that she could actually pray for her father. And maybe — oh, maybe! — because of her prayer her father would some day, when she had prayed for him a great many years, come to know of this experience by personal knowledge. Would more happiness ever come into Dorothy's life than surged over her at that thought?

Still, Deacon Belknap troubled her. When was she to expect all this brightness to go away? And why must it go? Why hadn't Lewis said something to her about it — warned her when she frankly admitted to him this morning that she had never been happy before in her life? And oh, how long had the feeling stayed with him? He knew about it, for he had told her that he understood just how she felt. He remembered well his own experience. Then a sudden, bewildering doubt of Deacon Belknap's theories came over Dorothy, for she did not believe the feeling ever left Louise. This was what made her different from others. Still, Deacon Belknap ought to know. Besides, what mightn't Louise have had to go through before the joy came to stay? Dorothy's brain was in a whirl.

It was well for her that Louise, standing at one side, had heard every word of Deacon Belknap's well-meant and honest caution. She saw the instant clouding of Dorothy's face and watched for her chance to remove the thorn. It came to her just after dinner, when Dorothy was upstairs hunting for her apron. Meeting her in the hall, Louise said, "So Deacon Belknap thought he ought to caution you against being happy in Christ?"

"What did he mean?" Dorothy asked, her cheeks glowing. "Does the happy feeling all go away? Must it?"

"What does it spring from, Dorrie, dear?"

"Why, I think," said Dorothy, hesitating and blushing violently, "it seems to me that it comes because I love Jesus and because He loves me."

"Yes. Well, if Deacon Belknap had told me that I must not expect to be as happy with my husband in the future as I am now because there would be trials and difficulties to encounter and that therefore his love and mine would not burn as brightly, I think I should have considered myself insulted."

"I should think so! Do you mean — oh, Louise, I mean do you think they are a little alike?"

"He calls the church His bride, dear. It is His own word. Of course. it falls far below the real, vital union that there may be between us and Christ."

"Then what did Deacon Belknap mean?"

"Why, if I should treat Lewis very coldly and indifferently, forget to notice him some of the time, go for days without talking with him, neglect his suggestions, disregard his advice, and all that sort of thing, I imagine that we would not be very happy together."

"Well," said Dorothy in bewilderment.

"Well, don't you know, dear, that that is just the way in which many Christians actually treat Christ? And Satan blinds their hearts into thinking that it is not their own fault that their joy in Him is gone, but that it is necessary because of this troublesome world. If I were you I would not tolerate any such insinuations. It is an insult to Jesus Christ, who deliberately says He will keep you in 'perfect peace' if your mind is stayed on Him."

"Then all that isn't necessary!"

"No more necessary than for me to have days of gloom and disappointment over my husband. It lowers the power and love of Christ to make that comparison, because, Dorrie, His love is infinite and, as He says, everlasting."

Dorothy went through the hall below, singing:

Mine is an unchanging love,
Higher than the heights above;

Deeper than the depths beneath,
Free and faithful, strong as death.

She had found that hymn in the morning, while
Mr. Butler was preaching, and had joined in singing
it until Deacon Belknap had banished it from her
heart. Now it came back in strength, and it would
take more than Deacon Belknap to shake it, for it had
taken root.

That Sunday had one more experience to be remembered. If Louise's little plan for the walk home
from the social had included rousing Lewis, she
could not more successfully have accomplished it.

He had walked ever since in a new atmosphere.
He had risen to the glory of the possibilities of his
life. He had heard Dorothy say — she had said it
that very morning when he met her early, out in the
back kitchen woodshed where the kindlings were
kept — that he had shown her the way to Jesus,
and now she had found rest in Him. Was a man
ever to forget such sweet words as those — a Christian, honored of God in showing another soul the
entrance way to the kingdom? Shall he sink to the
level of common, everyday things after that and
forget that he has a right to work with God on work
that will last to all eternity? Lewis Morgan, Christian man though he had been for years, had never
heard those words before. But do you think that
something of the honor which he had lost and the
shame of having tamely lost such honors did not
sweep over him? Surely it would not be the last
time that he would hear such words — at least it
would be through no fault of his if it were.

Low motive, do you say? I'm not sure of that.
There is a higher one, it is true. Every Christian who
can feel the lower will sooner or later grasp the

higher. But since God has called us to honorable positions, even to be co-laborers, "shall we not rejoice in the honor?"

Well, Lewis Morgan had worked all day in the light of this new experience. He thirsted for more of it. He felt roused to his very fingertips. He longed to be doing. He had taught that class of girls put into his care, as he had not supposed that he could teach. Now he walked up and down their room thinking, while the twilight gathered.

Louise, who had been reading to him, kept silence and wondered what question he was evidently deciding. She knew his face so well that she felt sure he was making a decision. At last he came to her side.

"Louise, I believe in my soul that we ought to go downstairs and try to have prayers with the family. Father might object to it. He thinks all these things are meaningless ritual, and I have been especially anxious to avoid anything that looked in the least like it. I have been too much afraid of what he would think. I believe I ought to try. What do you say?"

Of course he knew just what she would say. Soon after that they went downstairs. Lewis possessed one trait worthy of imitation: when he had determined on a course, he went straight toward it with as little delay as possible. So directly they were seated in the clean and orderly kitchen, Neelie cuddled in Louise's lap — a spot which was growing to be her refuge.

Lewis began: "Father, we have been thinking that perhaps you would have no objection to our having family worship together downstairs. We would like it very much, if it would not be unpleasant."

Mrs. Morgan seemed suddenly seized with the spirit of uncontrollable restlessness. She hopped from her chair; drew down the paper shade with a jerk; then finding that she had made it disagreeably dark, drew it up again; set back two chairs; opened and shut the outer kitchen door; and took down the dish towel and hung it on another nail. Then she came back to her seat.

As for Father Morgan, he sat, tongs in hand, just as he had been when Lewis addressed him, and stared into the glowing fire for the space of what seemed to Lewis five minutes. In reality, it was not more than one. Then he said slowly and impressively: "I'm sure I have no objections, if it will do you any good."

It was Dorothy who rushed into the other room before her father's sentence was concluded and brought out Grandmother Hunt's old family Bible. In the Morgan household, after forty years of life together, the father and mother met for the first time at the family altar, although neither one bowed the knee but sat bolt upright in their chairs. But Dorothy knelt and prayed and dropped some happy tears on her wooden chair the while.

As for John, he would not go to church. He would not come to dinner with the family but took what he called a "bite" by himself when he chose to come for it. And he would not stay in the room during the reading and the prayer but strode off toward the barn the moment the subject was suggested by Lewis.

Yet despite these drawbacks the voice of prayer went up from the Morgan kitchen from full and grateful hearts.

CHAPTER XIX

"Whatsoever"

 am not sure I can explain to you the state of mind in which Dorothy opened her eyes to the world on Monday morning. Unless you've had a similar experience you will not understand it. She had always been a repressed, rather than indifferent, girl. Under the apparently apathetic exterior there had boiled a perfect volcano of longing. She hadn't known what she wanted. She hadn't felt the least hope of discovering how her thoughts had taken new shape. She was in another world. She was another person. Old things had passed away; all things had become new.

She stood before her bit of mirror and tried to arrange her heavy braids of hair as Louise wore hers. She was in a very eager, very unsettled state of mind. What was she to do? Where was she to begin? The bare walls of her uninviting little room had always seemed to shut her in, and she had always hated them. Now it seemed to her that she had a right to get away from them — get outside somewhere and do something. How was it all to be accomplished? She looked with disdain upon her life. She felt her years thus far to have been wasted ones. Now she was ready to make a fresh start; only she could not imagine which step to take first. You see her danger. Many a young life has shipwrecked its usefulness on just such rocks.

She threw down the covering of her bed and, opening the window to let in the crisp winter morning, smelled of the frosty, sunlit air. She looked abroad over her little world, shut in by hills and far-stretching meadows and homelike farms, and wondered just what she should do. The longing to get away from all this, where there seemed to be nothing to do, was the strongest feeling that possessed her, unless the determination to accomplish it was a shade stronger.

She stepped out into the narrow little hall and came face to face with Louise, who was bright and smiling in a fresh calico and ruffles.

"Louise," said Dorothy, a whole world of repressed eagerness in her voice, "what am I going to do?"

"Ever so many things I hope, dear," was Louise's prompt and cheery reply, and she emphasized it with a kiss.

"Yes," said Dorothy with shining eyes, "I mean to, oh, I mean to. But I don't know where to begin. What is there to do — I mean, for a beginning — and how shall I find it?"

"I think," said Louise, with smiling mouth and eyes and sweet, decided voice, "I think, my dear, if I were you, I would begin with that black kettle."

You should have seen the sudden change in Dorothy's face. Surprise, disappointment and intense mortification — all struggling with a sense of

being misunderstood and wronged showed in her
eyes and the quiver of her lips.

"You think I am teasing you, Dorrie." Her new
sister's voice was very tender. "Nothing is farther
from my intention. I honestly mean what I say. That
very kettle which gives you Monday morning
trouble can help you to a first victory. It's a symbol
of all the other things, which are small in themselves
but amount to much when counted together, that can
be used to serve you today."

"I did mean to try to do right, but I wanted to do
something for Christ." Dorothy's voice was subdued.

"And you think that Jesus Christ has nothing to
do with the black kettle or the boiler or the sink or a
dozen other things with which you will come in
contact today? That is such a mistake. Don't begin
your Christian life by thinking that all these duties
which fall upon us in such numbers consume just so
much time that must be counted out. Then with the
piece that is left we are to serve Him. Remember that
it is He who said, 'Whether therefore ye eat, or drink,
or whatsoever ye do, do all to the glory of God.'
Doesn't that 'whatsoever' cover the pudding kettle,
too, Dorrie?"

New light was struggling on Dorrie's face — just
a glimmer though, shadowed by confusion.

"It sounds as if it ought to," she said slowly. "And
yet I cannot see how. What can my dishwashing have
to do with serving Jesus? It seems almost irreverent."

"It can't be irreverent, dear, because He said it
Himself: 'diligent in business, serving the Lord.'
There is no period dividing these. I long ago discov-
ered that I could make a bed and sweep a room for
His sake, as surely as I could speak a word for Him.
It is my joy, Dorrie, that He has not separated any

moment of my life from Him, saying, 'Here is so much drudgery each day, from which I must be entirely separated; then, when that is done, you may serve Me.' Work so divided would be drudgery indeed. I bless Him that I may constantly serve, whether I am wiping the dust from my table or whether I am on my knees."

"Well, how?" said Dorothy. She had a habit of flashing a question at someone in a direct, firm way that meant business. The tone of this one said, This is all new to me, but I mean to get at it — I intend to understand it and do it.

"Louise, how could I be doing one thing for Jesus while I was washing the pudding kettle?"

"Did you ever hear of the young servant-girl who was converted and presented herself to the pastor desiring to be received into the church? He asked her what proof she had that she was a Christian, and she answered, 'I sweeps the corners clean now.' I always thought that the poor girl gave good evidence of a changed purpose. I don't know whether she knew that verse, 'By their fruits ye shall know them,' but it is true, Dorrie, with pudding kettles as well as with everything else."

That simple little talk in the upper hall on that Monday morning actually changed the whole current of Dorothy Morgan's future life. Up to that time religion had had nothing whatever to do with pudding kettles or Monday mornings in the kitchen or with the thousand little cares of everyday life. She had regarded them as so many nuisances to be pushed aside as much as possible for actual work. I may as well admit to you that this young girl hated the neatly painted kitchen in which most of her life was spent. She hated the dishpan and the sink and the dish towels with a perfect hatred. She hated

brooms and dusters and scrub brushes and all the
paraphernalia of household drudgery; it was liter-
ally drudgery to her.

Her new sister's wise eyes had singled out the
thing which she perhaps hated most for illustrating
this germ of truth that she had dropped into the soil
of Dorothy's heart: a heavy, black kettle which had
been handed down as an heirloom in the Morgan
family for generations and in which the favorite
Sunday evening dish, hasty pudding, was invariably
cooked.

Simmering slowly over the fire all Sunday afternoon, the pudding was eaten at supper time. The
kettle was filled with water and left to soak overnight. It appeared with relentless regularity every
Monday morning to be scraped and scrubbed by
Dorothy's disgusted fingers. Dorothy hated hasty
pudding. Dorothy almost never washed that kettle
with the nicety that Mother Morgan demanded. She
invariably left little creases of scorched pudding
clinging to the sides and a general greasiness about
it. Many sharp words came forth from the mother
and sullen defiance from Dorothy. That her religion
actually had to do with this pudding kettle came to
Dorothy like a revelation. She went downstairs
thinking it over. She realized that the thought gave
new interest to life. If the fruits of Christian living
were actually to be looked for in pudding dishes,
then where couldn't they show? There was a dignity
in living, after all. It was not simple drudgery and
nothing else. She thought of it when the foaming
milk was brought in.

John set the pail down with a thud and said: "Tend
to that, and give us the pail. And don't be all day
about it, either."

Dorothy was more or less accustomed to this form

of address, and it always irritated her. She was apt to reply, "I shall be just as long as I please. If you want it done quicker, do it yourself." Then other cross or sullen words would follow, with neither John nor Dorothy meaning fully the words they used; yet both felt crosser when they parted. It was a sad state of living, but it had actually become a habit with these two — so much so that John looked at his sister in surprise when she lifted the pail silently and returned it to him, remarking only that Brownie was giving more milk than before. He gave no answer and went away actually surprised at the quietness of the kitchen.

Monday morning is a time that tries the souls of many women. Mrs. Morgan was no exception. For some reason she was particularly tried this morning. Nothing went right, and nothing could be made to go right. The fire would not burn enough, and then it burned too much and sent the suds from the boiler sputtering over on the bright tins that Dorothy had arranged on the hearth to dry. Mrs. Morgan said that a child ten years old would have known better than to have put tins in such a place. Despite Dorothy's earnest care, the starch presently lumped. Worse than that, cloudy-looking streaks came from no one knew where and mixed with its clearness. The mother affirmed that Dorothy ought to have her ears boxed for being so careless.

Try as the daughter would, the mother was not to be pleased that morning. And Dorothy did struggle bravely. She made the smooth, black sides of the hated pudding kettle shine as they never had before on any Monday morning on record. She scoured every knife, even the miserable little one with a nick in the end and a rough place in the handle. She had longed to throw away that knife, but her mother had clung to it stubbornly. She rubbed at the hated sink until it shone like burnished steel. She scrubbed the dishcloth, for which she had a special and separate feeling of disgust, until it hung white and dry on its line. She neglected no cup or spoon or shelf corner, and she moved with brisk step and swift fingers.

But it was only to hear the metallic voice say, as it entered from the outer kitchen where the rubbing and rinsing were going on: "I wonder if you are going to be all day washing that handful of dishes! I could have had them all put away and the kitchen swept an hour ago. I can't see how I came to have such a dawdler as you!"

Dear me! Have you been so fortunate as never to have heard mothers speak in this way? Good, honest mothers, too — mothers who will sit with unblinking eyes and patient hands night after night, caring for the wants both real and imaginary of their sick daughters, and then stab them with unthinking words all day long! The words were not true. Mrs. Morgan knew perfectly well that she could not have finished all this work an hour before. Yet to be just to her, energetic woman that she was, she actually believed that she could have accomplished it all in much less time. For that matter perhaps she could. Certainly Dorothy had not her mother's skill; it was a wonder the mother should have expected young hands to be as deft as her own.

So the day wore on. A trying one at every turn to poor young Dorothy, who had just enlisted and was trying to buckle her armor on. She kept up a brave struggle and went steadily from one duty to another, doing not one of them as well as her mother could have done, but doing each one as well as she could. Could an angel do more? A hard day, both over the dishes and the dust and at the washtub. Yet it was not as hard as it might have been, but for that bit of talk in the upper hall in the morning. The new idea had put a song in her heart, despite all the trials — so much of a song that occasionally it flowed into words. Dorothy's untrained voice was sweet and clear. She rarely used it over her work, but on this Monday twice she sang, clear and loud:

> Mine is an unchanging love,
> Higher than the heights above.

Mrs. Morgan heard it. She heard the tune, caught no words and wanted to hear none. The spirit of song was not in her heart that morning. All she said was: "Don't, for pity's sake, go to singing over the dishpan. I always thought that was a miserable, shiftless habit. There is a time for all things."

Dorothy, wondering when it *was* her time to sing, hushed her voice and finished the melody in her heart. So it seemed to her, when the day was done, that it had been an unusually hard one. Many steps were added to the usual routine. A dish had broken; a leaking pail sent water all over the clean floor. John's muddy feet tracked through the kitchen just after the mopping was done. John's hands left traces of them on the clean towel. Then, in trying to do two things at once at her mother's bidding, she actually allowed the starch to scorch! In truth, when she sat down in the wooden chair in her own room for a moment's breathing space before it was time to set the table for tea, she looked back over the day with a little sigh. What had she done this day for the glory of God? How could He possibly get any glory out of her honest efforts to do her whole duty that day? True, she had resisted the temptation to slam the door hard, to set down the teakettle with a bang, to say in an undertone: "I don't care whether it is clean or dirty," when some undone task was pointed out to her. Yet what had been the result? Mother certainly had never been so hard to please.

She has found more to blame me for today than she ever did in the days when I only half tried, thought poor Dorothy.

So where was there any glory for the Master to be found in the day? Even then came the mother's voice, calling: "Well, are we to have any supper tonight? Or must I get it with all the rest I have to do?"

Then Dorothy went down. I'm afraid she set the cups and saucers on the table with more force than was needed. Life looked full of pin pricks that hurt for the time being as much, or at least she thought they did, as though they had been made with lancets.

What was the trouble with Mother Morgan?

She did not understand herself, to be sure. It had been an unusually trying day to her. Aside from the burden of domestic cares — which she along with many other housekeepers made twice as heavy as they should be — her nerves or her heart or her conscience or all of these forces had been stirred within her by the words of prayer in the twilight of Sunday.

She recalled an old hillside farmhouse surrounded by fields less rich and fruitful than those nearby. In an old armchair an old man sat morning and night, and by his side in another chair an old woman sat, morning and night. Together they read out of the same Bible; together they knelt and prayed. This cold-faced mother had heard herself prayed for many times by both the old man and the gray-haired woman. They were her father and mother, both asleep now side by side under the snow. And being

dead, yet speaking, they were speaking loudly to her
on that very Monday. As she looked at Dorothy she
felt as though she were wronging her of a birthright.
Dorothy had never heard her mother pray, as she had
heard *her* old mother many times. Dorothy's mother
had never said to her: "Dorothy, I want you to be a
servant of God more than I want anything else."

That was what *her* mother had said to her when
she was Dorothy's age and many times afterward.
She was not a servant of God yet, and her conscience
reproached her. Her child had never heard such
words, and her heart reproached her. She pitied
Dorothy! Yet this very feeling actually made her
voice sharper and her words more impatient when
she spoke to her. The human heart unchanged is a
very strange and contradictory thing.

But I want to tell you what Dorothy Morgan did
not know.

Her mother did discover the immaculate condition of the pudding kettle and said aloud: "I declare,
for once this is clean!"

CHAPTER XX

CLOUDS

I have been tempted to linger over these weeks of Louise Morgan's homecoming to give you a clear view of the surroundings and a true idea of the family life. Now, however, I shall have to take you into the spring. The long, cold, busy winter with its cares and opportunities passed forever from their grasp, and the buds and blossoms which foretold the coming summer were alert on every hand.

Many changes, subtle and sweet and strong, had been going on in the Morgan household. Dorothy had held steadily on her course. The first lesson in her Christian experience was ever present with her — that in the very smallest matters of life her light might shine for Christ. She was learning the important lesson to be "faithful over a few things." Little did she realize the importance of this faithfulness. She had no idea of the times her mother had regarded her curiously, as she looked in vain for careless ways or forgotten duties. She admitted to herself that "something had come over Dorothy, and she only hoped it would last." Oh, yes, it would last. Dorothy believed that. She had anchored her soul after the first hours of unrest on the sure promise of His "sufficient grace." She had no idea of doubting Him. She had not been able to take up much outside work. Yet, little by little, changes came. Carey Martyn figured in these changes, for he was full of schemes.

"See here, let us do thus and so" was a favorite phrase of his. And he was growing more and more fond of saying it to Dorothy.

The bright curtains in the parlor had not been taken down again. The old-fashioned sofa still held its place in the coziest corner. Now that the sun was getting around the corner, peeping in at the most pleasant window, the room took on a still more cheery look. Dorothy had fallen into the habit of touching a match to the carefully laid fire almost every evening just after tea, and one by one the different members of the family dropped in.

The long-neglected brass knocker often sounded during these days. People who had never called on the Morgans, chiefly because of the fear that they would be coldly received, discovered that Mrs. Lewis Morgan was a very pleasant woman and was very glad to see her friends. The mother was not so disagreeable as they had supposed. And "really, that shy, silent Dorothy had improved wonderfully."

So it was when spring opened, only a few months since the newcomer's first entrance. As far as outward eyes could see, nothing remarkable had transpired. Yet in a hundred little ways things were different. But on this particular May morning in the family circle, the prevailing atmosphere was gloom.

It rained — a soft, sweet, spring rain when the buds swell and leaves seem to grow while you watch and the spring flowers nod at one another. The world though in tears seems to the happy heart to be celebrating a holiday. Yet as Louise Morgan stood at her window and watched the dripping eaves and listened to the patter on the roof and saw the low, gray clouds sail by, a rainy day seemed to her a dreary thing.

The truth was, the Morgan family was in trouble. During the passing months Louise and her husband, joined by Dorothy and afterward Carey Martyn, had carried John Morgan on their hearts as a subject of constant prayer. Louise had often been eager, persistent and steadfast for a soul before, but it seemed to her that the desire had never been as intense as this one or that she had ever had so little encouragement.

From the time she walked home with him in the moonlight and tried to speak earnestly, John had seemed to withdraw more into himself. He carefully avoided Louise. He refused all invitations to attend church on Sunday. He informed Lewis that he was wasting words in trying to talk religion at him and would consider himself honorably excused from any such attempts. To Dorothy, who with tearful eyes and trembling lips said simply to him one night in the darkness, "Oh, John, won't you give yourself to Jesus?" he unceremoniously and roughly answered, "Shut up!"

In every respect during the last few months John had seemed to travel rapidly backward. The corner grocery now saw him more frequently than ever before. Indeed, almost every evening, late into the night, was passed there. The smells of tobacco and liquor lingered about his clothing and pervaded his room. In vain Louise struggled to keep that room pure. Gradually it had changed its outward appearance. Christmas and New Year's and then John's birthday had been helpful anniversaries to her plans.

The bed was spread in spotless white. The twisted-legged stand had its scratched and paintless top concealed under a white and delicately crocheted doily. A little rocker occupied the corner by the window with a bright-colored doily fastened securely to its back. The space between the hall door and the clothespress was occupied by a stand with all the convenient toiletry accessories arranged neatly on it. The walls were hung with two or three choice engravings and an illuminated text. On the white-covered stand there daily blossomed in a small vase a rose or a bunch of lilies-of-the-valley or a spray of delicate wildflowers — some sweet-breathed treasure from the woods or garden, which struggled with the tobacco-scented air. They were placed there by Louise's tasteful fingers.

Once she ventured on a gift in the shape of a nicely bound Bible. She had John's name put on the flyleaf and made a place for it on the white-covered stand. The very next morning she found it had been placed on the highest shelf in the clothespress, along with a pile of old agricultural papers that reposed there from one housecleaning to another. All of these patient, little efforts had been greeted with nothing but frowns or sneers or total indifference.

John Morgan seemed determined to ruin his prospects for this life and the next and to forbid anyone to hold him back. Yet these four did not give him up. The more hopeless the case seemed to grow, the more steadily they tried to hold their grasp on the arm of power.

But on this rainy morning all four were plunged into more or less anxiety and gloom. Apparently, not only had their efforts failed, but the subject — John — had resolved to remove himself from all further influence or molestation from them. His threat to leave home and go where he pleased he had now determined to execute. A week earlier he had suddenly and fiercely announced his decision, and no amount of persuasion had effected the least change. He was likewise indifferent to his father's advice or threats.

"You needn't give me a red cent if you aren't a mind to," he had said sullenly during one of the stormy talks. "I'll risk that I can take care of myself. I can beg or I can steal or I can drown myself, if I feel like it. Anyhow I'm going, and there's no use in talking."

"But where are you going?" pleaded the mother.

And one less indifferent than John could not have failed to notice that her face was pale and her voice husky with pent-up feeling.

"Just exactly where I like, and nowhere else. If I knew where that was I might tell you, but I don't. I never did as I pleased an hour since I was born, and I mean to do it now or kill myself — or maybe both. I've often thought I'd like well enough to do that."

What was the use of talking to one in such a mood? Yet they talked and argued and threatened, and they used sharp words and bitter words and words that were calculated to leave lifelong scars on hearts. The talks were frequently renewed and lasted away into the middle of the night. At last John declared that he wouldn't stand this sort of thing another hour. He wouldn't take any money, not a cent of it, even if it was offered. And he would not take his clothes along, not a rag.

"You can sell them to the first ragman that comes along and build another barn with their value, for all I care," he said to his father in a pitiful attempt at sarcasm.

And then, without another word or a glance at his mother or a pretense at good-bye, he strode out of the room, closing the door after him with a bang. That was the evening before, just at supper time. His mother did that night what she had never done before in her life — put some of the supper down, carefully covered to stay warm for John — but he came not. The next morning's milking was done without him. As the long, rainy day waned, it became evident to each heart that John was gone.

The worst of this is that, for the past week, the mother's heart had been wrung with such anxiety that she had humbled herself in a manner that she would not have imagined possible a few days before. She had followed Louise one morning up to her room with a slow and doubtful step. She closed the door after her and looked behind her in a half-frightened way, as if to be sure no one else would hear her humiliation. Catching her breath she said to Louise, "You know how I feel about John. I have heard you talk about praying over everything. If you believe that it does any good, why don't you pray to have him kept at home?"

"Mother," said Louise, coming close to her and taking the hard, old hand in hers, "I do pray for him — every hour in the day, almost every minute, it seems to me — and I believe it will do good. I believe He will hear our prayer. But there is no one who could pray for John as his mother could. I do so desire to have his mother's prayers enfold him like a garment. Won't you pray for him?"

"I'm not a praying woman," said Mrs. Morgan, trying to keep her voice steady. "Still, if I believed in it as you do, I would pray now if I never did again."

Then she turned and went swiftly away. She had actually humbled her proud heart to ask her daughter-in-law to pray for John! She could not get away from the feeling that Louise's prayers would be likely to avail, if anyone's would. There was more to it than that, but at the time this was known only to her own heart and to the One who reads the heart.

In the silence and darkness of her own room, after Neelie was asleep and before Farmer Morgan had drawn the last bolt in preparation for coming to his bed, she had gotten down on her knees and had offered what in her ignorance she thought was prayer. "O God," she said, "if Thou hearest human beings in their need, hear me, and keep John from going away." There was no submission in her heart to the divine will, no reference to the only name by which we can approach God, no realization of anything except John's peril and a blind reaching out after some hand that had power. Yet it was a nearer approach to prayer than that mother had made for fifty years!

The rainy day wore on. Mrs. Morgan could not help a feeling, which she told herself was probably superstition, that something somehow would prevent John from carrying out his plans. Yet the days went by, and no unseen arm stretched out its hand of power and arrested John. The feeling settled down hopelessly on the mother's heart that her son had gone from her with hard words on his lips and with the echo of hard words from her sounding in his heart. How strange a thing is this human heart: Mrs. Morgan had never seemed more hard or cold to her son than she did during the week that her heart was torn with anxiety for him.

As the days moved on, it became evident to all that John had carried out his threat and was gone. The mother's grief and dismay found vent in hard and cruel words. She turned in bitterness from Louise and from Dorothy, indeed from everyone. To Louise she said plainly, it was not strange that John had wanted to get away. She had given him no peace since she had been there. She was always tormenting him to go to church or to prayer meeting or to do something that he didn't want to do. For her part, she thought he was quite as good as those who were always running off to meetings. He couldn't even have any peace in his own room. It must be cluttered up with rubbish that any man hated — vases to tip over and doilies to torment him!

She flung the doilies on a chair in Louise's room and folded and packed away the spread which she said she had been "fooled into buying." She restored every corner of that little hall chamber to its original dreariness. And, worse than that, she declared that she hoped and trusted she would hear no more talk about prayers in that house. She had not been able to see that the kind of praying being done in these days accomplished any good.

To Dorothy she declared that if she had had the spirit of a mouse she might have exerted herself, as other girls did, to make life pleasant for her brother. She had never tried to please him in anything, not even mending his mittens when he wanted them. She would rather dawdle over the fire roasting apples with Carey Martyn than to give any thought to her own brother.

All this was bitterness itself to poor Dorothy, whose own heart reproached her for having been indifferent to her brother's welfare for so many years. She had honestly tried with all of her heart to be pleasant and helpful to John ever since she had been doing things from a right motive.

Mrs. Morgan did not spare her husband. She wouldn't have let a boy like that go off without a cent in his pocket — no, not even if she had to sell all the stock to get him ready cash. He had as good a right to money as Lewis ever had, and he had been tied down to the five barns all his life. No wonder he ran away. He showed some spirit, and she was glad he had.

Do you suppose Farmer Morgan endured this in silence? Not he! Sharp words grew sharper, and bitter feelings ran high, until the once quiet kitchen was transformed into a babel of angry words. Poor Louise could only run away and weep.

The very worst of this was in this Christian woman's own sore heart. The awful question *why* had crept in and was tormenting her soul. She had been sincere in her prayers, honest in her desires and unwavering in her petitions. Why had God permitted this disastrous thing to come? Had she not tried — oh! had she not tried with sincerity to live Christ in this home ever since she came into it? Why then had she been allowed to fail so utterly? Wouldn't it be to God's glory to save John Morgan's soul? Wasn't it evident that the mother might possibly be reached through him? Wasn't it evident that John at home under her influence and Lewis's and Dorothy's would be in less danger than away among strangers, wandering wherever he would? Wasn't it evident that this conclusion to their prayers had caused Mrs. Morgan to lose faith in prayer — to grow harder and harder in her feelings toward God and Christians? Why was all this allowed?

She had prayed in faith — or, at least, she had supposed she had. She had felt almost sure that God would answer her prayer. With a steady voice and a smile in her eye she had said to Dorothy only the night before John went away, "I don't believe John will go away. I don't think God will let him go."

And Dorothy, half-startled, had answered: "Oh, Louise, I don't mean to be irreverent, but I don't understand. How can God keep him from going, if he *will* go?"

And Louise, smiling outright now, so sure of her trust, had answered: "I don't know, dear. He has infinite resources. I only know that I believe He will do it."

What had become of her faith? It grieves my heart to have to confess to you that this young servant of Christ, who had felt His "sufficient grace" in her own experience again and again, allowed Satan to stand at her elbow and push before her that persistent and faithless *why*.

That word in all its forms was crowding into her heart on that May morning, as she looked out at the dripping eaves and the leaden clouds.

CHAPTER XXI

"HEDGED IN"

s for John, perhaps he was quite as much astonished at the turn of events as the members of the family were. He had threatened for many weeks to turn his back on the old homestead. But it is doubtful if during that time he had really intended to do it. No plans as to where he should go or what he should do had taken shape. He had only a vague unrest and a more or less settled determination to get away from it all sometime.

John turned his back on the familiar barns and long-stretching fields and went out from them in the darkness of that May evening. And not one of the family was more in a fog as to what he would do next than John himself was. Instinctively he turned his steps to the village, spending the evening in his old haunt. Only a more reckless manner than usual showed that anything in his life had changed. In fact, John realized no change. He turned toward the family road leading homeward, as he came out from that corner grocery at a later hour than usual. But he stopped abruptly before he reached the top of the hill, thought a moment, then turned and retraced his steps and presently struck out boldly on the road leading to the city.

The great city, only sixty miles away, was of course the first objective of an enterprising young man about to start out in life for himself. About midnight he reached the station where the express train stopped. By the depot lamps John discovered that the eastern-bound train would be due in five minutes. He drew from his pocket the handful of silver and copper coins that constituted his available means, slowly counted them, entered the depot and inquired the price of a ticket to the city. He smiled grimly to himself to discover that, after purchasing one, he would have just ten cents left. "I guess I can live on that for a week or so," he muttered. "Father could. If I can't, I can starve. I'm going to the city anyhow." And the ticket was bought.

Presently the train came. Our reckless young traveler sauntered into it, selected the best seat he could find, settled himself comfortably and went to sleep, apparently indifferent to the fact that his mother was at that moment shedding bitter tears for him. No, he was not indifferent, nor would he have been had he known it. Nothing in all his young life would have amazed him more. He didn't understand his mother. That isn't strange, when one considers that she had spent years in learning how to hide her heart from those she loved best. John Morgan actually did not believe that he had ever caused his mother to shed one tear. He didn't believe that she loved him!

What did he know about mother love, except what she revealed to him?

It is not my purpose to take you wandering with John Morgan. Even if we had time for it, the experience would be anything but pleasant. He went into many places where you would not like to follow. He did many things that were better left undone and are much better left untold.

Yet I will be just to poor, silly, wicked John. He held back, or rather was held back by a force which he did not in the least understand, from many a place that otherwise he would have entered. He had plenty of chances to sink into the depths of sin and folly. Nothing in his own depraved heart kept him from sinking into them; yet into them he did not sink. He would have smiled scornfully over the idea that the incense of prayer which had been rising day and night for him during the passing weeks had anything to do with the unseen force that held him back when he would have plunged headlong into those depths. Still he was held. He is not the first one who has been saved from self-shipwreck by a power outside himself, unrecognized and unthanked.

Still John Morgan took long enough strides on the way to shipwreck. He did what he could for his own overthrow, goaded by an exasperating and ever-increasing sense of failure. Here he was at last, his own master and able to work if he could find anything to do or to let it alone as he pleased. There was no one to direct him, or as he had always phrased it, to "order" him about; no one to complain, no one to question — a life of freedom at last. Was it not for this he had pined?

It was humiliating to discover that it didn't satisfy him. Not even for an hour could he cheat himself into believing that he was happy in the life he had chosen. He led a very vagabond life. He tried working and loafing and starving, and the time dragged on. It was more than humiliating; it was exasperating.

But he could no more get away from the memory

of that clean, sweet-smelling, sweetly kept room in which he had lately passed his nights than he could get away from his own miserable self. The very smell of the wildwood violets which had nodded on him from the tiny vase that last morning at home and which he had pretended to despise seemed to follow and haunt him. How perfectly absurd it was of him, here in the very center of this great center of life, actually to long for a whiff of those wild violets! He sneered at himself and swore at himself and longed for them all the same.

So passed the days, each one bearing him steadily downward — yet each one holding him back from the downward depths into which he might have plunged. The summer heat came in all its fierceness and wilted him with its city-polluted breath. He had been accustomed to the free, pure air of the country. At times it was hard for him to believe that this crowded, ill-smelling city could belong to the same earth on which the wide-stretching harvest fields lay and smiled. The summer waned, and the rich, rare October days, so beautiful in the country, so barren of all interest to the homeless in a great city, came to him.

John Morgan had actually become a tramp! The work which he had at first despised and hated he could not find now. If he wouldn't carry out his early threat and starve, he must tramp and beg. Starving had lost its charms somewhere among the parchings of those summer months. He had so nearly tried that way as to shudder over it. To ask for a bite at the back door of country-looking houses was more to his mind.

One never-to-be-forgotten October day he shook himself out from the shelter of a wrecked car, under which he had passed the night, and resolved to find a breakfast of some sort. His own mother would not have recognized him. His clothing in the old days hadn't been the finest, but whatever passed through Mother Morgan's hands was clean and carefully mended. This bundle of rags and dirt would have been in danger of being spurned from her door without a second glance. "There is no excuse for filth!" she would say grimly. John had heard her say it many times. He thought of it this morning as he shook himself; yet how could he help the filth? He had no clothes. He had no place in which to wash. He had nothing with which to brush, and very little left to brush! True, he had brought himself into this very position. He did not choose to think of that. Besides, everybody knows it is easier to get into certain positions than to get out of them.

John didn't understand his own mood. He was not in the least repentant. If anything, he was more bitter and defiant than ever. But he was disappointed. Bohemianism was not what he had supposed it to be. Assuming control of one's own actions was by no means so comfortable or desirable a lot as he had imagined. Some days he believed that to milk the gentle cows and care for the fine horses would have been a positive relief. John had not shirked work. Yet he had no idea of going home. His proud spirit and defiant nature would not let him even consider that.

On this particular morning he had resolved to try again for work. He managed to get on the last car of an outgoing freight train and was thus whirled a few miles into the country. At the first station he jumped off and began searching for work. He found a farmer who was compassionate and gave him wood to carry into the already well-stocked shed to earn his breakfast.

Presently the farmer came to the door and called:

"We are about ready for breakfast now. You can come in while we have prayers and then to breakfast."

"I don't want prayers," said John, stopping about midway between the door and the woodpile, his arms full. "I asked for something to eat, not for praying."

"I know that, and you shall have something to eat. But a little praying won't hurt you. Why, man, you can afford to be thankful that you have found a chance to eat again!"

"No, I can't," said John fiercely. "If I can't have the breakfast without the praying, I'll go without the breakfast."

"Very well," said the farmer. "I'm bound you shall then. I declare — if a fellow has got so far that he can't even listen to a word of prayer, he doesn't deserve to eat."

"Then I'll starve," said John in anger. He threw the wood on the floor and stalked away.

"Oh, I don't know about that, Father," said a motherly voice, and a motherly face looked out after angry John. "Seems to me I'd have given him some breakfast even if he didn't want to come to prayers. May be he was ashamed to — he looks so much like a ragbag."

"Why didn't he say so then?" said the disturbed farmer. "Who expected him to fly off in a passion at the mention of a prayer? He's a hard case, I'm afraid."

That was true enough. But the incident was not so much against John as it sounds. Poor John, he was angry for remembering with a certain tenderness that prayer in the kitchen at home in the Sunday evening twilight. He wanted no experience that would call it up more plainly. No breakfast this morning and no supper last night! There had always been plenty to eat in his father's house. How bitter it was to think that, now that he was independent, he was actually a dependent on the chance charities of the world!

He tramped on. He was growing hungrier. He felt that he really could not work now until he had a chance to eat. It was actual pauperism this time. A neat-looking house, a neat kitchen door — he knocked at it and asked for a bit of bread.

A trim, elderly lady answered: "Yes, to be sure, come in. And so you're hungry? Poor fellow! It must be hard to be hungry. No home, I suppose?"

John shook his head.

"Poor fellow! You look young, too. Is your mother dead, did you say?"

All the while she bustled about getting a savory breakfast ready for him: a cup of steaming coffee and a bit of meat and generous slices of bread and butter — bread that looked and butter that smelled like his mother's. And this was a farmhouse with a neat, clean kitchen and a yellow-painted floor.

At that last question a strange feeling came over John Morgan. *Was* his mother dead? No, he almost said. He wouldn't have liked to nod his head to that. And yet here he was among the October days, and it had been early May when he left her. How many funeral processions he had passed on the streets since, and he had had no word from his mother!

Down in the pasture lot one day his father had said to him: "Don't plow that bit up. I've never made up my mind to it. In spite of me it looks as if it was meant for a kind of family burial ground." There was a great tree there and a grassy hillside, and a small, clear stream purled along very near. How did he know a grave hadn't been dug on that hillside since he went away? His heart gave a few sudden thuds and then for a minute almost seemed to stop beating! Could it be possible that John Morgan really loved his mother! He was eating his breakfast now — a good breakfast it was, and the trim, older lady talked on.

"Well, there are a good many homeless people in the world. It must be hard. But then, you know, the Master Himself gave up His home and had no place to lay his head. He did it for our sakes, too. Wasn't that strange! Seems to me I couldn't give up my home. But He made a home by it for every one of us. I hope you've looked after the title to yours, young man."

No answer from John. The old lady sighed and said to herself, as she trotted away for a doughnut for him, He doesn't understand, poor fellow! I suppose he never has had any good thoughts put into his mind. Dear me! I wish I could do something for him besides feed his poor, perishing body!

But John did understand — perfectly. What was the matter with all the people this morning? Why were they so persistently forcing that subject on him? In all the six months he had been wandering, he had never encountered so many direct words concerning it as he had that morning. Isn't it possible, John Morgan, that God's watching Spirit knows when to reach even your heart? The little old lady trotted back, a plate of doughnuts in one hand and a little card in the other.

"Put these doughnuts in your pocket. Maybe they'll come in handy when you are hungry again. And here is a little card. You can read, I suppose?"

The faintest suspicion of a smile gleamed in John Morgan's eyes as he nodded assent.

"Well, then, you read it once in a while, just to remember me. Those are true words on it, and Jesus is here yet trying to save, just the same as He always

was. He wants to save you, young man, and you
better let Him do it now. If I were you, I wouldn't
wait another day."

As he tramped down the street, his body so wonderfully refreshed by the good coffee and bread and
butter, he could not help looking at the card. After
that breakfast, he could not help taking the card,
although he wanted to throw it in the cheery fire. It
was a simple enough card, with these words printed
on it in plain letters: "This is a faithful saying, and
worthy of all acceptation, that Christ Jesus came into
the world to save sinners." Then underneath: "I am
the bread of life. He that cometh to me shall never
hunger." Still lower on the card in decorative letters
were the words: "The Master is come, and calleth for
thee." Then a hand pointed to an italicized line: *I
that speak unto thee am he.*"

"Queer mess, that," said John. He thrust the card
into his pocket and strode toward the village depot.
He meant to board the next train, get a little farther
into the country and continue his search for work. It
was another freight train, and he succeeded in slipping on it. But it was hardly under way when he
discovered that he had miscalculated and was being
carried back toward the great city instead of farther
into the country.

"I don't care," he said. "I don't know what I want
of the country. On the whole, I may as well try my
chances in the city. I'll go up Greenwich Street and
try my luck in the warehouses. I can roll boxes now,
since I've had another breakfast."

But the freight train presently switched off and ran
off into another depot into another part of the city,
where John was as total a stranger as though he had
just dropped from the clouds.

"Where on earth am I?" he asked bewildered,

swinging himself down from the top of the car and
looking around. "Just my luck! I'm nowhere. East,
west, north, south — which way shall I go? I'll go
north. Which is north? Or — no, I won't. Winter's
coming. I guess I'll go south and walk as long as it
looks interesting and see where I'll end up. What
difference does it make which way I go?"

All the difference in the world, John Morgan. It is
a thread in the cord that is reaching down to you. It
is one of the apparently trivial movements which
will have its silent, unnoticed, unthought of part in
helping you decide which way you will go for the
rest of your life and where you will finally land.

CHAPTER XXII

CORDS UNSEEN

he morning service was just finished in the great church on Lexington Avenue. A large group of men and women lingered in the broad aisles, shaking hands with each other and saying a word here and there in subdued, happy tones. A looker-on, who was familiar with religious meetings but had not been at this one, would have known by the atmosphere lingering in the church that the worshippers had been having a joyous time. They were reluctant to leave. They gathered in little knots and discussed the events of the hour and the prospects of the evening.

Large numbers of the ladies held packages of white cards not unlike calling cards in size and texture and as carefully written on as calling cards were. The handwriting was peculiar: delicate, gracefully rounded letters with skillful flourishes. Somebody had considered the work important and had bestowed their time and skill to doing it.

"Estelle, dear, won't you go forward and get some

of the cards? I see very few here who will go up Fairmount Street, and you may be able to reach some who will be otherwise neglected."

One of the lingerers, a fair-faced woman with silver-tinted hair, spoke to a very graceful bit of a girl. She was evidently her daughter and evidently lingered, not so much from her own personal interest in the scene as because her mother did. She turned full, wondering and yet deprecating eyes on her mother at the question.

"Oh, Mama! I can't offer those cards to people. I'm not one of the workers, you know. It isn't expected of me. You have some, and that will be sufficient for our family."

"I am not going up Fairmount Street," the mother answered quietly. "I have only enough cards to meet my own opportunities, daughter. If Louise were here, dear, can't you think how she would scatter those little white messengers?"

"Louise is good, Mama, and I am not, you know. You mustn't expect me to be Louise. I can no more take her place in that way than I can in a hundred others."

"Oh, yes, you can, my child. It doesn't require any special skill to hand a card of invitation to a passerby or even to speak a word of encouragement to those who are half-persuaded."

"But, Mama, how would it look for me to invite people to the meetings? I am not one of the church members. It wouldn't be very consistent, I think."

The mother's eyes were sorrowful and questioning, as they rested on the face of her fair young daughter. She didn't seem to know just how to answer. At last she said: "Estelle, dear, even though you refuse Christ yourself, don't you wish that many others might come to Him? Poor, sad hearts, who haven't had your opportunities nor know the way as you do — shouldn't they have their chance to choose, and aren't you willing to extend the invitation?"

The young girl's cheeks flushed a deeper pink, and her eyes drooped, but she answered steadily: "Certainly I am, Mama."

Then she went forward and received from the pastor a package of the beautiful cards. She turned them over curiously in her hand, wondering how it would seem to pass them out to people and whether the cards would be accepted or refused.

They were simple little cards — nothing pretentious or formidable about them. They just announced daily religious services, giving the hours of meetings and the name of the preacher. On the reverse side in the most exquisite penmanship was this simple quotation: "The Master is come, and calleth for thee."

Estelle read it, and the glow on her cheeks did not lessen. There was certainly something very solemn in the suggestion. Estelle could hardly help giving a moment's attention to the question of whether the Master really was calling for her. If she could have brought her heart to the point of believing that it was so, it would have been well with Estelle, for she could not have said no to the Master. The sin in her case was that she would not study the subject long enough to be able to believe that she was personally included in the call.

Nevertheless, she made her way up Fairmount Street on her unusual errand. She was a little vexed over the thought that Louise would have done all this so well and would have delighted in it, while she must bunglingly try to fill her place. It was about this time that John Morgan turned into Fairmount Street, wondering where he was and what he should do next.

"Will you have a card, please?" A vision of loveliness fell on his astonished gaze, and a delicately gloved hand was stretched forth with the tiny bit of pasteboard. "It is just an invitation to the meetings. We hope you will come." Still the card was outstretched, and still John stood and stared. What was there about that face and voice that seemed familiar to him as one whom he had met in a dream or in the faraway unreality of some other existence? It bewildered him so much that he forgot either to decline or accept the card but stood looking and wondering.

Estelle felt the need to say something further to this silent starer. "They have very good singing, and great crowds come every evening. I think you will like it. Will you take the card?"

Thus petitioned, John was roused from his bewilderment and put forth his hand for the proffered card. For the moment he couldn't decide what else to do.

Then Estelle, her mission accomplished and her embarrassment great, flitted away from him around the corner. "What a strange acting fellow!" was her comment. "How he did stare! One would suppose he had never seen a lady before. Dear me! He looks as though he needed a friend. Somehow I can't help feeling sorry for him. I really hope he will go to the meeting, but of course he won't." And Estelle Barrows actually realized that for such a dreary, friendless-looking person as he, the love of Christ would be a great transformation. She did not mean that she, Estelle Barrows, in her beauty and purity and surrounded by the safety of her high position in life, had no need of Christ; neither did she realize that this was the logical conclusion of her reasoning.

"What in the name of common sense has got into all the people today? They are running wild on cards!" This was John Morgan's comment. He was ashamed and vexed to think he had forgotten his sullenness and indifference so much as to stare at the fair young face. He read the card carefully — more to get away from his present thoughts than from any interest in it. But the verse on the reverse side held his attention longer; the words were the very same as those on the card given him by the old lady who had provided his breakfast. It struck him as a strange coincidence. Presently he thrust the bit of pasteboard into his pocket and dismissed the incident from his mind. It didn't occur to him again until later that same evening when he was passing a brightly lighted building, from which came sounds of music. He didn't know how or why, but something in the strains recalled the morning's incident and the invitation card.

"I wonder if this is the place?" he asked. "It would be rather odd if I had blundered on the very building without the least notion of doing so." He paused before the door, listening to the roll of the organ as it sounded on the quiet air.

"*That* organ doesn't squeak, anyhow," he said grimly. He remembered the organ scene in the old church at home and Louise's pleasure in its improved condition after he worked on it. Thoughts of her suggested the card again, and he brought it forth from his pocket. By the light of a friendly lamp he compared the name on the card with the name on the building before him. Yes, they agreed. Chance or Providence, according to how you are accustomed to viewing these matters, had led him to the very spot. Still, he had no intention of going in.

"Pretty-looking object I am to go to church!" he said, surveying himself critically with something between a smile and a sneer on his face. "I would create a sensation, I imagine. I wonder if the bit of silk and lace that gave me the card is in there? And I wonder if she expects to see me? And I wonder where I have seen her before and why her face haunts me?"

The organ had been silent for some minutes. Now it rolled forth its notes again, and voices that to John seemed of unearthly sweetness rang out on the quiet:

> Come home! come home! you are weary
> at heart.
> And the way has been long,
> And so lonely and wild!
> Oh, prodigal child, come home! oh, come
> home!

Was John Morgan homesick? He would have scorned the thought. Yet at the sound of these tender words, a strange, choking sensation came over him, and something very much like a mist filled his eyes. He felt rather than realized how long and lonely and wild the way had been. Still, he had no intention of going in. He would step nearer and listen to that music; those voices were unlike anything he had heard before. He drew closer under the light of the hall lamp. He could see into the church; the doors stood invitingly open. Even the aisles were full. Some people were standing, not all of them well-dressed by any means, but some so roughly clad that even he would not attract attention by the contrast. One well-dressed young man with an open hymnbook in his hand stood by the door, almost in the hall. He turned suddenly, and his eyes rested on John. He beckoned him forward, then stepped toward him.

"Come right in, my friend. We can find standing

room for you, and the sermon is just about to begin."

"I'm not dressed for such places," said John, imagining that he spoke firmly.

"Oh, never mind the dress. That is not of the least consequence. Plenty of men are here in their rough work clothes. Come right in."

"Come home, come home," sang out the wonderful voices. And John Morgan, still with no intention of going in, was impelled by a force which he no more understood than he understood his own soul. He stepped forward and followed the young man into the crowded church.

The singing ceased, and the minister arose and immediately announced his text: "Friend, how camest thou in hither, not having on the wedding garment?"

The sentence was spoken so much like a personal question that John looked about him, startled. Could it be possible that the man was addressing him—actually referring to his uncouth dress? This lasted only for an instant. Then he discovered that no one was paying the least attention to him and that his dress, rough as it was, was not worse than some of those around him. But the preacher's manner was so new and strange and so unlike anything that John Morgan had ever met before that, despite his own half-formed determination to get out of this, he stayed and looked and listened.

If I could I would tell you about that sermon. But sermons on paper, reported by a second party, are so very different from the words that come burning hot from the heart of the preacher; so on second thought it is better not to make the attempt.

To John Morgan the entire service was like a revelation of mysteries. What had seemed to him confusing and contradictory in the plan of salvation and finally exasperating, was made as clear as the sunlight. One by one his own daring subterfuges were swept from him. Before the sermon closed, he felt that he did indeed stand unclothed and speechless before the King. What next? Where should he go now? Where could he run? Was he wretched enough before? Did he need to feel these truths in order to make his condition less bearable?

The sermon closed, the few words of solemn prayer followed, and the choir took up the service. Strangely clear to John's ears were the voices that spoke the tenderly solemn words:

> Oh, do not let the word depart,
> And close thine eyes against the light;
> Poor sinner, harden not thine heart;
> Thou wouldst be saved, why not tonight?

He had no difficulty in singling out among the singers one face and voice. The voice held unusual sweetness and power, and the face haunted him. He could not yet tell why. There she was, the fair young beauty who had given him his card. How strange it was that he had accepted her invitation after all! After the song, instead of the expected benediction, came another invitation.

"Now I know," said the preacher, "there are some in this room tonight who feel that they are without the wedding garment. They believe that, if the King should ask them why, they would be speechless. Don't all of those wish to settle the question? You intend to settle it sometime. You do not intend to go up to that guest chamber unclothed. Why not settle it tonight? Why not come up here, all of you who think the question is unsettled and who believe that it is important enough to be attended to? Come, and let us ask the Holy Spirit to help you settle it tonight."

Did John Morgan intend ever to settle the question? For almost the first time, he looked the thought squarely in the face. He believed that the man who had been speaking was in earnest. He believed that he knew what he was talking about. Somehow the unbelief in which this foolish young wanderer had entrenched himself so long would not bear the piercing light of one solemn Bible question, one gospel sermon. It slipped away from him and left him without a hiding place.

"Come," said the preacher. "Be men now, and be women. Be worthy of your position as reasonable beings. Take steps toward understanding this important matter better. Do what you can. Rest assured that the King will see to it that the rest is done for you. Come now."

Had John Morgan the least idea of going? He told himself that he hadn't. He told himself that he didn't believe in these things, that they were not for him. Even while he said so his heart said back to him, "That is not true." How did he leave his place back by the door and follow the throng that was moving up the aisle and kneel down there before that gray-haired man? Neither then nor afterward did John Morgan understand it. He hadn't intended to go — at least he didn't think he had — and yet he went. He didn't believe that he had any feelings on the subject. He believed that he hated religion and all religious people.

No, not all — there was Louise. He had tried to hate her and failed. There was that fair girl who gave him a card and that wrinkled old woman who had given him a card. Why hate them? He didn't believe that he did. Then this gray-haired, earnest, clear-brained preacher — no, he found nothing like hatred in his heart for him.

But why go up there? He didn't want to be prayed for. Yes, he did — maybe. He wanted something; he wasn't sure what it was. Before it was reasoned out, before he understood what or why, he had been impelled — he could almost have said pushed forward — by a something or someone stronger than himself. He felt impelled to yield to that force.

The city clocks were striking the hour of nine. At that hour, unknown to John, four people in three separate rooms were kneeling and presenting his name before the King, begging the wedding garment for him: Louise and Lewis in the quiet of their room, Dorothy in John's chamber and Carey Martyn in his own room over the kitchen. According to the covenant into which they had entered, each one breathed the same name, united in the same desire. "While they are yet speaking, I will hear." Did the King say that of them that night? Did a message go from the palace that night, "Clothe John Morgan in the wedding garment, and write his name among the guests who have accepted the invitation"? Some, even in the so-called Christian world, would fail to see the connecting link between this conference held nightly with the King and the strange inclinations which John Morgan had called chance.

Yet isn't it wonderful, after all, to remember that the witnesses are daily increasing who can testify to just such cords. These cords stretch to the Infinite Arm and move that Arm to reach down and lift the feet of a stranded soul, surrounded by sin, from the mire and set them firmly on the Rock, even the Rock of Ages?

CHAPTER XXIII

"Forbid Them Not"

uring the long, golden summer months time moved slowly for the Morgan family. The first actual rift in the household had occurred. None of the family had realized how hard it would be until they confronted it. Trial either softens or hardens the human heart. Certainly Mrs. Morgan's heart was not undergoing the softening process. She brooded over her first great anxiety until it seemed to her that no sorrow was like her sorrow; she chafed under it as a cruel thing.

Farmer Morgan, though he said little, had aged because of the trouble; he seemed at times like a broken-down man. Yet he steadily resisted any effort to be comforted and sternly forbade any attempts to search for the missing boy.

"He has chosen to cut himself off from us," he would say coldly. "Let him get the full benefit of it."

At times he hinted in the presence of the mother that if the home atmosphere had been less hard and cold John might have stayed. And she more than hinted very coldly that if his father had not treated John like a little boy and made him work like a slave, there would have been no trouble. Of course those two could not help each other and only grew further apart in their common sorrow. Altogether, the summer was one full of bitterness to the new bud that had been grafted onto the gnarled old tree.

Sometimes Louise's brave heart sank within her, and she cried to the Lord for relief. She was not unwilling to bear the heat and burden of the day, but her poor heart so longed for fruit. Was her Christian effort in vain? she questioned. Then her thoughts went away from the old farmhouse back to her own lovely home and her lovely sister, Estelle. How long she had prayed for her! How earnestly she had worked to bring her as a trophy to the Master! Yet the bright, winsome girl was fast blossoming into womanhood, her life still uncrowned by this commitment. Thinking of her and of John and of the steadily aging father and the hard mother in this new home, could Louise be anything other than sad at times? "If ye had faith as a grain of mustard-seed...." Yes, it was true; her faith was weak. But whose is strong?

There were bright spots. With the example ever before her, it was strange that she should so often forget it.

Dorothy moved steadily on her upward way. She had given herself entirely to the Master's service, and daily He was showing her that He accepted the gift. Occasionally, Louise found joy in admiring the rapid strides that Dorothy had taken, as well as the avenues for work opening at every turn. During the summer months, a Sunday school had been organized in the little brown schoolhouse just above them. No one quite remembered how it got started — except Louise. She knew it grew out of Dorothy's sud-

den, startled comment, "What a pity those children
are not being taught anything!" as she watched half
a dozen boys and girls playing together raucously
one Sunday afternoon. The Sunday school had been
in progress three months and was flourishing. Lewis
was superintendent, much to his astonishment.
Louise, Dorothy, Carey Martyn and the young lady
whose father employed him were the teachers.

Louise had organized a Bible class composed of
some of the mothers and was working faithfully
among them. Yet she had not seen the fruit that she
longed for. Mr. Butler himself had lately developed a
habit of walking out on Sunday afternoon and talking
to the children for a few minutes.

Once he overheard a conversation which was in
no way intended for his ears: "Mr. Butler's talk to the
children was real good, wasn't it?" Carey Martyn
said to Dorothy.

She had answered heartily: "Yes, it was. When he
talks, without having it written down on paper, it
sounds as though he means it. I wonder why it makes
such a difference to read things."

The minister, just at their elbows, had intended to
join them for a little talk, but he turned away with
heightened color and went home to ponder the question. Perhaps that had somewhat to do with the fact
that two Sundays thereafter he *talked* to the people
who gathered in the dreary little church.

They may not have discussed the sermon much
during the week, but I know that several said among
themselves: "I must try to get to prayer meeting
Wednesday evening. I declare it is a shame to have
so small an attendance. We ought to go, if for nothing
else than to support the minister. He seems to be in
earnest." But he had not preached about the prayer
meeting. Its evident growth the next Wednesday

evening encouraged his heart and was related to certain earnest thoughts that he expressed in his next sermon, which was simply "talked" again, not read. Perhaps he would have been discouraged had he known that these wise people, who were not used to preparing sermons, did not call these efforts sermons at all. And he had toiled over them as he never had over written work. They imagined that he had been late in preparing and simply had opened his mouth and let the words flow out.

"We haven't had a sermon in two weeks now," said one wise person to another.

Surely the minister who had sat late nearly every night, trying to sort out what he meant to say, would have been discouraged had he heard it — especially if he had not heard the answer: "The fact is, I like these talks better than the real sermons. I get better hold of them. They seem somehow to do me more good. I don't care how many times he leaves out the sermon, I'm sure!"

Now this comment came from one of the most thoughtful minds belonging to the little company that gathered once a week in the old church. On the whole, wouldn't the minister have felt somewhat encouraged if he had known it all?

But I began this chapter with the special intention of telling you about little Neelie Morgan. She has been kept very much in the background of the story. She was a quiet sort of a child, who kept herself pretty much out of hearing, though she listened well.

On this particular autumn afternoon, the world was in gloom. The glory which had possessed the country for the past few weeks seemed to have departed in a night. It left in its place clouds and wind and dull, withered leaves flying about and then a chill, depressing rain.

The Morgan household felt the depression. Mrs. Morgan senior knew, when she first opened her eyes on the dreariness, that it was one of her black days — John's birthday. She was sorry she thought of it; she struggled all day with memories of the past. She saw John's curly head nestled in her arms. She saw him trotting, a beautiful two-year-old bit of mischief, always at her side. She saw his little shoes; they were laid away in the bottom of her old trunk in the attic, but they seemed to stare at her all day, haunting her with the dreams that she had had and that had faded. Every hour in the day her heart grew heavier, and her outward demeanor grew harder. Why couldn't those around her have realized that she suffered bitterly? Whether the knowledge had helped her or not, it would have made the day easier to them.

Soon after the early dinner, Neelie took refuge in her new sister's room. Drawing the small rocker close to the cheery fire, she turned over for the hundredth time a volume brightened by many pictures. She remained silent, leaving Louise to the sadness of her thoughts. They *were* sad; the atmosphere of the house was growing at times almost too much for her. She did not seem to be succeeding with her mother-in-law. Yet she felt that on Dorothy's account she would not be elsewhere.

Neelie's soft voice broke the silence: "Sister Louise, what do you think He said to them when He took them in His arms?"

She was bending her fair head over a familiar picture. She seemed to love to study Jesus, holding a sweet-faced child in His arms with many others clustered around Him.

Louise tried to collect her thoughts enough to answer: "Why, you know, dear, He blessed them."

"Yes, I know. But just what do you think He said —

the exact words? I wish I could have heard Him."

The voice expressed intense emotion, but Louise's preoccupied heart did not notice.

"I don't know just the words, Neelie. Only I suppose He prayed for them that His Father would take care of them and make them His own children."

Silence again filled the room, and Louise went on with her broken thread of thought. The child's eyes were still riveted on the picture.

Suddenly she spoke again, and this time the voice was so eager, so intense, that it called her sister back quickly and entirely from all wandering: "If I could only have been there...."

It was the echo of more than a passing fancy of a child. Louise saw that her soft blue eyes were brimming with tears, and the large drops were staining the page before her.

"Why, my darling little sister, what is the trouble?" Her voice was full of sympathy now, and she dropped the work she had been sewing listlessly. Drawing the little rocker toward her, she put loving arms around Neelie.

"What makes the tears come, little sister?"

"Oh, Louise, I don't quite know. But I think and I think about it, and I wish I could see Him and hear Him speak. If He would only say, 'Neelie, come here,' I would run so fast. I can't make it seem as though He cared now for me. My teacher in the Sunday school says I must give my heart to Him, but I don't know how. If I could see Him and ask Him about it, as they had a chance to do, I think it would be so nice; then I can't help crying."

Louise remembered that Jesus had said, "Suffer little children, and forbid them not, to come unto me," after His disciples had rebuked those who brought the children to Him.

Is it possible, thought Louise, that I have been one of those faithless disciples, rebuking or at least ignoring the presence of one of His little ones, while I reached out after fruit that I dared to think was of more importance.

I cannot explain to you what a chill her heart took in this thought. She gathered Neelie to her, and her voice was tenderness itself.

"You poor little lamb! Would no one show you the way to the Shepherd? It is just as easy, darling, as it was when He was on earth, and He calls you just as surely. You don't know how to give your heart to Him? I shouldn't wonder if you had done it without knowing how. Do you think you love the dear Savior, Neelie, and want to try to please Him?"

"I'm sure I do," said Neelie, brushing back the tears and looking with earnest eyes into her questioner's face. "I do want to, but I keep forgetting and doing naughty things, and then I'm sorry. I think I won't ever again, and then I do. Oh, dear! I don't know what to do."

The old sad cry of the awakened human heart: "The good that I would I do not: but the evil which I would not, that I do." The little heart had not learned the triumphant chorus, "Thanks be to God, which giveth us the victory *through our Lord Jesus Christ!*"

"Poor darling!" said Louise, and she held her close. "I know about that. But see here, if you love Him, then you have given Him your heart. Whomever you love has a piece of your heart. If you love Him very much, so that you are determined to please Him just as well as you can, then you belong to Him, and He has blessed you. Neelie, dear, I know what you have been thinking about. You would like to have been there so that He could pray for you."

"Yes, I would!" exclaimed Neelie.

"Well, now, let me tell you. I felt just so when I was a little girl. A lady found a verse for me in the Bible which showed me that He prayed for me while He was here on the earth. Then I was glad. Listen: Once when Jesus was praying and had asked His Father to take care of His disciples and keep them from sin, He said, Father, I do not pray only for these; I pray for everyone who shall ever believe on Me, because My disciples have told them about Me."

"That means me!" said Neelie, with a flash of intelligence in her bright eyes. "Oh, Louise, that does mean me!"

"Of course it does, my darling little sister. Now let me tell you what I said when I was a little girl, not much older than you. I determined that I would belong to Jesus all my life and that I would try in everything to please Him. My papa taught me a little prayer to say to Him, telling Him what I meant to do. This was the prayer, 'Here, Lord, I give myself away, 'tis all that I can do.' Do you want to give yourself to Jesus, Neelie, to belong to Him forever?"

"Yes," said the child, with serious face and earnest eyes from which the tears had flowed, leaving only solemn resolve. "I do."

And the two of them knelt down beside the little rocker, and the rain pattered from the eaves outside, and the fire crackled in the stove inside. Aside from these sounds and the low, murmured words of prayer from young lips, silence filled the room. And the deed of another human soul was "signed, sealed and delivered" to its rightful owner.

It was a radiant face that was raised to Louise a few moments later. The child's voice had a note of triumph in it.

"He took me," she said simply. "I belong to Him now. I didn't understand it before, but it's very easy.

He took me."

Could any elaboration make the story of the mysterious change simpler?

How do you think that older disciple felt about the matter of fruit? Here she had been looking right and left of her for sheaves to take to the Master, and behold, just at her feet, a bud had grown and swelled and burst into bloom before she had even discovered signs of life! It taught her a lesson that she practiced among the lambs afterward. And she remembered that possibly His disciples today often occupy unwittingly the position of rebukers, even while the Master's voice is calling, "Suffer little children, and forbid them not."

Two hours later Louise and Neelie were down in the kitchen. Louise had been called down by a message from a neighbor, and Neelie had followed. The errand was taken care of, and the daughter-in-law lingered in the kitchen, her hungry heart looking for a bit of cheer.

On that day Dorothy and her mother were rearranging the kitchen and cleaning out the shelves, including a certain corner cupboard. Dorothy, perched on a chair, was organizing the upper shelves. Her mother, with a face that had grown harder every hour because she was determined nobody should suspect her conflict, was sorting through boxes of spices, bags of dried seeds and other treasures. Dorothy found a niche which she believed would hold one of the treasures, a large, covered dish of china. The dish and its pattern dated back nearly a hundred years. It was valued by the Morgan household, as such pieces generally are, for a dozen times its worth.

Dorothy glanced about her. Louise had moved to the distant window and was looking out upon the dull sky and earth. Her mother was absorbed and looking as if she didn't want to be disturbed. Little Neelie was standing very near the treasured dish. Her quick eyes saw what was wanted. Her eager fingers grasped the treasure.

"I'll hand it to you, Dorrie. You needn't get down."

"Oh, no!" said Dorothy, aghast but not soon enough. The small hands that were so anxious to help had seized the dish and were carrying it safely to Dorothy when the metallic voice of the mother startled her.

"Cornelia Morgan, put that dish down on the table this instant!"

Poor, frightened Neelie was so eager to obey and anxious to show her mother and Dorothy and, above all, Louise that she meant to do right. She turned to obey, but, alas, her nervous little hand misjudged the height of the table. She hit the rare blue dish against its edge. The treacherous cover toppled over, and — well, how did it happen? Who ever knows just how dire accidents happen? Such a second of time in which they do! What Neelie and the other surprised spectators knew was that the family heirloom lay in a dozen pieces on the yellow kitchen floor!

CHAPTER XXIV

STORM

ilence filled the kitchen for the space of about one minute. Mrs. Morgan senior crossed the room with swift steps and a stern face and caught the trembling Neelie by the arm. She whirled her into the little bedroom nearby and shut the door with a bang. Then sounds followed which cannot be endured by those with refined and sensitive nerves, sounds of rapid blows, mingled with pitiful pleadings for mercy.

I have often wondered if those people who are given to administering such punishment would not change their views on the subject if they were to watch or listen while another dealt the blows. Is it possible under the circumstances to avoid losing respect for the administrator or to escape from the idea that one is degrading oneself?

The two sisters looked at each other in utter dismay!

"Poor little Neelie!" gasped Dorothy at length. "She hadn't the least idea that she was doing anything wrong. How can Mother punish her?"

Louise gave no answer. There seemed to be nothing safe to say.

"Oh, Mama, don't — please don't!" wailed Neelie. "I didn't mean to do anything wrong."

Then Dorothy's courage rose to the point of action. She hurried over to the closed door, pushed it open and spoke with a tremulous voice: "Oh, Mother, don't whip Neelie. I know she didn't mean to do anything wrong."

"Dorothy Morgan!" said the firm, stern voice of her mother, which had never been colder or firmer than at that moment. "Leave this room and close the door immediately."

Dorothy immediately obeyed. She always obeyed her mother. But is it likely that at that moment she respected her?

Louise leaned her head against the rain-spattered window pane, looked out into the dreariness and waited. Dorothy got back on her perch and leaned her head against the cupboard door. She wiped a distressed tear from her face with the back of her hand and waited. Neither of those misery-stricken waiters feared injury to Neelie — at least not physical injury. Mrs. Morgan was not cruel in that sense. They knew the punishment would not be unduly severe. Nevertheless, there was a sense of degradation. Could they avoid concluding that the mother was angry and was venting the pent-up irritations of the day on her defenseless child

Each wail of Neelie's sank the mother lower in the estimation of both daughter and daughter-in-law. The latter struggled with the feeling and tried to believe that Mrs. Morgan must know what was best for her child. At the same time she wondered if she could ever respect her again. Dorothy was not aware of why she felt so miserable but she knew that life seemed very horrid just then. All these stages of misery took little time — one's heart works rapidly.

Quiet came to the little bedroom and was broken only by an occasional sob. Presently the administrator of "justice" came out, closing the door after her.

"Pick up those pieces and throw them away" was her first command to Dorothy. "One would have thought you'd have done that without waiting to be told. And don't climb up there again. I'll finish the work myself. If I had done it in the first place, instead of giving it to you, I'd have saved myself a great deal of trouble."

"Can't they be mended?" Dorothy asked, horrified at the idea of throwing away the bits of treasured blue china.

"No, they can't. I don't want my mother's china patched up. It would be a continual eyesore. I'd rather put it out of sight."

"Poor Neelie!" said Dorothy, stooping to gather the fragments. She was astonished at her own courage. "She was so eager to help."

"It was not for trying to help that she was punished," explained the mother coldly, betraying the fact that she felt the need to justify herself. "She knows very well that she has been forbidden to touch any dishes without special permission. That she forgot it only proves that she pays very little attention to commands. And you, Dorothy, are trying to help her pay less attention. I was shocked at your interference! Don't let me ever see anything of that kind again."

And Dorothy hated the blue china pieces and would rather throw them away than not. Still Louise lingered in the kitchen. The atmosphere was far from pleasant, but she pitied Dorothy, who was evidently still distressed. She could not go away and leave her, perhaps to be conquered by the tempter.

Then Dorothy had a new source of anxiety. The early autumn night was closing in. The rain was increasing, along with the wind and the dampness. In the kitchen Mother Morgan poked the fire and added another stick, and the glow and warmth were welcome. The bedroom door was closed, and Dorothy was almost sure that the bedroom window was open. Occasionally there came a dry little cough from the little girl shut in there, deepening the look of anxiety on the sister's face.

Her mother grew more gloomy as the moments passed, but Dorothy ventured yet again: "Mother, shall I shut the bedroom window?"

"No. Let the bedroom window alone."

Moments later the mother descended to the cellar, and Dorothy seized the opportunity to express her anxieties. "Neelie will catch her death in there. She must be real chilly. It is growing damper every minute, and she has a cold now. What can Mother be thinking of?"

Then Louise noticed the dry little cough and grew anxious also. She debated about whether she would help or hinder by speaking but finally decided to try.

"Shall I open the bedroom door, Mother?" she asked, in as indifferent a tone as she could assume. "Neelie seems to be coughing."

The mother turned to face her from the cupboard where she was still working. "Mrs. Lewis Morgan, can I be allowed to manage my own family, or must I give it up to you?"

Then Louise went upstairs and shut her door and locked it. She sat down in the little rocker so recently vacated by Neelie and gave herself up to the luxury of tears! It was not merely this event but a good many

little events that had been piling up during the many
trying days. The night was cold, and the world outside was in gloom. Lewis was gone all night and for
two nights to come. It seemed to the young wife as
though two nights represented years, and it seemed
a long time since she had seen her mother. She was
sorry for poor, little banished Neelie. All these events
and more brought the tears.

Louise had some vindictive thoughts also. She
told herself that this struggle to belong to the family
was perfect nonsense. She had borne it quite as long
as any human being could be expected to. Lewis
would insist on a separate home whenever she
dropped the hint. Why try to endure this sort of thing
any longer? Mrs. Morgan had insulted her — why
should she bear it? She would not go down to supper.
She would not go down again tonight. She would
send word that, as long as her husband was absent,
she would remain in her room and not irritate the
mistress of the house by her presence. She would
write to her mother and tell her just what a hateful
world this was and how disagreeable a person
named "Mother" could be. She would go home.
She would leave tomorrow morning and telegraph
Lewis to take the westbound train instead of the
eastbound and meet her there. They would stay until
Father Morgan was willing to give them what was
her husband's right — a plot of land.

To be sure, she meant to do none of these extreme
things. But it was a luxury of sorts to rehearse them
in her heart and imagine what she *could* do and the
sensation she could create, if she chose.

This is one of the awful snares Satan uses to trip
the feet of unwary saints. He leads them to feel that
it does no harm to relish bitter thoughts they really
do not intend to carry out. He lets them forget that

relishing those thoughts even for a moment weakens their spirituality and cuts off their communion with Christ. In this case it was only a partial victory, for Louise felt the weight of gloom on her heart too heavy for her to struggle under. She looked about her for relief. Being accustomed to seeking it in only one place, she dropped on her knees and carried the whole dreary scene to Him who bears our sorrows and carries our griefs. Almost an hour afterward, she answered Dorothy's summons to tea. Her face was serene and her heart at rest.

Neelie was at the table, a trifle more quiet than usual, although she was always a meek and quiet little mouse. Her face was a shade paler than usual. Her eyes sought Louise's with a questioning gaze, as if Louise would determine whether she had been considered naughty. When Louise answered the question with a tender, reassuring smile, the little face became radiant.

I want you to be just with Mother Morgan. She was by no means intentionally cruel. She would not have kept Neelie in the cold five minutes had she realized the situation. Her own blood was fairly boiling in her veins; she could not have conceived of anyone's being chilled that day. She honestly believed that Dorothy was a simpleton and that Louise was trying to interfere with her duties as the mistress of the family. Therefore she did not have a self-condemning spirit when she met her family at the tea table; she was poised and dignified. Louise, in her half hour of communion in that upstairs chamber of peace, had found strength enough to bear any amount of dignity and carried herself sweetly and helpfully through the hour.

Into the gloom of that rainy night came a guest that dispelled all the dignity and made each isolated

member of the household feel as one. Louise was the
first to hear it, even before Dorothy. That strange,
hoarse cough, which has fallen in so many house-
holds almost like the sound of earthclods on a coffin,
has too often been but the forerunner of that very
sound. Louise had heard it from her little sister at
home often enough and understood the signal so
well that it brought her to her feet with a bound.
When Dorothy a few moments later knocked hesitantly at her door, she answered with a quick "Yes,
dear" and threw it wide open. She was nearly
dressed.

"Oh, Louise! Do you hear Neelie? Isn't she very
sick?"

"She has the croup, Dorrie. I'm going right down."
Louise dug into her trunk and lit instantly upon the
package, for she knew what she wanted and where
it was. Dorothy shivered.

"Oh, Louise! What if Mother doesn't think there is
much the matter with her and won't do anything?"

"I wouldn't borrow trouble, dear. Your poor
mother is more likely to be overwhelmed with anxiety. Come down. We can find something to do." And
she sped swiftly downstairs.

Dorothy's courage returned. She followed and immediately attacked the stove. She arranged kindlings
with her skilled fingers, struck a match, lifted the
large kettle and filled it with water. Louise pushed
her way into the bedroom none too soon, for the
white-faced mother needed help.

The terrible disease was rapidly taking its toll, and
there were no young men to hasten for a doctor.
Concern gave haste to the old father's fingers, for he
was even then saddling a horse with what speed he
could.

"Have you tried hot water?" was Louise's first

question, as she hurried to raise the head of the struggling, suffering child.

"No," said Mrs. Morgan, unable to conceal her anxiety. "There is no hot water and no fire. There isn't anything, and the doctor will never get here."

"Yes, there's a fire," said Louise, who had heard its brisk snapping. "Dorrie is there. We will have hot water in five minutes." She dashed to the kitchen.

"That's right, Dorrie — just a little water so we can have it at once. Then set the other kettle on and fill it half full. As soon as it heats, fill it up. And, Dorrie, get a tub. I'll run for blankets. But first where's a spoon?"

"Do you have the medicine you use?" Louise asked Mother Morgan, for she was back again beside her.

"No," she said, in that same distressed tone, "I haven't *anything*."

Then Louise produced her package and untied it quickly. "This is what my mother uses for my little sister."

Mrs. Morgan senior seized the bottle, gave one glance at the label and returned it. "Give her some."

The spoon was produced and the medicine dropped just in time, for it was growing harder for Neelie to swallow anything.

How those three women worked for the next hour over that child! For those who have not experienced such suffering, there is a dire need of haste. All remedies at times are utter failures. Louise blessed the past experiences that had prepared her for this night. Mrs. Morgan's usually cold, strong nerves were shaking. A terrible fear of what might come blanched her face and made her limbs tremble beneath her. She yielded herself completely to Louise and Dorothy's lead. The moment Dorothy found something to do, she sprang into action. The hot-water bath was ready almost before it had seemed possible.

In the midst of her sufferings Neelie had strength to greet Louise's presence with a smile. It was difficult to speak at all, but she murmured, "He took me." Louise's face recalled the earlier events of the afternoon.

"What does she say?" asked the mother, pain sharpening her voice.

Louise hesitated a moment. Struggling to keep back the tears, she answered steadily, all the while smiling on Neelie: "She is referring to a little conversation she and I had this afternoon. She gave herself to Jesus, and she is telling me that He took her. Yes, darling, I know He did."

A sharp cry, almost like one from a wounded animal, escaped the tight lips of the mother. Then with renewed energy she gave herself to fighting the disease.

The clock was watched closely and the drops administered at just the right moments. The bath water was replenished, the rubbing of Neelie's feet and hands continued, and the compresses were changed constantly. Just then Dorothy gasped with relief, "There's the doctor!" when she heard voices in the hall. And Louise and her mother-in-law said, in the same breath, "She breathes easier!"

"Well," said the doctor, after examining the patient and the drops from Louise's bottle and having his questions answered, "you have done all that was needed. The little woman is past the crisis for tonight, but it was a tough case, I guess. That medicine works like a charm sometimes, and sometimes it doesn't. It helps when there is hot water along with speed and good judgment."

The Morgan family was not likely to forget that night's experience. To each member it had been different. No one can describe the emotions that tugged at the heart of the father, as he galloped through the gloom of that night. For all he knew the death angel, who evidently hovered near, might have taken his youngest born before he could get back to her. No one perhaps but the Searcher of hearts will ever know what the mother felt as she strained every nerve to hold back the destroyer; she thought she saw his grim steps approaching.

Through all the work the strongest feeling of Louise's heart had been pity for the mother. All the events of the dreary afternoon presented themselves before her with startling clarity. What must they be to the mother? As swiftly as she worked, she seemed to give her mind entirely to the needs of the hour. But with every motion a prayer went up to the great Physician to speak the word of healing for the mother's sake. And then went up a prayer of grateful acknowledgment.

Fair little Neelie, as she lay back at last, white and exhausted with her hard hours of suffering, seemed to have the same feeling of pity for her mother. But she expressed it in a way that almost broke her mother's heart. She put up her weak little hand as the mother bent over her and patted the white, wrinkled cheek tenderly. "Dear Mama, I didn't mean to be naughty," she said in the most loving and penitent of tones.

The strain that had been upon the mother's heart, not only for that afternoon but for days and weeks, gave way suddenly. With a bitter cry she burst into a passion of tears. "Oh, Neelie, don't!"

CHAPTER XXV

UNCONDITIONAL SURRENDER

second time in her life Mrs. Morgan senior sought her daughter-in-law's room. It was not unsolicited, however. Louise, without knowing, had planned the way for an easier approach.

"Mother," she said, toward the evening of the day that followed that night of watching, "won't you just slip up to my room and lie down for an hour or two? You look so tired, and you know you had no rest at all last night. Dorrie and I will take the best possible care of Neelie. Indeed, she looks so bright that she hardly needs care."

She had repeated this invitation at intervals during the day. Mrs. Morgan had quietly but steadily resisted every suggestion, though not ungrateful for the thoughtfulness.

"Perhaps I will by and by," she had said to Louise's last suggestion. An hour later, when Louise had despaired of succeeding and had sought her room, Mrs. Morgan tapped at her door.

"Oh, good," the daughter-in-law said briskly when she entered. "Let me bring a spread and arrange the pillows comfortably. You'll get a nice rest before Neelie misses you."

"Wait," said Mrs. Morgan. "Don't fix the bed. I haven't come to lie down. I don't feel like resting. I want to talk with you. Sit down here by the fire. I suppose I need your help. I need something — I don't really know what. I've been having a very hard time."

"I know it," said Louise sympathetically. "Last night was a heavy strain, but you can rest safely now. She is so much better. I never saw anyone rally so rapidly."

"I don't mean that. My hard time did not begin last night. I don't feel sure that I can tell you when it began — away back. I have made some of my hard times — I can see that. I have been disappointed in my children. John disappointed me long ago. I had ambitions for him. I had plans, and everything happened to thwart them. I felt hard toward Lewis some of the time, because he seemed to get in the way. I felt hard — well, at everything. I've thought that John's father didn't treat him just as I would have if I'd been a father. So I have just gone through life being out of sorts at everything.

"For a while after you came here I had hoped that John would take to you and that he would come out all right. When I saw how much emphasis you laid on prayer, I began to feel glad that you were praying for John and to sort of expect that good would come of it. You know how awfully disappointed I was and how things went from bad to worse. After he went away, it seemed to me as if my heart turned to stone. I didn't feel that I cared much for the other children, and I didn't want to. Dorothy provoked me, and

Lewis provoked me, and you provoked me worst of all. I have grown more hard and bitter every day. I was rebellious toward God; I thought He had treated me badly. I got down on my knees once and prayed for John. I said to myself that He ought to have heard me, and He didn't, and I couldn't forgive Him.

"Then came last night. I was hard on my poor little girl. I didn't punish her hard — I don't mean that. I just gave her three or four slaps. If they had been given in sport, she wouldn't have minded. It was her heart that I hurt, and I knew it. I knew at the time that I was punishing her unjustly. The child didn't mean to be disobedient — didn't know that she was — but I had been having a dreadful day, and it seemed an actual relief to have some escape for my bitterness. So I whipped her. But I have been punished for it.

"Last night was an awful night! If she had died I believe I would have lost my reason. And I thought she would die. I believed that God had sent for her in retribution. Yet I cried to Him. I told Him I had been bitter and severe and rebellious and was yet. But if He would spare my baby I would try to serve Him. I would do anything that He told me. Now He has taken me at my word, when I didn't expect it, and I am a woman who has always been noted for keeping a promise. I mean to keep this one, but I don't know how. I don't even know what He wants of me. It seemed to me that you ought to know and could tell me, so I've come to you for help."

Throughout the telling of this story Louise had not interrupted with a word or even a movement. But long before it was concluded, the sympathetic tears were dropping on her mother-in-law's hand. When the steady, unnaturally quiet voice ceased, this servant of Christ was ready with His message.

"Oh, Mother! What He wants of you is to lean your head upon His bosom and tell Him all your fears and cares and disappointments. Let Him whisper to you, 'Daughter, be of good courage.' He loves you, Mother, and He loves John and Neelie and all your flock. He wants to save you all in His everlasting arms and bring you, an unbroken family, to His Father's house. I believe He will do it. In return He asks your love. You know, Mother, when we stop to think of it, it would be simply impossible to help loving someone who waits to do all this for us and ours."

Mrs. Morgan looked at her daughter-in-law with grave, sincere eyes and slowly shook her head. "It may not be possible for you to help loving Him, but I don't feel a bit of love in my heart. It feels as hard as flint. I believe that He is willing to do a great deal for me, and yet I don't seem to care."

"Mother, tell Him so." Louise's voice trembled with the earnestness of her desire. "He is unlike any other friend. To a human friend we couldn't say simply: 'I know I *ought* to love you, but I don't. Show me how.' But to the tender Savior we can come with even these words. Mother, do not wait to feel as you think you ought. You have promised to serve Him. You say you mean to keep the promise; then just give yourself to Him. He will accept the gift and fill your heart with joy in return."

"But, Louise, that would be mockery. He asks for love, and I cannot love Him. I feel as though I have no love for anybody."

Louise shook her head. "No, if you are sincere you cannot mock Him. He made the heart. You cannot make your heart love Him, but you can resolve to give yourself to Him, to obey His directions, to follow His voice. I assure you, He will see to all the rest. Will you keep your promise?"

There was silence. Mrs. Morgan was evidently puzzled, as well as painfully embarrassed. The way was darker to her than it had been to Neelie. She had not the faith of a little child to rest upon.

"How much does the promise mean?" she asked at last. "What would I have to do?"

"It means everything," said Louise solemnly. "You would have to do just exactly as God directs. He has promised to guide you, and you are to promise to be guided every step of the way, to lose your will in His. Will you do it?"

"But if He directs what I cannot do?"

"There is no possibility of such an 'if,' Mother. He will be sure to give you the power to do what He commands. Unless you mean 'will not' by 'cannot,' there is nothing in the way. The world is full of people who say, 'I can't,' when in their hearts they know they mean, 'I won't.' But you are an honest woman. You will not say, 'I cannot,' to God when you know that you could, if you *would*. Mother, will you redeem your promise? See here, only yesterday your little Neelie sat in that chair where you are. She knelt beside me and prayed this prayer:

Here, Lord, I give myself away,
'Tis all that I can do.

"When she arose from her knees she said, 'He took me.' Will you use Neelie's prayer, Mother? If you will I'm sure you'll receive her answer. Will you kneel down with me here and now?"

I can't assure you that the daughter's faith was strong. She was startled at her own heart's beating, and a great deal of the emotion was the result of anxiety. It was evidently the turning point in Mrs. Morgan's life, but how would she decide it? Would she kneel down and deliberately give herself away to Christ, even in this darkness, declaring that she had no love in her heart for Him? Louise was afraid. The silence lasted. She did not know what else to say; she was afraid to speak again, so she kept silent.

Oh, how her heart sped to the throne with its errand. How she blessed the King that at this crisis hour she didn't need to petition for an audience and then await His leisure. Instead, without introduction or explanation, she pressed her petition. "Oh, Jesus, save her now." Again and again and yet again these desires were presented. Thinking of it later, it seemed to her that she almost felt the presence of the King and whispered yet again in His waiting ear, "I will not let You go." So strong grew the feeling that Louise was not surprised when suddenly in the quiet and darkness the little rocker was pushed back with a resolute hand, and her mother-in-law went down on her knees before it.

Louise slipped down beside her and, changing the tone of her prayer, said aloud: "Dear Jesus, here is this soul come to redeem her promise. She's giving herself to You now, to be Yours forever. She's going to follow wherever Your hand points the way. Now, Jesus, accept the covenant and make her Yours, even as You have promised."

And then from that room, only a little over twenty-four hours away from its yesterday's baptism, went up the words of Neelie's little prayer:

Here, Lord, I give myself away,
'Tis all that I can do.

The tones were firm, without emotion — almost stern. In truth, an iron will was bending now but with a definite purpose. Only those words were spoken, then silence. Louise waited, praying softly. She broke the silence then, sealing the offering with a tender prayer of petition that the Lord might now reveal His smiling face to the waiting soul. Finally, almost alarmed at the stillness, lest the feelings might be too much for the wearied body of this iron-willed woman, she arose. Mrs. Morgan quietly followed her example and sat down again in the little chair.

Louise waited then spoke: "Mother, you'll rest here now awhile, won't you? I'll go down to Neelie. When she awakens and wants you we'll call you immediately. I've made the bed comfortable, so perhaps you can get a nice rest. Will you have a light? No?" as Mrs. Morgan shook her head. "You like the firelight best. I'll make it just a little brighter."

Louise stirred the embers and added another stick. She stepped softly back to the little chair and touched her lips for just one second to the mother's cheek, then slipped out and left her.

Mrs. Morgan sat a few moments as if spellbound, gazing into the glow that sprang up on the hearth. Then she rose suddenly, crossed to the door and turned the key in the lock. Instead of lying on the bed she knelt before the little chair.

With her first words of surrender this woman had already felt a touch of the mighty hand that leaves its imprint upon the heart. She could not say now what she had fifteen minutes before, "I cannot love Him. I feel as though I have no love for anybody." She did not know what to name the strange new feelings that were surging through her. But for the first time in her life she could say, "I want to pray." And so she dropped on her knees, and the old, yet always new, continually repeated miracle of transformation occurred. "If any man will do his will, he shall know of the doctrine, whether it be of God." Why don't honest unbelievers apply the test of the Lord's own promise?

"What's the matter?" Dorothy asked in half-startled and wholly wondering tones, as Louise came once more to the little bedroom.

"Nothing. Why?" Louise asked, as she took her place beside the bed and smiled at the pale little face on the pillow.

"I don't know. You look — I hardly know how — a little as though you had seen an angel."

"Perhaps I have." This she said with gladness in her eyes and a bright, reassuring smile.

Then the father came to look in on his sleeping baby and to ask of Dorothy in a half whisper: "Where is your mother?"

"I don't know," said Dorothy. She turned inquiring eyes on Louise, who answered: "She is up in my room, Father, resting."

"Resting!" Father Morgan repeated the word in awe. Rest was something that Mother Morgan never took. The word seemed foreign to her nature. Even when she slept you hardly thought of her as actually resting. "She must be sick!"

"Oh, no, she isn't. I think she feels better than usual. She will have a nice rest and be down presently."

And then the farmer looked wonderingly at his daughter-in-law. He detected the lilt in her voice and the brightness in her face. It was always a bright face, but here was positive joy. What was there to be joyful about? Farmer Morgan did not define the question, nor did he think of angels. He had not been reading about the shining of Moses' face after he communed with God, as Dorothy had. But he told himself for perhaps the thousandth time that "Lewis had an unusual kind of a wife, somehow."

It was nearly midnight. Farmer Morgan was asleep on the old settee in the parlor when Mrs. Morgan opened the door quietly and entered.

"Did you get any rest, Mother?" It was Dorothy who asked, as Louise glanced up.

Her voice was calm as usual, but was it Louise's imagination that the hard ring had disappeared from it? "Yes," she said, "a good rest — better than any I've ever had in my life. You girls may both go to bed now. I'd just as soon sit up all night as not." And then she looked at Louise and smiled.

"What were those words Neelie said to you last night?" she asked Louise a little later, as Dorothy moved about, tidying up some last-minute things for her mother's comfort.

"She told me that *He took her.*"

"It is a strange thing, but I believe He has taken her mother, too. Good night, and God bless you."

And Mother Morgan folded her arms about Louise and kissed her twice — before the astonished eyes of Dorothy, who had just come in from the kitchen.

She then asked: "Mother, couldn't you lie down beside Neelie and sleep and let me stay awake to watch her?

"No, Dorothy, I don't need it. I am rested. I've found such rest that I knew nothing about. Louise will tell you."

It is very peculiar that kisses should have been such a rare thing between a mother and a daughter. But when Dorothy felt one on her cheek, the rich blood rolled into her face in waves. She was utterly bewildered until she heard Louise repeating: "Come unto me, all ye that labor and are heavy laden, and I will give you rest."

"Mother has just been to Him with His promise and received its fulfillment, Dorrie," she said. As they climbed the stairs together, she added: "Dorrie, dear, I believe you and I could sing the long-meter doxology with good effect tonight. Meanwhile, dear, we mustn't for one moment let go of John."

Ah, but stronger arms than theirs had hold of John!

CHAPTER XXVI

DORRIE'S AMBITION

as the progress in the Morgan family been unusual — the fruit more than the earnest Christian has a right to expect? Unless one gives a year of patient endeavor and constant prayer to the work which lies all around him or her, how can one possibly know what the results of such a year might be?

Did Louise Morgan have faith equal even to a grain of mustard seed? If she had, would she not have seen greater mountains than these removed? She was frequently discouraged and asked why. But such faith as she had the Lord honored, and as much real prayer as she was able to send up into the golden vials, He kept before Him.

From the hour when Mrs. Morgan knelt before the little rocker in Louise's room and gave herself unconditionally to God, she was a different woman. I'm not in sympathy with those who say conversion makes no radical change in character, that a person who is selfish or malicious or penurious before conversion is selfish or malicious or penurious after conversion in the same degree. Conversion is a change of heart. A heart given up to the rein of Christ, with the supreme desire being to please Him, will at the outset beat in a very different way from one that was given up to the reign of self. Mrs. Morgan's changed heart showed in her life; it showed promptly and decisively.

On that very next evening after tea, with Neelie among the pillows in the rocking chair that had been brought from Louise's room, the mother said: "Now, Lewis, I have made up my mind that I want family prayers in this house from now on. On Neelie's account we will have them right after tea, if it is just as well for you. Dorothy, get Mother's Bible. Sing a hymn, if you like, before reading. I like singing, even if I can't help, and your father used to be a good singer when he was young."

Farmer Morgan made no remark about this change in the family arrangements. If he was surprised he gave no sign. She had probably been talking with him about it — his wife was a straightforward woman. But Lewis's voice was very unsteady as he began the solemn hymn:

> Now I resolve with all my heart,
> With all my powers, to serve the Lord.

It seemed almost too wonderful to be true that those words should actually embody the resolve of his mother's heart! Besides, he had another reason for an unsteady voice. He had an absorbing desire for his father to understand and adopt that language. I haven't had a chance to say much about Lewis Morgan during these latter days, but I can tell you this briefly: Each day began in the morning with

"Lord, what will You have me to do?" and ended in the evening with a note of triumph.

> How sweet the work has been!
> Tis joy, not duty,
> To speak this beauty:
> My soul mounts on the wing!

and then the consecration,

> Lord, if I may,
> I'll serve another day.

When a Christian reaches such a plane, it is what a blessed saint of God describes as "the graded road."

How I would like to linger over those autumn days, to tell how rich they were. What a fresh, new spirit pervaded the home. Mother and daughters drew together. One afternoon they established a little female prayer meeting; Mother, Louise, Dorothy and little Neelie prayed in turn for John — such prayer that reached after him and drew him steadily, even though he did not know it. They prayed constantly and persistently with a measure of faith for the head of the household and watched eagerly for signs of life in his still soul; as yet they saw none. They enjoyed the rides to church and to prayer meeting on Wednesday evening. Mother Morgan, who had never been used to going anywhere in the evening astonished them all by getting ready as a matter of course. She answered Dorothy's wondering look with the statement: "Of course I am going, child. I need all the help I can get." All these and so many more experiences I would like to give you in detail, but time will not wait for me. The days fly by.

They bring us to a certain Thanksgiving evening. It was cold without but very pleasant upstairs in Louise's room. Dorothy was lingering with her brother and sister, having a confidential chat as she was now so fond of doing. They had grown to be wonderfully in sympathy, these three.

"Dorrie," Lewis said, "what do you think about a neighborhood prayer meeting this winter? Don't you believe we could sponsor one?"

Dorrie flashed a pair of glad eyes on her brother.

"Of course we could. We have enough in our family to support it, and Carey Martyn would make one more. Where could we have one? At the school-house? How could we warm it up? Could we furnish wood, do you think? Of course we could, if Father would think so, and I guess he would?"

Lewis laughed. "You take my breath away," he said pleasantly. The three laughed their way into talking about the neighborhood prayer meeting and from that to their individual efforts and specific cases.

"What about the Graham girls?" Lewis asked.

"Well, the Graham girls are progressing steadily. I'm wonderfully interested in Delia. Have you talked with Delia, Louise? Don't you think she is an unusual girl?"

Then Lewis laughed again. "You think each one of those girls is unusual, don't you, Dorrie? I think I have heard you make a similar remark about half a dozen of them."

"Well, they are remarkable, every one of them, to me. I didn't know they were such girls. They are getting on nicely with their grammar, those Graham girls are, and are so interested in it. Mr. Butler thinks they would have been fair scholars if they had had a chance."

"You would make a good teacher, Dorrie," Lewis said, his mind evidently more on Dorrie than on the girls of whom she was speaking.

Her cheeks, as well as her eyes, glowed now. "Do you think so, Lewis — do you honestly think so? I'd like it so much. Since I began studying this last time, I've thought about it a good deal. At first I thought I couldn't prepare myself without going away from home, but that was before I knew what a wonderful teacher I had at home." She glanced lovingly at Louise.

At that moment the clang of the old-fashioned knocker sounded through the house. Dorrie arose promptly.

"I suppose that's Mr. Butler," she said, stopping a moment before the mirror to arrange her hair. "He was to come this evening to see about the German class. Shall I speak to him about the neighborhood prayer meeting? But you'll come down presently, won't you?"

To this they nodded, looking after her as she left the room with a quick, eager step.

"Speaking of changes," Lewis said, "how wonderfully that girl has changed! I don't think I ever saw anything like it before. Don't you think she has developed very rapidly?"

"It's steady growth," Louise said. "But I'm not sure that there is so much actual change in her as there is development. Evidently she always had plenty of energy, but it was slumbering — she didn't know what to do with it. I think she was in the apathy of disappointment when we first came home."

"She is certainly a remarkable girl," Lewis said, "and I never knew it. I believed her to be more than ordinarily commonplace. The influence she has gained over the young people in a short time is really wonderful. I'm glad she has an ambition to become a teacher. I believe she'll be a good one. Louise, don't you think Mr. Butler will help her perfect her education?"

"I think he has been helpful in many ways and will be," Louise said, with smiling eyes.

Downstairs in the kitchen Mrs. Morgan sat at the table with certain unused implements before her — namely, pen and ink and paper. She had resolved to spend this Thanksgiving evening writing to John — not that she knew where he was, but she imagined that the great city such a little distance away held him. She had no address. She'd simply decided to send the message out addressed to John Morgan in the forlorn hope that somehow it might fall across his path. True, it was extremely doubtful, but what if it should happen! The mother's heart thrilled at the thought. She bent over the paper and carefully began her letter. She had wonderful things to tell John!

Farmer Morgan dozed in his chair behind the stove. He opened his eyes when the knocker clanged and kept awake long enough to discover that Dorothy appeared to answer it, then dozed off again.

"It's Mr. Butler," Dorothy said, appearing again to exchange the candle for the lamp which now belonged to the front room. "Louise and Lewis will be down pretty soon. Will you come in, Mother?"

"Not tonight — I'm very busy."

The writing and the sleeping continued, and Dorothy returned to the brightness of the front room. Writing was slow and laborious work to Mrs. Morgan. And this was an unusual letter, a subject which was new to her. She chose her words with special care. Farmer Morgan, enjoying his many naps in the cozy corner, was unaware of the passing time.

Lewis and Louise were enjoying a quiet hour together in their room, when they suddenly remembered they were expected downstairs.

"That couldn't have been Mr. Butler," Lewis said,

glancing up at the clock. "Dorrie would have been after us before now, if it had."

"Perhaps they're busy over their German," Louise answered. "But we ought to go down, Lewis. Father must be tired of waiting. Mr. Butler is probably gone by now. I didn't know it was so late."

But in the kitchen the writing and the dozing were still going on. Mother Morgan, flushed with her unusual work, glanced up as the husband and wife entered.

"Where is Dorrie?" Lewis asked, speaking low so as not to disturb his father.

"She's in the front room with Mr. Butler," the mother said. "Mr. Butler came in a few minutes ago. Dorothy said you were coming down to see him."

"A few minutes ago!"

Lewis and Louise exchanged glances. By the clock it was an hour and a half since they had been expected in the parlor, and it was an hour past the usual bedtime! But the slow-moving pen moved on, so Lewis turned the knob of the parlor door. The two occupants of the room were standing near the large fireplace and were engaged in an earnest conversation. Dorothy's face was flushed, and her eyes were shining. And the minister's face revealed something that arrested Lewis's steps. An exclamation escaped his lips before he knew it. Andrew Butler held Dorothy's hands in his own, and the light in his eyes and the flush on Dorothy's cheeks were not caused by the glow of the firelight.

"Come in," he said, turning suddenly at the sound of the opening door. In no other way did he alter his position. "Dorothy and I were just speaking of you and wishing you would come down. We want to ask your advice. I want to ask Mr. and Mrs. Morgan for a Thanksgiving present. I'd rather ask for it tonight,

but Dorothy prefers to wait until tomorrow. What do
you say?"

"Dorothy!" said her brother. He himself couldn't
tell whether his tone meant surprise or doubt or
what! "I don't understand."

The red glow that spread over Dorothy's face indicated that her old embarrassment was overcoming
her; she could not explain.

"It is a simple matter." The minister was unembar-
rassed and dignified. "I've asked Dorothy to be my
wife, and she has said yes. Now I need to ask her
father and mother. I had hoped that you would not
be displeased at the news."

Lewis Morgan recovered his wits. He was
amazed, but he did not want to be misunderstood.
He waited to close the door after Louise, then
stepped forward eagerly and held out a hand to each.
"I was very much astonished," he said. "I'm sure I
may be excused for that. Who imagined such a thing!
But to say that it is not a glad astonishment would
not be true."

Women, at least some women, know what to do,
even when they are very much astonished, and
Louise was not that. She slipped over to Dorrie and
put both arms around her and bestowed tender,
sisterly kisses on her flushed cheeks.

A few minutes later, after the first feelings of bewilderment had subsided, Lewis said suddenly,
"Dorrie, I thought you had an ambition to be a
teacher."

"She has," said Andrew Butler cheerfully. "I've
engaged her, but the school is a private one — with
the number of pupils limited to one."

CHAPTER XXVII

HEARTTHROBS AND COMMONPLACES

I don't mean to relate in detail what was said in the Morgan family when that evening in the parlor was revealed to them. You can hardly doubt that the revelations were astounding — at least to certain members of the family. The father and mother would hardly have been more amazed if an angel from heaven had descended and claimed their daughter Dorothy for a friend. Not that they regarded the young minister in an angelic light. They didn't admit it even to themselves, but they had much of that staunch loyalty to the profession, which seems to be born of New England soil. A minister was a person to respect, not so much because of himself as his profession. Farmer Morgan felt this. Sneer as he might in a good-natured, tolerant way at the inconsistencies of Christians — ministers included — he never went beyond certain general phrases, and he disliked hearing others go even that far.

The family genuinely liked Mr. Butler, but they

didn't know it. Farmer Morgan would have been amazed if anyone had told him he liked Mr. Butler. He would probably have thought the person mistaken. But it was true.

Along with her respect for the minister and pride in the fact that he had actually sought her daughter for a wife, Mrs. Morgan senior was utterly astonished that *anybody* wanted Dorothy! Why Dorothy was nothing but a child! The idea of her being married! For several days she studied it and tried to understand it. It had never occurred to her to consider this daughter as one who was growing into a woman. She had seemed to stay somewhere between twelve and fourteen at best — a girl to be directed and managed, to be told what to wear and where to go and where not to go — in short, a child, to obey without questioning. She was older than Neelie, of course, but still a child.

Now in the space of one night, or so it seemed to the mother, she had sprung into young ladyhood — no, sprung over it entirely and was standing on the verge of womanhood! Engaged to be married! What an unaccountable state of things! Dorothy was actually planning to leave home, to be gone overnight, many nights — every night! Dorothy would have a home of her own and be a housekeeper, a planner, a manager — a minister's wife! The story grew more perplexing.

The mother turned on her pillow, overwhelmed with it. She arose in the morning with a strange sense of confusion. She looked doubtfully at Dorothy in her brown calico. It was the same brown calico she had worn every morning that week. She appeared to be much the same in every respect. Yet by the light in her eye and the spring in her step — and a certain throbbing of her mother's heart — she would never again be the same.

Look at the matter from any angle. Let the circumstances be as favorable as they will. Let the congratulations be as sincere and as hearty as possible. There is always a sad side to this kind of story — change. It always occupies a heavy corner in a mother's heart. Still the new order of things worked well for Dorothy. If her mother was sad, she was also glad. Along with the sense of pride was a feeling of dignity in being Dorothy's mother, though at first the respect for her that accompanied it was nearly overpowering. It seemed hardly the thing to send the prospective wife of her minister down to the cellar after the bread and butter and to skim the cream! Gradually this feeling wore away. But the fact remained that Dorothy was a young woman, and not a child, and was to be consulted and conferred with and, in a measure, deferred to. And that benefitted both Dorothy and her mother. The following year would be one that mother and daughter would in future years remember pleasantly.

Lewis was sincerely glad and thankful. Andrew Butler had grown rapidly in his estimation, especially since he had realized Lewis was not merely a critic but a fellow laborer who was committed to work with and support his pastor. That his sister Dorothy should be the one chosen astonished Lewis. But since she was chosen, he was glad. Every day he grew more convinced that Mr. Butler was a sensible man and had made a wise choice. He had underrated his sister nearly all her life; he was almost in danger of overrating her now. But that is such a pleasant and easily forgiven failure, and such a rare one between brothers and sisters, that I find myself liking Lewis the better for possessing it.

As for Louise, she was a young woman with wide-open eyes and a sympathetic heart; she was not surprised at all. Matters had progressed more quickly than she had expected. She was even a trifle sorry that Dorothy had not gotten just a little further with her German before her teacher turned into her lover. She feared that little German would be taught or studied now. But then she reflected that possibly the lessons he had to teach were more important than German. At least the matter was not in her plans. The studies in which she was teacher and in which Dorothy had progressed so rapidly during the year would still continue. All things considered, Louise was happy.

I find myself lingering longer over this explanation than is needed. I meant to tell you about something else — a winter evening near Christmas time. The day's farm work was finished. The early evening had closed in upon the Morgan family and found them in the bright, clean kitchen at their plentiful supper table. They were a cheery group; somehow this family was learning to have social suppers and joyous times together. Lewis was recounting an interesting matter that had occurred in the village. He was interrupted by a decisive rap at the outside door.

"Another tramp?" asked Lewis, as Neelie slipped from her corner to answer the knock. "This is the third one today, isn't it? Those fellows are increasing."

"Strange that they straggle away out here," the mother said. "I would think they'd stay in large towns."

Neelie gave a startled little exclamation, possibly out of fear or perhaps only surprise. But it caused each member of the household to turn suddenly toward the door. Then *they* exclaimed — not in fear certainly, for there was nothing in the young man to awaken fear.

The mother was on her feet and at the door while the others stared and waited and all talked at once. She had both arms around the intruder and her lips to his cheek for the first time in years and years. And her heart cried out: "Oh, my boy! My boy!"

Now I'm sure you don't expect me to tell you what the Morgan family said to each other and to John for the next ten minutes. They don't even know. They couldn't remember later what they did or said or who spoke first after the mother. And if I would tell the tale, it probably would sound strange and unnatural; the words would be trite and quite unsuited to the occasion. There is even a chance the speakers would declare: "I don't believe I said any such thing; it doesn't sound like me." Such scenes are better left untold. The heartthrobs, the quivering lips and chins, and the glances exchanged from wet eyes cannot be described and, in fact, describe much more than mere words can.

This much Dorothy remembered: Before the initial surprise had subsided, she hurried to the pantry and brought out a knife and fork and plate. She motioned to Louise, who had taken the hint and arranged John's old seat near his father. Dorothy set his place and said, "Come, John," and they all settled into their places again.

Farmer Morgan remembers now with a curious, half-embarrassed smile that he filled John's plate to overflowing with the cold beans that he remembered John used to like. Unmindful of what he did, he reached forward and added another spoonful after the plate had been passed! Well, what did it matter, whether expressed in beans or some other way, that his heart wanted to give even to overflowing to the son who was lost and is alive again!

The familiar sentence hovered in Louise's mind,

Was he alive? She watched him closely, tremblingly, while Lewis talked. His face looked older, much older — worn and grave, not hard. The eyes were clear and steady, and his dress was that of a clean, respectable working man. But how much hope was there that he would bring joy with him to the old home? A joy that would stay?

"Well," John said, pushing his chair forward so that his face was more in shadow. The tone of the simple little word sent a thrill of expectation through the family group that something important was coming. The tea things had been cleared away, and the room had assumed order and quiet. Not that there had been much bustle in cleaning up that evening. Mrs. Morgan had done what was for her a surprising thing: She pushed her chair back from the table and sat still during all the moving to and fro from pantry to cellar. For the first time in her life, she was unmindful as to whether the milk went down in the right pitcher or the bread went down at all. Louise and Dorothy had moved softly, putting back their chairs noiselessly, and dried the cups and plates without a sound so as not to lose a syllable of the conversation. But it was not until they were seated that John spoke that little opening word.

"I have a long story to tell — a very long one. I don't know where to begin or how to begin — only that I've decided to strike into the middle of it first. Father and Mother, I want you to forgive me for everything I've done in the past that has hurt you, and I know that is a lot. I want you to know that I've started life again — at the beginning. In short, I feel I can honestly say that this your son 'was dead, and is alive again...was lost, and is found.' " And he turned to his mother with a smile that evidently she understood.

"Did you really get my letter?" she asked him, her

voice so full of eagerness and so unlike her that
Louise could not keep from wondering.

"Yes," John said. He launched at once into the
details of the apparent accidents that brought him his
mother's letter.

"I was signing for a package for Mr. Sloan. I had
to sign my own name so that in case of loss, you
know, it could be traced to me. As I wrote my name,
the carrier, who stood by, said: 'A letter's been lying
in the office up here at Station D for a person of that
name. I remember it because it doesn't have a street
or number — just the name and the city. We thought
it was intended for John Y. Morgan, the mason, but
he brought it back to the station. He said it was none
of his, that it began, "My dear son," and the two
people who used to begin letters that way for him
had been in heaven for a dozen years.'

"I don't know what made me go after that letter,"
said John, after a moment's silence, his voice breaking. "I'm sure I had no reason and no right to expect
that it was for me. But it seemed to me that I must
have it, so I went for it. And, Mother, that letter
brought me home. I meant to wait to do certain
things before I came — for one, I meant to earn some
money. I wanted to wait until I could feel that my
coming would not disgrace you. But after I read that
letter I knew I ought to come right away, and after I
decided it, I could hardly wait for morning.

"Now, Mother, Father, will you take me back? Will
you let me try to be to you the son I ought to have
been and never was? I don't know that I should dare
say that to you, except that I've been to my heavenly
Father and found out that He can forgive. And I've
found that He says: 'Like as a father pitieth his children' and 'as one whom his mother comforteth.' And
that has given me a notion of what the love of a father

and mother is. And then, Mother, that letter of yours — I went down on my knees before God with it and blessed Him for it."

They were crying now, every one of them, except Farmer Morgan, and what he felt no one knew. He drew out his red silk handkerchief and blew his nose twice, then he leaned forward and snuffed the candle. When he presently found his voice it was husky, but all he said was, "We won't talk about them days that are gone. I guess most of us are willing to bid good-bye to them and begin again. There's a chance for improvement in us all; like as not we better try for it."

The Morgan family actually sat up that night until nearly eleven o'clock! It was an unprecedented thing for them to do. I can't tell you what they said; I even doubt much whether I would if I could. Don't you hate to see some things attempted on paper? A little of the commonplace might be mixed in with it. In fact, I doubt whether there could be a true home scene without touches of what we call commonplace.

For instance, in the course of the evening Louise remembered the little dismantled hall chamber and slipped away and brought comforters, quilts, a spread, clean linen and towels. She worked quickly until the room took on a sense of home and being occupied again. She even set out the doilies and the vases to make it all seem as he had left it. Then she climbed to the upper shelf and took down that Bible. What a rush of glad emotions swelled in her heart as she thought of the tender way in which John had quoted those two Bible verses. That Bible would be to him now something besides a burden.

Down in the kitchen the mother — her heart filled with the most precious thoughts that ever throbbed in a mother's heart — remembered suddenly that

John had been very fond of a certain kind of griddle cakes. He and Lewis were talking, and their father, with his elbows leaning on the arms of his chair and his head bent forward, was listening as though ten o' clock had not been two hours past his bedtime for more than half a century. Mother Morgan, meanwhile, gave quiet directions to Dorothy to sift flour and "bring a yeast cake, a little warm water, the big yellow bowl, the batter spoon and a little salt." With skillful fingers and such a light in her eyes as the yellow bowl had never seen before, she prepared to make the breakfast table abound with good cheer. These commonplace attempts to create pleasant memories of the home do bear good fruit.

I find myself wanting to linger over that evening in the Morgan household. It was such a wonderful hour; it became for them a time from which they dated events before and after. Years after that they said, "The moonlight tonight reminds me of that evening when John came home, you know," and then a thoughtful silence. Such sentences were never spoken except in that innermost circle and those who in later years grew into the circle and had an interest in the family history. Yet there is little to tell about it. How often that's the case when there is so much to feel!

One train of thought intimately connected with it ought to be told. There was something in the evening's story which silenced Mr. Morgan — in fact, it bewildered him. Until now he had professed to be — and I think believed himself to be — a skeptic regarding supernatural change in human hearts. He believed conversion meant simply to make a firm resolution, a decision of character — willpower. Louise was by nature and education different from most others; so in his way was Lewis. Thus Mr.

Morgan had reasoned. Dorothy needed waking up, and Louise and Lewis and Mr. Butler between them had awakened her. The sudden and marked change in his own wife had perplexed him not a little. She certainly had always possessed will enough. But, he told himself, after all, what had she done but determine to be interested in the Bible and in the church and all that? All it needed was determination.

Now here came his strong-willed son — so strong indeed that his will had been his one great source of trouble even from babyhood. As a wee boy he had hated to give up one inch. He had been unable to say, "I'm sorry," or "I won't do it again," or "forgive me," or any of the penitent phrases which fall so readily from baby lips. A scowl and a stubbornness to go his own way had characterized John's babyhood. What power had brought him home to say not only, "I was wrong," but "forgive me; I want to begin again"? For John to say, "Father, Mother, forgive me" — to say it without being ordered or compelled by circumstances — his father was amazed! Here, at last, was something — some strange change that could not be explained by any power of the will whatever, except by admitting that something — somebody — had changed the current of the willpower.

Late that night Father Morgan sat down on the edge of his bed and slowly and thoughtfully removed his boots, while Mother Morgan went to see if John didn't need another comforter. I believe, said Father Morgan to himself, I believe in my soul that somehow — I don't know how, but somehow — God has got hold of John!

CHAPTER XXVIII

"I DON'T KNOW"

une brought the roses and Estelle, the fairest rose of all.

There had been much planning in the Morgan household in preparation for her coming. Things had changed in the farmhouse since Louise first came home to it. Many of them were subtle changes brought about too slowly to be recognized as changes. The family had gradually slipped into these new ways without even noticing them — little refinements here and there, trifles every one of them. They probably wouldn't have recognized them unless they had suddenly dropped back to their old ways for a week. That experiment no one seemed inclined to try.

Louise took great pleasure in making the large front room with its quaint furniture into a very bower of beauty for the sweet rose that was to bloom there. She smiled joyfully when she thought of what blissful surprises the wealth of June flowers and the smell of June clover would be to the city maiden. She had many plans for Estelle, many hopes related to this two months' sojourn in the farmhouse. She did not indulge in these hopes, however, without weaving in anxious little sighs among them.

She had hoped so long and waited so eagerly and in vain. She told John about it one evening, as they sat on the vine-covered porch together, waiting for Lewis and Dorothy to conquer the problem in algebra that was vexing the latter.

"John, I have such a strong hope that you will be able to help Estelle this summer. It has a lot to do with my joy in her coming."

John turned anxious eyes on her for a moment and was silent. After a moment he said: "Once I would have thought you were saying that for effect, but I've learned that you never say things simply for effect. So you must mean it, and it makes me anxious. I can't see how I could influence your sister in any way, to say nothing of the foolishness of hoping to help her. I don't understand what you can mean."

"She isn't a Christian, you know, John."

"I know, and I understand you're talking about that kind of help. But what puzzles me is, how could you possibly expect me to do or say anything that could influence her, when she has had you all her life."

"That is easily explained," Louise said smiling. "In the first place, you are in the mood just now to overrate my influence over people. I have some with Estelle, but that it is not great is plainly shown in the fact that, in this most important of all matters, she has chosen her way and I have chosen mine, and we have walked separately for a good many years. Don't you know, John, that sometimes the people we meet but once, with whom we really have very little to do, are given a word to say or an act to perform that will influence all our future lives?"

"Yes," John said, with sudden energy. He certainly knew that as well as any person could. He immediately remembered the young girl who had held out her hand and whose winning voice had said: "Won't you have a card?"

"Well," Louise said, "I can't help hoping that the Holy Spirit will give you a word or look that will influence Estelle. It doesn't seem to me that I can have her wait any longer."

There were tears in her eyes. Then John felt hostile toward Estelle. He told himself that he didn't believe he could endure her; she must be a little simpleton. To have grown up under the influence of such a sister and yet to have chosen a course that would grieve her argued ill for her heart or her sense or something. Although he wanted to help, Louise was not awaking much hope in him that he could. This brother and sister had established a good understanding.

For that matter, the rebuilt household understood each other well during these days. They had begun to realize something of what the family relationships meant. John was certainly "a new creature in Christ Jesus." The new life doesn't always have so plain a chance of showing itself as his former life had given. No Christian doubted the presence of the unseen guest who had come to abide with him. The father kept silent on the matter, but he also kept keen eyes on his son. He told himself a dozen times a day that whatever had come over John, he was a different person.

By slow degrees the Morgan family had settled into definite plans for the future — plans that were not developed without some soreness of heart and even on Louise's part a touch of tears. Giving up future prospects for usefulness in the church had been a trial to Lewis, and he had given up those prospects by inches. At last, however, it had become obvious that, if he would keep his health and strength, he must be content with an active, outdoor life.

Once this was settled, the father was entirely willing to loose his hold on John and give him the desire of his heart — a medical education. At least, he said it was for this reason he was willing; those of the family who watched him closely strongly suspected there was very little the father would not have been willing to give John during these days.

The father himself was somewhat changed. One bright winter day, he invited Lewis to take Louise out and pick out the spot where he would like to build a house. They would see what kind could be built one of these days.

Strange to say, the desire to have a home of their own was less intense than it had been. They talked it up; they said it would be "nice," in fact, delightful. Then, in the same breath, Lewis wondered what Mother would do when Dorothy went away. Louise wondered whether Dorothy wouldn't need her help right there at home for the next year or two before she left the home to become the minister's wife. Finally, though they made no objection to picking out the lot and even planned the house — built it, indeed, on paper a good many times — they unanimously agreed they could do nothing definite about it until spring. In truth the need for their own home was not as great to this young couple as it once had been. Now that spring, yes, even summer, was fairly upon them, the question of a house arose again, brought forward by Farmer Morgan himself.

"Not that I am in a hurry," he said, with a little embarrassed laugh. "In fact I hope it will be about five years in getting built and you five more or so in getting moved. I've no notion of what this house would be without you. But I've made up my mind it is your right to have your own house, and I mean you shall have it."

The house was a settled fact. Lewis and his wife were undeniably pleased, yet nobody hurried. The necessity for haste was past.

So they had journeyed into June, when Estelle was to make her first visit to the farmhouse. She was to have come the summer before, but home matters had detained her. As Louise arranged roses in the white vases of her room, she rejoiced that it had been so and smiled over the different dress the home and family wore from that which they would have worn had Estelle come only a year before.

These were the closing touches to the preparations, for Lewis, accompanied by Dorothy and little Neelie, had already gone to the train to meet his sister. Louise declined the ride with the plea of escaping the afternoon sun; in reality, she felt that when she got that bright young sister in her arms again she might disgrace the welcome by crying outright.

Who would have imagined that the months of separation would have stretched themselves out so! Louise was to have gone home at the latest a year from the date of her departure, and yet she didn't. It often happens in this world that with all our planning our lives move in exactly different lines from how we have prepared. So Louise had not even gazed upon the face of her beautiful young sister since that morning when she became a bride. It is surely no wonder that her heart beat faster at the sound of the carriage wheels, and she had some difficulty getting down the stairs.

Just as daylight was fading, John came to be introduced to the newcomer. He had planned differently, but unexpected business had detained him in the village until a late hour. He had taken his supper alone and came out to the piazza to meet Estelle, just as they were adjourning to the house.

John had decidedly dreaded this ordeal. He had spent so much of his life in shadows that before certain creations he was unreasonably timid — among these were young ladies. And to meet one he was expected to help was formidable. Still John's strong point was decision of character; what had to be done was to be done promptly and with as little appearance of hesitation as possible.

"Come," Louise said. "These bugs must be shut out, and you must be shut in. Oh, here comes John."

At that moment Dorothy brought the large lamp. The glow of it fell on Estelle's face. John stepped forward boldly and raised his eyes to her fair, bright face.

But instead of the friendly greeting he had planned, he stared hard at her. At last, the words exploded from him in astonishment: "You are the very one!"

"Of course," said Estelle, mischief shining in every line of her beautiful face. Undaunted by this strange greeting, she held out her hand graciously, while Louise stood by amazed. "Did you think I was some-body else? Shake hands, won't you?"

"Don't you remember me?" John said slowly, as one awaking from a dream. He looked from Estelle to Louise, then back again to her. He studied the two faces, like one who had been puzzled over a riddle but had just found the answer.

"Not in the least," Estelle said promptly. "I don't think I ever saw you before in my life. But since you seem to be acquainted with me, I thought I would be friendly."

"You *have* seen me before," John said. He recovered his usual manner and gave the small white hand a cordial grasp. "It is partly your resemblance to Louise which gave me such a vivid impression of your face and a feeling of having seen *you* before somewhere. And it was your picture. I hung it myself in the front room when Louise first came here. I have looked at it since, thinking it seemed familiar," John said, still very much in earnest.

Then Estelle laughed. "What an idea!" she said. "I don't look the least in the world like Louise and never did. What is more trying, I am not in the least like her, as you will find to your sorrow." She had nothing but bright, thoughtless mischief in her voice and manner.

"Louise," he said, turning to her for sympathy, "isn't it strange that it should happen so? She is the very young lady who gave me that card on that miserable and memorable night and invited me to the meeting."

A vivid blush spread over Estelle's face. She had given some curious thoughts to the forlorn specimen of humanity she invited to the meeting. It was her only attempt at evangelism, and it stood out in her memory. She had commented on his appearance to her mother; she had given a laughing description of him to her young friends. Now it seemed most unlikely that this well-dressed, nice-looking young man and her forlorn tramp were one and the same!

"Are you adept at masquerades?" she asked at last. "You certainly played the character of a woebegone street wanderer to perfection — or else you are playing the well-dressed young man very well. Which is the assumed character anyway?"

John saw no humor in this episode. He answered

her gravely: "The street wanderer was a real and dreary wanderer; he thought he was a hopeless case. But he will never cease to thank God for sending you to put out a rescuing hand that night."

The flush that had been fading from Estelle's face became vivid again. How was she going to jest with one who took matters so solemnly? She didn't know what to say to him and turned away embarrassed.

Now John was stirred. Intensity was part of his nature; what he did at all, he did with all his might. Louise was anxious as to what this revelation would produce. She was soon satisfied that it had roused his interest in her as nothing else could have done. It filled him with pain to think that the one who had brought him into the light of Christ was herself walking in darkness.

From that hour she was the subject of his constant prayer. He brought her before his Master only as one can who has learned the sweetness of being a servant of Christ and who longs to call in others. Now and then he had a word with her, as the opportunity arose, but he spent most of his strength on his knees.

On the way to the neighborhood prayer meeting — which, by the way, had been started and had flourished — John was Estelle's companion. It was actually the first time he had seen her alone. He didn't have to waste time in trying to make up his mind to speak to her on the subject; he was eager to speak. "I was so surprised. I was so used to praying for the one who gave me that card, as one would for a saint almost. I hadn't considered that you might not be a Christian."

"And now all those prayers have been lost! So much wasted strength — what a pity!" Estelle did not really mean to be wicked, although her tone was mischief itself. She was in the habit of parrying personalities on this subject in a jesting way. She usually shocked the person addressing her into silence, thus giving her freedom for the time being. She did not even mean irreverence by it; she meant simply to have fun — and to be let alone.

John, however, was not used to nonsense in conversation. Since he began to converse at all, he had nearly always talked with earnest people and had been tremendously in earnest himself. So he answered her as if the remark had been serious. "No, I don't think that. Of course God knew just where you were, and He accepted the spirit of the prayer. But isn't it strange that with Louise for a sister you have lived so many years without Christ?"

Louise was a person about whom Estelle did not jest. She could be flippant *to* her but not *about* her, so to this sentence she had no answer at first. After a moment she rallied: "Come now, isn't it strange that with Lewis for a brother and Mrs. Morgan for a mother, you lived so many years without paying any attention to these things? Didn't you ever hear that people who live in glass houses shouldn't throw stones?"

"Ah, but," said John eagerly, "I didn't believe in it. I didn't think there was any such thing as conversion nor any reality in religion. I was a fool, to be sure, but I was an honest one. I really didn't believe in these things. But you had a different upbringing. My mother is a young Christian, you know. You had no such doubts to trammel you, had you?"

"No," said Estelle slowly. She was obliged to be honest before this honest young man. She thought of her mother, of her father and of her sister, Louise, and she had to say no.

"Then why haven't you been a Christian these many years?"

"I don't know."

"Then why don't you become one now?"

"I don't know."

John could not hold back an exclamation that was not unlike the half sneer which used to express his entire disapproval of an act. Then he said significantly, "Seems to me if I were you, I'd find out."

Estelle was silent. This was an entirely new way of approaching the subject. This serious young man gave her something to think about. She had struggled with skepticism, although she didn't know it by that name. In her heart she had believed that some persons were by nature religious in their youth: Mama was, and Louise was like her. Mama said that when Louise was just a baby, she would lie quietly by the hour to be read to from the Bible, while she, Estelle, never lay quietly at any time for anything but sleep. She was not by nature religious, she argued. Sometime, when she was old and gray, it would become natural to her to think about these things. Some people were called in their youth, and some in later life. It must be that she was designed to be a middle-aged Christian.

Into the face of this theory came John; he was young, keen, intense, fierce, as irreligious by nature as a man could be and as far away from even outward respect for the cause as a scoffer could be. Louise, who intuitively understood some of Estelle's line of reasoning, had taken pains to explain in detail John's past life and his intense nature. Estelle must work out this problem for herself. She showed that she had begun to work at it by her grave, sincere answer, "I don't know."

CHAPTER XXIX

THE OLD AND THE NEW

A stretch of years I am passing in silence — not because there is little that would be pleasant for me to tell concerning the Morgan family. The lengthening chapters simply remind me it is high time to have done with them; yet I must tell certain things.

I am dropping you into the midst of June roses again, after a lapse of five busy, earnest years, back at the old farmhouse. It really was not the old farmhouse at all; it was in a new dress. A corner had been put on here, a bay window there, a piazza at the south side and a wide porch at the east, until the house would not have recognized itself. Inside, not a single room from the yellow-painted kitchen onward remained the same. Was this the new house, which had been planned years before? Well, not exactly. The new house was built with bricks and mortar, just as it had been planned on paper. A gem of a house it proved to be. But its location was next to the church in the village, and Dorothy and the minister were the occupants.

"It isn't exactly a parsonage," Father Morgan said, "and yet it is. At least the minister lives in it and is welcome to, of course, for it belongs to his wife. But if another minister should come in his place, why then I suppose it couldn't be called a parsonage."

At present there is no prospect that another minister will come in Andrew Butler's place. The people like both him and his wife. That's a strange statement, I know. Yet there are a few parishes left in which the people continue to stand by a faithful pastor, even after a lapse of years.

Dorothy had certain advantages. To be sure, Mr. Butler had done what is supposed to be an unwise thing: He married the daughter of one of his parishioners. But you will remember that in her early girlhood she had almost no acquaintances among the people of the village. She had not mingled with them in any capacity. They knew no more of her character, and almost as little of her life, as they would have had she lived a thousand miles away. Somehow, the one they had spoken of as "that Morgan girl" on rare occasions seemed to the people entirely different from their minister's wife, as in truth she was. As if to confirm the promise about "all things working together for good," the very obscurity in which Dorothy had spent her girlhood worked well for her in her present sphere. So Dorothy reigned in the new house and ruled it well, and her mother grew used to looking upon her as a married woman and a housekeeper, yes, and a mother.

Lewis Morgan had not a little to do with the successful ministrations of his brother-in-law. After being discouraged by his health and the change in his life's plans, he rallied at the time of Dorothy's conversion and tasted anew the joy of working for

Christ. He took what perhaps I may reverently term a new lease of spiritual life and gave himself up to joyful service. Since then he had been busy for the Master, and the refrain of his song was still "How sweet the work has been!" Imagine how helpful such a wide-awake, prudent, faithful Christian could be to a pastor. Imagine the alert eyes he could have to the needs and the wishes and the whims of the people. Imagine the kind suggestions he could offer to a younger pastor, who not only thoroughly respected him, but loved him as a brother. As heavy as the cross had been to give up what is called active work for Christ, Lewis Morgan was active in his way and perhaps just as successful as if he were preaching the gospel from the pulpit. I make that distinction because in his class, in the prayer meeting and in his daily life, Lewis Morgan was assuredly preaching the gospel.

The renovated farmhouse was still large enough for the two families. Yet the new house — the other new house — was in the process of being built.

It was Louise's plan again. One of the prettiest of houses, it, too, was in the village and was planned with special reference to the needs of Dr. John Morgan. Yes, he was going to settle down in the little village! No, I forgot — the word "little" doesn't apply to it anymore. During these years in which I have said almost nothing, the village sprang into life, aided by the junction of another railroad and a large machine shop. Dr. John had accepted a partnership with the gray-haired physician who had held the practice in the village and outlying hills for forty years. Just as soon as the new house was finished and furnished (and it was nearly complete), he was going to keep house.

Every cheery, sweet-smelling room in the Morgan farmhouse had a gala look on this afternoon. They were such pretty rooms! I wish I could describe them

to you — simple, quiet in tone and in keeping with
the wide-spreading green fields and the glowing
flowers. Bright, clear carpets covered the floors with
tasteful hues and graceful patterns. Sheer muslin
curtains, looped with ribbons to match the carpets
decorated the windows. Nearly every easy chair had a
design of its own. Wide, low couches with luxurious
pillows invited you to lounge among them. Books and
papers and pictures were plentiful. Louise's piano and
guitar were poised in convenient places, ready for
service, and her light touches were seen everywhere.
Who can describe a simple, pretty room? It is easy to
tell the color of the carpet and the position of the
furniture, but where are the words to describe that
spirit of comfort and ease and home that hovers over
some rooms and is utterly lacking in others?

Upstairs, in the room that was once Louise and
Lewis's, and which they had vacated now for the
sunnier side of the house, special care had been exercised. It was a fair, pink and white abode. The carpet
was sprinkled with pink moss-rose buds on a mossy
ground, and the white curtains were tied with pink
ribbons. The cool, gray furniture, of that peculiar tint
of gray that suggests white, was adorned with delicate touches of Louise's skill in the shape of moss-rose
buds that matched the carpet. The dressing table was
a mass of delicate white drapery through which
glowed a hint of pink, and the very china had been
deftly painted in the same pattern. Easy chairs and
large, old-fashioned rockers occupied cozy nooks.

Louise, her face aglow with merry satisfaction,
had enhanced each one with the veritable doilies
which she had brought from home as a bride and
with others, made in a pattern similar to hers. She
was arranging fresh roses generously in the mantel
vases, on the little dressing table and wherever she

could find a spot for a vase.

Neelie came and stood in the door. She herself was a vision of beauty in flowing curls and spotless white garments, made according to the latest and most desirable style for young misses of thirteen, and a flutter of blue ribbons about her, from the knot fastened among the curls to the dainty bows perched on her slippers. With a little exclamation she indicated how delightful everything appeared to her.

Louise turned. "Will this do for a bride?" she asked, her smiling eyes taking in Neelie as a very pleasant part of the picture.

"It is too lovely for anything," Neelie said in genuine girl parlance, "and it looks just exactly like Estelle."

Louise laughed. Something like that had come to her mind, too. Don't imagine that I think I have startled you now with a bit of news. I have given you credit for surmising long ago that the gala day was in honor of a coming bride — and the bride none other than Estelle herself. I didn't mean to say much about it. Such things occur so often in all well-adjusted families that you would have been naive, indeed, not to have foreseen it.

But Louise didn't. She had been as blind as a bat about it, though the old story was lived right before her very eyes. Glad eyes they were, however, when they took in the facts. Louise loved her brother, John. Wasn't he the one God used at last to bring her darling Estelle to know His love?

"Louise," said Neelie, coming back to commonplaces as soon as she had taken in all the beauty, "Mother wants you. She wants you to see if you think the table looks overloaded and whether you think the turkey platters haven't too much dark meat on them and half a dozen other things that I have forgotten. Won't you come right away?"

"In three minutes," said Louise.

But she had hardly time to attend to all these important matters when Neelie's voice shouted through the house: "There they come! There's the carriage! It has just driven through the archway. Oh, I wonder what John thought of the archway?"

When I tell you that it was wound with evergreen on which there glowed the words "Welcome Home," in roses arranged by Neelie's own fair hands, you will be sure that John liked it. Then the family gathered on that south piazza to greet the bride and groom. The aroma of coffee was stealing through the house, and the spacious dining table, spread its entire length in the large dining room, looked almost burdened with its weight of dishes for the wedding feast. Mother Morgan stayed a moment to cover a cake basket before she hurried to the piazza.

Let me give one moment's time to her. Her face had grown younger; it was smooth and fair and set in calmness. Her dress was a holiday one of soft, neutral-tinted silk, and her white lace cap, which Louise's fingers had fashioned, was perfectly suited to her pleasant face. Dorothy had seated herself in a matronly manner in one of the comfortable easy chairs, which abounded on the piazza. The fair bundle of muslin and lace, bobbing around in her lap, was too restless to allow her to stand, although she admonished, "Do, little Miss Louise, sit still, and receive your new auntie with becoming dignity."

Little Miss Louise's papa had just dumped her ladyship out of his arms and hastened to open the gate for the family carriage, which was just emerging from the shade of the evergreens with Lewis driving. At this moment Father Morgan came from the small room at the right of the piazza with a pompous specimen of three-year-old boyhood perched serenely on his shoulder. He was little John Morgan and liked no place so well as his grandfather's shoulder.

The carriage wound around the lawn and drew up before the piazza door, and they all crossed over to meet it. Estelle's bright and beautiful face, which still held its rare beauty but had matured a little since we first knew her, appeared in view. She threw her eager arms around Mother Morgan's neck.

That lady gave back hearty, loving kisses. And in a voice which I am not sure you would recognize, so little have you known of her in these latter days, she greeted her: "Welcome home, my daughter."

I haven't told you that the carriage contained others beside the bride and groom. Louise's own father and mother had actually come to pay the long-promised visit. They had arranged to meet the young couple at a designated place as they returned from their wedding trip and travel with them homeward. Louise had been home several times in the last five years, but her father and mother were just fulfilling a promise to visit her. Here at last they were all gathered under the Morgan roof, the two families unbroken.

They gathered in the dining room and sat down to the bountiful wedding feast. Among them all only two had vivid recollections just then of the contrast between that homecoming and the greeting Louise and Lewis received on that winter night. Mrs. Dorothy Butler remembered it, it is true. But such important matters had filled Mrs. Dorothy's mind in the intervening years, and everything was so utterly changed to her that she doubted sometimes whether or not she really had dreamed all those strange earlier experiences and only *lived* through these latter years. To Estelle the house was new, of course, and handsome, and everything was delightfully improved. But Estelle did not know that hearts and faces had greatly improved. She could not imagine Mother Morgan in her straight calico without a collar. She could not see John in his shirtsleeves, his pants tucked inside his boots, as Louise remembered him at that moment.

Ah! there were sweeter contrasts than those. When the bright evening drew to its close Neelie wheeled the little center table close to her father's chair and set the student lamp on it. Farmer Morgan opened the old Bible which always held its place of honor on that center table and read: "Bless the Lord, O my soul: and all that is within me, bless his holy name. Bless the Lord, O my soul, and forget not all his benefits: who forgiveth all thine iniquities; who healeth all thy diseases; who redeemeth thy life from destruction; who crowneth thee with lovingkindness and tender mercies."

And then Farmer Morgan said reverently, "Let us pray." The two families, joined by ties that reach into eternity, bowed together, and Father Morgan commended them all to the care of the God whom at last he and his house served.

They talked about old times just a little the next morning, both upstairs and down.

Louise lingered in Estelle's room and listened with pleasure to her lavish praise of all its adornments. Suddenly she asked, "Do you remember this, Estelle?"

"Yes, indeed I do! The very doily that Fannie Brooks made for your wedding present — and there is that white one I made. Oh, Louise, isn't it funny? Do you remember my asking you what you were going to do with all those doilies?"

"Yes, dear. I told you I would find some use for them, and you see I have. Do you remember also that

you assured me that morning how impossible it
would be for you ever to leave Papa and Mama and
go away with a stranger, as I was doing?"

"Well," said Estelle, with an amused, half-
ashamed little laugh, "I didn't go away with a
stranger; I came with John. You see I didn't know him
then."

And again Louise wondered what Estelle would
have thought of him if she had.

Downstairs, an hour or so later, she tarried in the
sitting room to say a few loving words to her own
dear mother. While they were there, Mother Morgan
passed the piazza windows with little John in hand.
He was discoursing loudly to her about the beauties
of a certain bug which he was eagerly dragging her
to see.

"Mother spoils him," Louise said, with a compla-
cent laugh, as the boy's shrill voice floated back to
them. "She will go anywhere and do anything that
he coaxes her to."

"The idea of Mother spoiling anybody!" said Dr.
John with incredulous voice and laughing eyes.

"Well, she certainly does. I suppose all grand-
mothers do."

Then she straightened the books and papers and
restored the sitting room to its yesterday's freshness.
"I'm glad mothers don't spoil their children," her
mother said with satisfaction in her voice, as she
watched Louise bring order out of confusion.

"I didn't spoil her, did I, Lewis? What a lovely
home you have had here all these years! I'm glad
you've demonstrated the folly of the saying that no
house is large enough for two families. How could
anything be better than the arrangement you have
here? Mrs. Morgan was telling me this morning that
when you talked of keeping your own house it al-

most made her sick. I'm very glad you didn't. Little John gives Louise enough care without the responsibilities of housekeeping, although your mother says, Lewis, that she takes a great deal of the work from her. I guess she has a rather exaggerated opinion of you, Louise. Perhaps she is trying to spoil you."

"She is a remarkable little woman, you will have to admit," Lewis said half laughing. But he regarded his wife with earnest, tender eyes. "I'm glad you brought her up so well, Mother. Not many would have succeeded with the problem of two families in one house as she has done."

"Yes," said the mother emphatically. "There is another thing to be considered. She had unusual surroundings. Anyone can see that your mother is an unusual woman! Probably Louise's experience has been exceptional. I really believe there are not many houses large enough for two families. I trembled for Louise. I used to watch every letter critically for signs of failure. You see, I didn't know your father and mother. I didn't feel so anxious about the father; they always get along well with daughters-in-law if the mothers do. But I worried a good deal unnecessarily now, I can see. Still it is, after all, an exceptional case. Don't you think so?"

Lewis turned slowly from the mantel against which he had been leaning and regarded his wife with a curious look. His eyes brimmed with a mischievous light, yet behind the light they held a hint of tears. His voice betrayed his deep feelings.

"Yes, it is an exceptional case. Very few daughters-in-law have such experiences. I do consider my mother an unusual woman and my wife an unusual wife! And I tell you in all honesty, Mother, that we of the Morgan family thank God every day of our lives for the vine from your branch that was grafted into ours."

If you enjoyed *A New Graft on the Family Tree*, we would like to recommend the following books by Isabella Macdonald Alden in the Alden Collection:

The King's Daughter
A young woman's faith and courage
in the midst of opposition

Ester Ried's Awakening
A young woman's spiritual awakening
and its effect on her family

As in a Mirror
A man's search for truth and honesty
and the price he pays to find it

Yesterday Framed in Today
What if Christ had come to
nineteenth-century rural America?

The Man of the House
A boy's struggle against poverty
while maintaining his integrity

Available at your local Christian bookstore or from:

Creation House
190 North Westmonte Drive
Altamonte Springs, FL 32714
1-800-451-4598